CHARLIE FOXTROT 101

CHARLIE FOXTROT 101

THE WARRIOR™ BOOK TWO

MARTHA CARR
MICHAEL ANDERLE

LMBPN Publishing
PMB 196, 2540 South Maryland Pkwy
Las Vegas, NV 89109

Version 1.01, January 2022
ebook ISBN: 978-1-68500-644-0
Print ISBN: 978-1-68500-645-7

THE CHARLIE FOXTROT 101 TEAM

Thanks to our Beta Readers

Larry Omans, Zacc Peltor, Paul Westman

Thanks to our JIT Readers

Dorothy Lloyd
Wendy L Bonell
Jackey Hankard-Brodie
Larry Omans
Diane L. Smith
Dave Hicks
Deb Mader
Zacc Pelter
Jeff Goode
Paul Westman

Editor

SkyHunter Editing Team

CHAPTER ONE

"Okay, soldiers. We have our mission." Private First Class Idina Moorfield looked at every face of Bravo Squad watching her intently and nodded. "There's an armored convoy heading toward our position. Strategic charges before the enemy arrives, and I want two gunners on counter-mobility to funnel them in. That convoy is *not* making it to the village. Got it?"

"Yes, Squad Leader."

She nodded, then tilted her head, listening to the rumble of heavy armored vehicles in the distance, the air peppered with the roar of aircraft and the occasional *crack* of gunfire. "All right. Timbers, take your position east of the road. Matthews, I want you in a nest on the west side. Everyone else with me. We're setting a hell of a trap."

Bravo Squad broke apart to carry out their squad leader's orders. Privates Timbers and Matthews shouldered their gear and hoofed it toward opposite sides of the dirt road cutting across the valley in the hills. By the time Idina and the rest of her squad made it down onto the road itself, the two machine gunners had already found the perfect locations to set up their nests. Their job after that would be to camouflage themselves within the tree line and establish their fields of fire before waiting for the target to arrive.

Idina slid to a halt in the middle of the dirt road and pointed at another soldier. "Pierce. What are we using here?"

The soldier looked down the road where they expected the enemy's approach and wrinkled his nose. "For a convoy of AGMVs? Claymores."

"Then get 'em down. DeLafor, we have an ETA?"

Private DeLafor glanced at his field watch. "T-minus four minutes. If they haven't stopped to fuck around."

She glanced at him sideways and snorted. "They're not stopping. Let's move. Claymores set and hidden, then everyone into position."

Her squad moved quickly and efficiently, as they'd trained. Pierce had already pulled two claymores from his pack and handed one to Hughs. The latter pressed his lips together as he went to his belly in the dirt to set up the mine. Pierce walked backward twenty paces north along the road toward the village, gauging the distance between Hughs' mine and where he wanted to place his.

DeLafor walked swiftly away from the village and raised his binoculars to peer around the corner of the hill where the road curved. "Target sighted. T-minus three minutes."

"Take cover. Let's go." Idina waved for the rest of her squad to get out of the road, pausing only to look up and check the surrounding hillsides for signs of her machine gunners in their nest. There were none.

They've gotten a lot better at laying low and staying *low.*

She made it to the trees off the road as DeLafor counted down with two minutes until enemy approach. "Hughs."

"Yes, Squad Leader." The guy's fingers moved nimbly as he inserted the firing wire into the mine's fuse well.

"Make sure you screw it in all the way this time, huh?"

The rest of her squad laughed at that, including Hughs.

If he hadn't gotten over his fear of explosives, he wouldn't be here anymore.

"Let's go. Let's go," Pierce shouted, signaling to his fellow soldier to hurry. Both privates stood and unrolled their firing wires as quickly as possible across the dirt road toward their positions in the trees. Each of them kicked loose dirt over the cords, and Pierce had already scattered a few branches from the fallen trees across the track to hide the claymores from the advancing enemy. It wasn't a clear path, anyway. Their mission was to defend this village at the end of this road, and during wartime, nobody cared about making the route look pretty.

Idina smirked as Pierce and Hughs hurried back into the trees, their faces set in grim determination as they visually checked the firing wires to be sure those claymores would go off exactly when they were supposed to.

Not like we need much cover for the mines anyway. A convoy barreling around that hill will be looking up at the mountains for an attack. Eight kilometers from the village, they'll think they're home free on this one. That's when we'll end this.

Beside her, DeLafor tapped his field watch twice, then lifted one finger and closed his fist.

T-minus one minute. They'll come around the bend in those AGMVs, and we'll have them right where we want them.

The rumble of the Army Ground Mobility Vehicles rose louder, and a puff of dust carried on the wind from around the bend in the road. Bravo Squad's visuals on the target wouldn't come into play until the convoy was almost right on top of them. That was the plan.

Idina glanced at Pierce, who felt his squad leader's gaze on him and nodded without looking away from the convoy's entry point around the bend. Hughs crouched beside the trigger of his claymore. He gripped it in both hands despite it resting on the ground in front of him.

Yeah. He has a love-love relationship with explosives, all right. Pretty mandatory for Twelve Bravo combat engineers.

The woods around them fell incredibly silent as the convoy vehicles rounded the bend. Clouds of dust rose behind the rumbling engines and the massively thick wheels. Pebbles sprayed in all directions behind them. Then the enemy target made a call Idina had half-expected.

The AGMVs slowed.

They're not idiots. Of course not. They want time to scout this part of the valley and the road for possible attacks. This is why we—

Her thoughts were interrupted by the sharp crack of machine-gun fire from the nests created by Timbers and Matthews. The constant *clack-clack-clack* ricocheted off the mountains and rocky hillside of the bend, making it sound a lot louder—maybe even like there were more than two gunners stationed somewhere above.

The driver of the first vehicle cursed and shouted something at his team.

Gravel sprayed behind the first of the two AGMVs as the driver stepped on the gas to outdrive enemy fire. The second vehicle was quickly on its heels, and now massive dust clouds filled the air to join the machine gun report.

Got them in a bottleneck this way, didn't we? And now...

Idina crouched farther into the underbrush, hidden by her camouflage netting like the rest of her team with her eyes fixed intently on the spot where Pierce had set the first claymore.

She fully expected the green lights of her strange, unexplained ability to flare up in her vision around that first set mine, so there was no surprise there. Despite the strange preludes to episodes that never quite fulfilled themselves during her Army basic training, she still trusted her secret abilities completely. They'd never steered her wrong.

What she didn't expect was for the first enemy vehicle to surge right past the first set of claymores without Hughs pulling the trigger to detonate.

What the hell?

She glanced at Hughs again, whose grin had become a sneer of concentration.

Pierce's focus equally consumed him, and still, the mines didn't go off.

I swear, if they think now's the right time to be a couple of smartasses on this mission...

Amid the constant crack of machine-gun fire from her gunners' nests, Idina heard Hughs puff out a light exhale in concentration. Then the thick *crack* and *whump* of his claymore filled the air as the mine detonated beneath the second vehicle.

Pierce detonated his a second later. The second explosion cut through the air, scattering pebbles, dirt, and smaller twigs from the branches all over the road.

With that spray came small, hardened chunks of white chalk, accompanied by the billowing explosion of a white chalk cloud that was visible for half a mile. Both AGMVs skidded to a stop on the dirt road. Timbers and Matthews stopped firing. The wind picked up to blow the chalk east, away from the enemy target and right into the faces of Bravo Squad.

Bingo. Idina didn't move as the chalk in the air tickled her nose and coated her mouth with a thick, dusty layer. Slowly, with her eyes fixed on the convoy vehicles, she raised a hand and signaled for her squad to move from their positions and close in on the enemy.

The other soldiers of Bravo Squad rose as one entity from their cover in the forest, M16 rifles at the ready. They moved swiftly, practically floating over the underbrush until they emerged from the tree line to soundlessly surround the enemy convoy.

Idina thumbed the radio strapped to her combat vest and muttered, "Target neutralized."

"Aw, shit." The lead vehicle's driver growled and angrily tried to brush the thick coat of chalk off his uniform. "I had to wait three fucking days to get my OCPs in the wash, and now you idiots are spraying chalk all over me. Fuck."

"That's blood, genius." DeLafor snickered. "Pretty sure dead men don't give a shit about their uniforms anyway."

"Fuck you, Private Asshat." The driver glared at DeLafor, then turned in his seat and shouted toward the other vehicle behind him. "Connors! You hit?"

"I'm—" A round of violent, choking coughs rose from

the second AGMV as the dust and chalk finally cleared. "Shit."

"Damn right, you are," Petrie shouted back, her rifle trained diligently on the second driver struggling to clear the chalk from the air. "Shit outta luck."

"Yeah, yeah. You killed us all." Connors snorted, spat a glob of chalky white phlegm into the dirt, then slid out of the driver's seat and raised both hands in surrender. "I'm dead. He's dead. The enemy's fucking dead. Now let us get back to what we were doing, huh?"

"Which is what?" Hughs wrinkled his nose and slightly lowered his weapon. "You're dead."

A few branches *cracked* in the forest behind them, then Staff Sergeant Andrew Remmington stepped through the tree line with a smirk. "*Their* mission, Hughs, was to get to the village and expect a team to ambush them somewhere between their starting point and their target. Yours was to stop them. So well done."

Bravo Squad lowered their weapons and turned to face their drill sergeant, who'd led them through the rigors of basic training for three months. None of them had known to expect Remmington as their instructor for the last two months of demolition training too.

Idina nodded at the staff sergeant and tried to hold back a smile.

Black Phase. Pretty fitting for the end of our training as official Army soldiers. Black is the end, right? Or the beginning.

Remmington nodded at the first vehicle's driver, who still struggled with swiping the thick chalk off his Operational Camouflage Pattern uniform as he muttered angrily to himself. "You'll live, Jolly."

"I know I'll fucking live." Sergeant Jolly stuck a thumb over his shoulder toward the second vehicle without turning around. "Connors might die from chalk inhalation, though."

"I'm not—" Connors let out another whooping cough again, choking on the still-dusty air before spitting again onto the road. "Fuck this." He started the engine again, shifted angrily into reverse, and drove the AGMV backward down the road until he turned wildly around to drive forward around the bend and the hillside that had hidden Idina and Bravo Squad from view.

Still grumbling to himself, Jolly started his vehicle again too. Only this time, he steered it in a fast, tight circle on the road, forcing Bravo Squad to step out of the way to avoid getting clipped. Dirt and pebbles sprayed from beneath the huge, thick tires, and the sergeant stuck his middle finger out the window as he sped away. "Congratulations, assholes!"

Bravo Squad snickered and shook their heads, many of the soldiers lifting their middle fingers in a good-natured reply as the AGMV raced off down the road again and disappeared.

They would've smoked us 'til we bled for flipping the bird at an E5 instructor. But we're not in basic anymore.

"All right, fall in." Remmington clasped his hands behind his back as Bravo Squad lowered their weapons and fell into their accustomed formation. Only now, they didn't have to stand at attention like recruits getting their asses kicked until the Army broke them and rebuilt them as soldiers. "PFC Moorfield."

"Yes, Staff Sergeant." Idina nodded, forcing herself not to shoot DeLafor a sidelong glance when he rolled his eyes.

He can keep pretending to be fed up with me all he wants. He knows I make a hell of a squad leader. I guess he's okay at his job too.

"Run me through your process for executing your mission," Remmington continued.

"Our mission was to ambush the convoy. Intel told us two AGMVs would approach around this bend in the road." She gestured at Timbers and Matthews hurrying down the hillsides with their machine guns and gear to join the rest of the squad. "I sent our gunners up to take their positions elevated in the mountains for counter-mobility."

The staff sergeant raised an eyebrow. "The enemy slowed in their approach."

"I expected it, Staff Sergeant. That's why the gunners were in place. It distracted the target from paying more attention to the road. Private Pierce suggested claymores, and I agreed with him."

Remmington turned his attention to Hughs and looked like he was about to burst out laughing. "And Private Hughs went through the entire four days of your final CEFTX without arming an explosive the wrong way."

The entire squad burst out laughing, soldiers clapping Hughs on the back and shoulders as he flushed and rolled his eyes.

Their platoon sergeant laughed along with them, then his smile disappeared instantly, and he stood at attention. "Bravo Squad, move out!"

The laughter died as Timbers and Matthews rejoined

the squad, breathing a little harder than normal after their quick descent from the machine gun nests. Bravo Squad still smiled and let out low chuckles as they fell in line behind Remmington for the ruck back to base.

Timbers double-checked her gear strapped to the front of her combat vest, then shoved DeLafor away from her when he purposefully stepped in front of her to make her stumble. "What'd we miss?"

"Hughs *not* screwing up," Petrie replied.

Hughs shook his head as they walked. "At least I didn't detonate a shitload of C-4 twenty seconds too soon."

"That was my first time, asshole."

"Doesn't make you special."

Idina couldn't help but laugh at the banter among her squad and the other soldiers she considered her friends by now. They'd all been through a lot together, including their last two months of training. Now that their final field exercises for their specific jobs and titles were almost at an end, there was no way to know exactly where they'd go and what they'd be doing after this. Or if First Platoon of Bravo Company at Fort Leonard Wood, Missouri, would see much of each other after they graduated their Advanced Individual Training.

I'm not even a little worried about what happens after this. I know I have options.

As the last thought entered her mind, a halo of glittering green light lit up in her vision around Staff Sergeant Remmington's head as he led the ruck out of the demo range and back toward base. Idina was still the only one who could see that light, and fortunately, it came without all the swirling visions of data and numbers and probabilities. Nor was there a roaring voice in her mind or the earth trembling beneath her.

Remmington's about to tell me exactly what's happening after we finish AIT. I have a feeling it's gonna be what I asked for this time.

CHAPTER TWO

"Moorfield," Remmington called after dismissing First Platoon for the rest of the day. "Front and center."

"Yes, Staff Sergeant."

Idina glanced sidelong at Amber Petrie, and the other girl smirked at her and shrugged before heading back into the barracks with everyone else. *This is it. He's calling me out in front of everyone, and I'm gonna hear whether or not I made it in. He wouldn't have offered to help me apply if he didn't think I* was *already in.*

"Oh, shit..." DeLafor pressed a fist to his mouth and cringed. "Is Moorfield getting kicked out before we even graduate?"

"Yeah, that's exactly what's happening," she shot back. "I'm such a good squad leader that they can't afford to keep me here with the rest of you. It makes everyone else look bad."

McCoy walked quickly past DeLafor, let out a startlingly loud guffaw, and slapped DeLafor on the back so hard that the shorter soldier stumbled forward with a grunt.

"Dude, go be a Neanderthal somewhere else," DeLafor snapped.

"And miss the look on your face? No way, man."

Idina tried not to let the comments from her friends distract her from catching up with her staff sergeant, who'd stepped aside in the yard behind the basic barracks where Bravo Company remained during their AIT phase. *It would seriously suck to start laughing at them only to get* bad *news from Remmington. He doesn't look happy, but it's not like that ever really meant anything.*

When she finally reached him, she stood at attention—more out of habit than anything else—and waited.

Remmington smirked. "At ease, Moorfield. Not sure how you're gonna feel about this, but there isn't really a better time between now and the graduation ceremony."

"That's this weekend."

"Yeah." He bit his lip and scanned the other soldiers milling around the yard at the end of the day. "It's about jump school."

Idina's stomach curdled into a sour knot. *It's not happening. That's what he's about to say. I haven't had an episode or weird green fog around me in months, but somebody saw something. Maybe it was Brock. He's the only one who's really seen it, and he freaked out and told somebody who wants to keep me from Benning so they can investigate—*

Remmington snorted. "You look like you're gonna hurl, Moorfield. You okay?"

"I'm fine, Staff Sergeant." She swallowed and nodded. "Just waiting for the news. I can handle it."

"Yeah, that's what they all say. Now that I think about it, that's what you said before basic started. Things didn't exactly turn out the way you expected after *that* either, huh?"

Shit. I didn't make it. He's about to drop a bomb on me. The kind AIT didn't *teach me how to diffuse.*

Remmington glanced around one more time like he didn't want anyone close enough to hear him letting Private First Class Idina Moorfield down gently, then leaned slightly toward her. "Your application was accepted."

Idina froze. "Accepted, Staff Sergeant?"

"Yeah. They have an opening at Benning for you in two weeks."

She stared at her platoon sergeant in mute shock. *Jump school. Accepted. This has to be some kind of trick, right?*

He chuckled. "Relax, Moorfield. It's good news. Hell, you earned the recommendation to apply, and you earned your slot. That is if you still want—"

"Of course I fucking want it," she blurted. Remmington's smile flickered at the corners of his mouth, and he tilted his head. "Sorry. Yes, Staff Sergeant. I want it. I want the slot."

"Good." He looked her up and down and nodded. "Then it's yours. I'll make sure the jumpmasters out there know you're ready to go. After graduation."

"Thank you." A belated surge of pride and excitement—and yeah, a small measure of adrenaline-pumped anxiety—flooded through her. "Shit. I'm gonna jump out of an airplane."

Remmington laughed. "More than one. You have to get

through the training first before jump week is even a possibility. No, I can't tell you any more about it, 'cause that's not in my training. I have a feeling jumping out of a C-130 won't be any harder for you than ambushing an enemy convoy with your squad, though."

Idina chuckled with him and had to look away quickly. "I hope so."

"Hoping didn't get you this far, Moorfield. *You* did. You deserve it. Now get out of here so I can go let Fort Benning know you're in."

"Yes, Staff Sergeant." She spun sharply and headed back toward the barracks for a hot shower and a change. She couldn't stop grinning.

I made it through Army basic, demo school for my new job, and now I have a spot in jump school. I can't believe all this is my job. *The Moorfield family would die if they knew how much I was making now as a soldier. That'd give Grandfather a bigger heart attack than knowing his youngest granddaughter is about to ship out to train as a paratrooper.*

After her shower and changing into civilian clothes now that she was officially off-duty, Idina returned to her bunk in the barracks' women's bay and sifted through her things. After the last phase of basic had ended, the new soldiers were allowed to have all their old civilian things back because this wasn't boot camp anymore.

So it didn't break any rules when Idina pulled out her cell phone and connected to the training barracks' spotty wireless Internet to check her emails.

It was a lot of the same junk mail in her inbox except for one that stood out like a beacon of her old life.

From: r.archibald@hotmail.com

Subject: RE: Army Update

Miss Idina,

As always, I was pleasantly surprised to receive your latest email. What an accomplishment to have come so far in the last five months, which I imagine have been remarkably rigorous in all aspects of the word. Your news regarding your application to attend Army Airborne school for training as a paratrooper had an even greater effect on those of us here with whom I've shared your correspondence. Mrs. Yardly nearly fainted, but when she came around, we shared a slice of her impeccable double-chocolate cake and found solidarity together in a renewed perspective.

I have no doubt you will excel at this next venture in your career, as you excel in everything else you set your mind to achieve. It's entirely fitting that jumping from military aircraft with nothing but your skill, presence of mind, and a working parachute would be the next step for you. I do hope for your sake the Army thoroughly inspects their gear for such an occasion.

Idina burst out laughing at that part, got a few strange looks from the other women in the bay going about their business at the end of the workday, and cleared her throat.

No, the Army throws us out and hopes their shit works.

She smiled, scrolled farther down in the email, and continued reading.

Per your request in your last email, I've investigated as much as possible into the likelihood of your parents and Mr. Moorfield Senior having received your previous electronic letters over the last two months. It should come as no surprise that everyone in your family remains diligent in their customary practices of reading all correspondence and clearing out their inboxes by the end of the day. They received your emails, and that is all I can say.

Whether you receive responses from anyone else here at the manor is entirely out of my hands, Miss Idina. Although I do encourage you to continue sending updates. Mrs. Yardly and I look forward to them almost as much as I look forward to the next immaculate dessert she brings to my room now that the nights have grown so cold and dreary, as they do in New Hampshire.

We missed you over the Christmas holidays. I daresay the Manor simply isn't the same without you here. I imagine that may have been very

much the point of you taking your leave, or at least part of it.

We eagerly await your next email with further reports on your progress and career. If you do receive this position in Airborne school, we will be rooting for you. Mostly in the hopes that you survive plummeting to the earth from over twelve hundred feet in the sky.

It's a privilege to be included vicariously in your adventures.

Respectfully,

R.

P.S. Since you began writing these emails to us, I've noticed a lack of any mention regarding your condition and any changes you might have experienced since leaving the manor. Avoiding the topic in mass correspondence sent to the rest of your family and myself is understandable and very likely the best course of action. I want to assure you that should you have any questions, concerns, or wish to discuss any changes or new experiences regarding your condition that you're always welcome to address them to me personally.

Know that I intend not to broach this topic with

you again in the future unless you expressly state your interest in such a conversation. Still, I would be remiss in not offering you the opportunity to share with me whatever might be happening as you navigate your new life as an Army soldier. Whatever the status of your episodes might be now, Miss Idina, it never hurts to reach out to a friend. One never knows how helpful a fresh perspective might be, even in matters seemingly impossible to traverse on your own or otherwise.

I am always here.

With a heavy sigh, Idina blinked away the few tears that had welled up halfway through Reggie's email and sniffed.

Not interested in talking about my episodes, Reg. No offense. I have it under control. A few flashing green lights and lines in the air and one *creepy voice in my head can't be all that bad if my family won't even bother to reply to a single email.*

She started a new email response, meaning to thank her family's butler and head of staff for the well-wishes and the strange offer of discussing her *condition*. She only managed to type, "Dear Reggie," before being interrupted.

"Moorfield!" Amber shouted from six feet away. "What the hell are you doing with contraband in the bay!"

Idina reacted instinctively and tossed her phone beside her onto the bunk before it fully sank in that she was getting jerked around by her friend and not a commanding officer. Amber burst out laughing, and Idina grimaced in mock anger before snatching up her phone again. "Very funny."

"Of course it's funny. You should've seen your face."

The other three women who'd made it through basic chuckled and finished going about their business beside their bunks.

"Yeah, okay. Fine. You got me." Idina locked her phone screen and stood to slip the device into the back pocket of her jeans. "Did you stop by just to screw with me or what?"

"Well yeah. That was first on the list." Amber folded her arms and looked her friend up and down. "The second part was finding you so I could tell you to scrap whatever plans you had for dinner. We're going out."

Idina stared at the other girl, hoping this wasn't another massive prank her fellow recruits had played on each other since they'd graduated from basic. "Out where?"

"Hell, I don't know. *Not* the barracks." Amber waved her forward. "Come on. The guys are waiting."

"Right. Waiting." After grabbing her jacket from the trunk beneath her bunk, Idina shrugged into it and hurried after Amber. "The guys as in..."

"DeLafor, Hughs, McCoy. Maybe Pierce, but he mentioned something about having to rub his ingrown toenail, and I didn't want the details."

They both laughed as they walked out of the women's bay and headed through the barracks toward the parking lot exit. When they stepped outside into Missouri's brisk January cold, they found the guys waiting for them. Except for Pierce.

"So Toe Boy's not coming, huh?" Idina asked.

DeLafor snorted. "I told him to forget about it. He has ten toes. Who gives a shit about losing one of them if he goes out for a night? But no. Apparently, his *toe* can't handle a little fun."

Hughs wrinkled his nose as everybody turned to head across the parking lot. "Can we talk about *anything* else? Pierce won't shut up about it, and now I have to hear from you assholes too?"

"Aw, come on, Hughs." DeLafor punched him in the shoulder. "I thought it got you off."

"Yeah, that's exactly what I'm into." Hughs shook his head and zipped up his jacket to the collar. "Dude's a hypochondriac. I can hear him talking about this shit in his sleep."

"Huh." McCoy scratched his head. "Seems pretty warm to me."

Everybody stopped and turned to stare at the tall soldier from Arlington, Kentucky. McCoy's thick southern accent hadn't diminished one bit since the start of basic, but his lankiness had since been replaced by as much lean muscle as Hughs had built over the last five months.

"Dude." Amber shook her head. "What the hell are you talking about?"

He shrugged. "I mean, yeah, it's cold *outside,* but if the heat's on, I didn't think you could get hypo…hypochondriac in your sleep. Shit, is that a thing?"

The group held their disbelieving silence for all of two seconds before Hughs and DeLafor cracked up laughing.

"That's *hypothermia,* dipshit!" DeLafor clapped McCoy on the back and snorted.

"Wait, what?"

"Don't bother trying to explain it to him," Amber added. "His head might explode."

"Well, hell. Then what's the other hypo?"

Hughs snorted. "Something you obviously don't worry about."

"I don't..." McCoy stopped in the parking lot and stared at his friends passing him, his eyes wide in confusion. "Come on, guys. What did I get wrong?"

Idina stopped beside him and patted his arm in sympathy. "A hypochondriac is somebody who worries about their health all the time or thinks they have every terrible disease they can think of."

"Well, damn." He scratched his head again. "Why the hell would someone want that?"

"Pretty sure they don't, McCoy. That's the point—"

"Hey, Rambo!" Amber called from beside a dented, rusting gray pickup truck. "Hurry the hell up and hand over the keys."

He scowled at her and spread his arms. "Why?"

"Let's see..." DeLafor propped an elbow on his opposite hand and stroked his chin. "Oh, yeah. Because you'll end up taking us all the way down to Florida instead of the pizza place on the other side of base."

"I can drive."

"It's not about your driving, man. It's 'cause you can't read."

Amber and Hughs cracked up at that, and Hughs slapped the side of the gray pickup. The truck let out a hollow *gong*, a grating *squeal* of metal, and a few *pops* like he'd dislodged something vital. He stopped laughing and quickly stepped away from the vehicle with both hands raised.

"Shit, y'all're just jealous I *have* a car out here."

"Jealous?" Amber looked the truck up and down. "Nope. But I'm hungry, so let's go."

McCoy rolled his eyes and strolled across the parking lot, his long legs making it harder for Idina to catch up as his leather cowboy boots *clicked* on the asphalt. "Nobody drives Bertha but me."

Hughs tilted his head and stared at the truck. "Maybe you should give her a break then."

Idina snickered as they approached the truck and DeLafor waved impatiently for McCoy to hand over the keys.

Can't blame them for not wanting McCoy behind the wheel. He's good at his job and an even better shot with a long-range weapon, but this is the same guy who thought he could drink the hot MRE water.

The truck's doors *squealed* when they opened, the entire cab rocking on a loose frame and bouncing when five soldiers climbed inside. Idina ended up in the back with Hughs on the other side, and McCoy smashed in the middle between them. DeLafor had taken over the driver's seat and violently cranked the ignition.

"Whoa, whoa, whoa, man. Take it easy!" McCoy lurched forward and reached for the ignition, which he probably could've touched with such long arms. "You break my car, asshole, and you're paying to get her fixed."

DeLafor looked over his shoulder to frown at him. "Might as well buy you a whole new car. It'd be cheaper."

Amber snorted.

"Man, just be gentle. You gotta caress her. Show a little love."

Idina shot him a playful frown. "Does that work on the ladies too, McCoy, or just the car?"

Everyone else burst out laughing, and McCoy thumped back against the seat beside her, hanging his head with a heavy sigh.

DeLafor finally got the engine purring, and the truck jerked out of the parking spot before racing out of the lot toward the road.

Idina grinned and looked out the window at the light quickly fading from the Missouri sky. *I guess it's a good night to go out for dinner with a couple of friends. Maybe I'll tell them about jump school, and we'll have something else besides graduation to celebrate.*

CHAPTER THREE

She waited until she and her friends were halfway through the two massive pizzas they'd ordered to spill the beans on her acceptance into jump school. Their reactions couldn't have been any more predictable after she'd spent the last five months studying her fellow soldiers like she'd studied their drill sergeants.

Hughs' eyes widened, and the half-eaten slice of pizza in his hand dropped onto his plate with a *thump*. Amber squinted at Idina so hard that she looked like she'd bitten into a lemon. McCoy—who'd turned twenty-one a month before enlisting and was the only one old enough to have ordered a beer—choked on that beverage and sent a spray of it across the table toward DeLafor sitting directly opposite him in the booth.

"Dude." DeLafor spread his arms and shook his head. "This is why we're not supposed to drink."

McCoy gulped and wiped his mouth with the back of a hand. "My bad. Same thing happens with water, though, so I don't think it has anything to do with—"

"Jump school?" Amber interrupted, leaning forward and staring at Idina sitting across from her.

"No." McCoy smacked his lips. "That's Moorfield's thing. I ain't—"

"She wasn't finishing your sentence, genius." DeLafor swiped off his jacket with a napkin and snorted. "Don't drink anything for a bit, huh?"

"Yeah." Idina ignored the guys and nodded at Amber. "Jump school."

"How the hell did you do that?" Hughs asked.

"Remmington said he'd recommend me if I wanted to go, and I figured why the hell not, right?" Idina shrugged. "It's not like I have anything to lose."

DeLafor snorted. "Yeah. Except for your brains when they splatter all over the jump zone because somebody got handed shitty gear."

Amber gave him a condescending glare. "That doesn't happen."

"Fine. Then it's your dignity. I heard everybody pisses themselves on the first jump."

Idina laughed. "I'm pretty sure everyone pisses themselves in basic too. So not that different than what we're used to."

"Moorfield's gonna be a paratrooper." Amber raised her Coke glass toward the center of the table for a toast.

"I won't technically be a paratrooper after this," Idina added.

"Same thing. We're stuck here with Hughs and bombs."

"Hey." Halfway through raising his drink, Hughs paused. "That was *one* time I almost didn't throw a live grenade."

"And the time you tripped yourself up in the fuse wire," DeLafor added.

"I didn't—"

"Plus the time you mismeasured ingredients," Amber added.

McCoy snickered. "And the time you tried to read the label upside down and almost blew us away with friendly fire instead of the... Oh, wait. Shit. That was me."

The guy's genuinely confused grimace made everyone laugh, and Idina raised her glass toward Hughs. "We've all fucked up. We're all still here. So I'll toast to that."

Everyone but Hughs *clinked* their glasses over the table. While McCoy glugged down the rest of his beer, Hughs scrunched up his face and tilted his head. "You can say shit like that, Moorfield, but when have *you* ever fucked up?"

"Come on, Hughs..."

"No, I mean it. Moorfield's, like, superhuman or something."

She met his gaze and tried to smile. "I have plenty of issues, okay? Maybe you weren't looking close enough."

I don't think anyone was looking close enough during basic, except for Brock. That was a close call when he saw my green light and the fog. Episodes or no episodes, I'm not perfect. My friends just have no idea how true that is.

"Dude." DeLafor stared at Hughs and shook his head. "We're celebrating, and you're the buzzkill trying to pick out what's wrong with Moorfield? I'll tell you what's wrong with her. She's a pain in the ass, and she'll ride you until your only choices are to be better or kill her in her sleep."

Idina laughed. "It fucking worked, battle buddy."

"You *would* try to take the credit for my successes, wouldn't you?" He raised his glass toward her again, then muttered to Hughs, "Just drink to Moorfield and shut up."

For a minute, Hughs looked like he was ready to crawl across the table and throttle DeLafor. Then he sighed, raised his drink toward Idina, and practically shouted above the noise of the restaurant, "Moorfield's gonna get her fucking wings!"

Laughing, everyone drank again, and DeLafor poured some of his soda into McCoy's empty beer glass so the guy wouldn't be toasting empty. McCoy grimaced in disgust but drank the sugary leftovers in his glass with everyone else.

This might be the only sendoff I get. You know what? It's a hell of a lot better than the sendoff I got from Moorfield & Associates when I left for basic. I'd take soldiers and friends over the rest of my family any day.

McCoy slurped down the last of his gross drink mixture, craning his neck back to get every last drop out of the glass. When he set the glass down, he let out a thoughtful hum and smacked his lips. "Well, hell. That's pretty good."

Amber scoffed. "That's the kinda dumbass remark you should keep to yourself, man. Makes it hard to take you seriously."

"I'm just sayin'."

Their server approached the table with a black checkbook in hand, smiling politely. "Anything else I can get y'all while you're here?"

"Naw, we're good." DeLafor nodded at her. "Thanks."

"You bet. I'll just leave this right here—"

"I'll go ahead and take that check, ma'am," McCoy interrupted.

"Oh. Sure—"

"No, don't give it to him." Amber reached across the table toward the checkbook. "Trust me. He gets his numbers screwed up as much as his letters."

"I can pay a bill, Petrie."

"With fake money?" DeLafor slapped the other man's hand away from the checkbook in the woman's hovering hand. "Nice try. I'll take it."

"Y'all play too much. Moorfield showed me how to save money. One hundred percent of my paycheck to— Wait…"

"See?" Amber shot the server an apologetic smile. "We got Private Gifted and Talented over here. I'll take that, and you bozos are just gonna have to deal with a woman treating you to dinner."

"Guys, let the lady go already," Hughs interjected, grimacing in apology at their server. "She has other tables—"

"So I'll take the check."

"The hell you will."

"Don't fucking grab my hand."

"I'll cut it off if you don't quit being such a dumbass."

"Jesus Christ," Hughs muttered, folding his arms and shrinking into himself in embarrassment.

The server kept trying to smile, not sure if the banter between off-duty soldiers was just that or an actual fight brewing in her section. "I'll leave this right here on the—"

"No, ma'am," McCoy said sharply. "I'm the one payin' for all this, and these idiots need to settle down!" He reached for the checkbook at the same time as DeLafor.

Both men grabbed a different corner, and when the server released it in the struggle, the checkbook launched out of everyone's hands to fly across the table.

"Shit." McCoy swept his hand across the table in an attempt to catch the flying check. Instead, the back of his hand caught his empty beer glass and sent that hurtling through the air.

Idina wasn't actively expecting her ability to jump into action over a pizza dinner with her friends. But it did.

Time slowed. The checkbook skittered across the surface of the table like a well-tossed stone skipping across a glassy lake. The beer glass soared through the air in front of her, tilting sideways and spilling two drops of Coke-beer on its way, heading right for Hughs' face at the end of the table. Both wayward objects blazed with shimmering green light, and the tingling itch of Idina's ability surged across her shoulders, down her arms, and into her hands.

She reacted instantly. Her left hand slapped down on the checkbook to pin it in place on the table, and her right hand shot up to catch the beer glass mid-flight. The glass smacked into her hand four inches from Hughs' face. A shimmer of sparkling green flecks pulsed inside the glass before they instantly disappeared.

Hughs launched himself against the back of the booth with a hiss, staring wide-eyed at the glass in Idina's hand.

Everyone else around the table fell silent in shock, also staring at her surprising and seemingly impossible reflexes.

Shit. That wasn't supposed to be a damn magic show. And that was not *my normal green light.*

Smiling sheepishly, Idina slowly lowered the beer glass

to the table and turned toward the server. "I guess I'm taking the check tonight. Thanks."

The woman looked like she couldn't decide whether to start laughing or run right out of the restaurant and never return. A nervous laugh escaped her. "That was... You have *some* reflexes."

Idina shrugged and slid the checkbook off the table before setting it in her lap. "Just a lucky catch."

"Uh-huh. I'll, uh...be right back to grab that." The server started to turn, paused, then spun quickly and headed to her next table of customers.

Staring at the table, Idina pulled her wallet from her jacket pocket and grabbed her bank card from Navy Federal Credit Union—definitely not Moorfield-&-Associates-approved. But it was all she had.

Act normal. Like you did with Brock. He thought it was the stress of constantly falling out of his harness for the practice tower, and they'll just think it's...what?

The whole time, she felt her friends' gazes on her like tiny needles piercing into her hands and face.

"Lucky catch my ass," DeLafor muttered. "What the hell was that?"

"Exactly what it looked like," she replied calmly, hoping she looked a lot more nonchalant than she felt.

"Damn, Moorfield." Amber huffed out a laugh that sounded way more concerned than amused. "You got some kinda Spidey-sense you never told us about?"

"Reflexes. We all have them."

"Not like *that*."

Hughs blinked hard three times, then shook his head. "I totally called it. Superhuman. You heard me call it, right?"

No one argued with him or made fun of his observation, and Idina set her card in the checkbook before sliding it toward the edge of the table. McCoy lurched away from her like she was on fire and looked her up and down. "Somebody tell me they saw that."

"Dude, we *all* saw it," DeLafor muttered. "That's what we're talking about."

"Yeah, but what about them green lights." McCoy pointed at his glass. "Y'all saw *those*, right? Like somebody threw a party in that—"

Idina barked out a laugh and shook her head. "Green lights, McCoy? Come on."

Her friends gave each other pointed looks around the table, all four of them waiting for some kind of explanation because they couldn't wrap their heads around what they'd seen.

They won't be able to wrap their heads around the fact that I have some weird ability that may or may not be a part of my family's genes from way back when in Scotland. I can't say shit about this to anybody.

She glanced around their table and sighed with overwhelming relief when she found the best excuse she could think of. Then she pointed at the neon beer sign hanging in the window above their table. "Look. There are your green lights. Reflection from the sign. Light refracted through the glass. Pretty simple."

"Uh-huh." DeLafor tilted his head. "Because you're only simple PFC Moorfield, right?"

"It's basic science, guys. What else could it be?"

"I don't know, Moorfield." Hughs squinted and leaned forward. "You tell *us*."

Idina raised her eyebrows and gave them all a crooked smile. "Oh, come on. What, you think I snatched a glass out of the air with a bunch of...I don't know. *Magic*? That's stupid as hell."

For a minute, she thought she'd botched the entire thing as her friends stared at her like silently condemning statues.

Shit. Why did I have to use the word "magic"? That's not what this is. I'm pretty sure.

The second she opened her mouth to try telling them how crazy they were all being—despite what she *knew* they'd all seen—DeLafor slapped a hand down on the table and let out a sharp, forced laugh.

"Damn, Moorfield. Your face right now. You look like someone just crapped on your bunk!"

Amber chuckled. "What do you think this is, huh? The *Witch Trials*?"

"Wait." McCoy turned toward Idina with an incredulous frown. "You're a witch?"

Everyone around the table groaned, and Hugh chucked a wadded-up napkin at McCoy. "You're a moron."

"What'd I say?"

Idina laughed and shook her head. "You guys had me going there for a minute. I thought I missed something."

"Yeah, we all got a few loose screws. Ain't that right, McCoy?" DeLafor flipped the middle finger at his friend sitting across from him, then laughed even harder. This time, it sounded like real laughter, as if everyone had decided to ignore the weird thing they'd seen Idina do because they didn't want to believe the other two options

—that they were all losing their minds at the same time, or that PFC Moorfield had *magic*.

That's not what it is. It can't be. We'll just all keep pretending this never happened because I don't have time for dealing with that.

The server finally returned to the table with a handheld card reader. She smiled like everything was fine but wouldn't look at a single soldier while she ran Idina's card and had her sign the device.

"Y'all have a good night. Thanks for coming in." The woman swiftly turned and hurried away before any of them had a chance to say anything.

"Huh." DeLafor slid out of the booth first and nodded at the retreating server. "You think she'd be used to dealing with soldiers by now on a damn Army base."

"Not soldiers like *Moorfield*," Amber added. "What'd you do for those reflexes, huh? Take some kinda superpowered mental enhancement drug or something?"

Idina choked on the question and tried to cover it up with a laugh as she followed McCoy out of the booth. "Nope. I left those at home."

"What?"

"Nothing." *Yeah, let's start talking about how I've been dosed with deadly nightshade my whole life and that the doc at MEPS thought I was full of shit about it.*

She grabbed her card and stuck it in her wallet before heading toward the door behind the others.

Hughs grunted and *thumped* against the edge of the table as he tried to scoot around the circular booth to get out. "Damnit. What's up with these stupid...tight...tables?"

"Look at that." DeLafor folded his arms and smirked as

he watched Hughs struggle with getting out of the booth. "Bet nobody would've said six months ago that you'd get stuck behind a table 'cause your *abs* are too ripped."

"Shut up." Hughs finally squeezed himself out of the booth, forgetting his strength for a moment as he pushed on the table and almost tipped it over on top of himself.

McCoy burst into hooting laughter and slapped his knee.

"What are *you* laughing at, smart guy?" Hughs muttered. "You ain't even the one who had a beer!"

"I didn't drink it with Coke either, so there's that."

"Sure. The Coke get you buzzed, Hughs?" McCoy ribbed the other on the way out of the restaurant, and Hughs stared straight ahead without saying a word.

Idina stepped outside into the parking lot with her friends and drew a deep breath of the crisp night air. *Okay. Celebration for me going to jump school aside, that was close. If I can't get my meds on base or from any other doctor who* doesn't *know my family, I need to figure out how to rein in my green lights. If I start glowing when I'm jumping from an airplane, they'll kick me out of the Army first and ask questions later. Maybe.*

CHAPTER FOUR

When the weekend arrived, the training barracks buzzed with excitement for the graduation ceremony to officially complete their basic training and AIT. Amid the banter of the other four women in the women's bay, Idina slipped into her dress blues for the ceremony and tied back her hair.

This is it. The end of training. The end of Fort Leonard Wood. We're graduating from AIT, and I ship out to jump school in two weeks. Whole new adventure.

"You look scared, Moorfield," Timbers muttered with a smirk as she buttoned up her dress shirt. "You scared?"

"Of what? Finally getting out of here?"

"Not without a little pain, though, right?" Amber snickered. "'Cause we're getting our castle tabs, and how much you wanna bet Moorfield's getting a blood castle tonight?"

Timbers clicked her tongue. "You think I'm an idiot? I'm not taking that bet."

"Blood castle?" Idina situated her dress cap on her head

before double-checking that she'd fully tied her dress shoes.

"Aw, that's cute." Amber exaggerated a pout although she tried not to laugh. "You don't have a problem with a little blood, do you?"

"Nope. But I have no idea what you're talking about."

"It means they like you," Timbers added as she checked her reflection in a handheld mirror beside her bunk. "I heard you got a slot to jump school. So they like you."

"You heard that, huh?" Idina met Amber's gaze.

"Hey, don't look at me." The other woman shrugged. "My mouth's not nearly as big as some of the others who heard what you're up to next."

"That's fucking badass," Stevens added. "No surprise you'd be crazy enough to be a paratrooper."

"Thanks." Idina shook her head. *Everyone thinks I'm insane for doing this. Maybe I am. At least I'm not afraid of heights.*

"It's good money too," Timbers added.

Amber scoffed and headed toward the bay doors. "They couldn't pay me an E6 salary to get up on one of those planes and throw myself out. Nope."

Idina headed after her with a crooked smile. "They almost couldn't pay you to jump off the Warrior's Tower."

The other women laughed, including Amber, who waved off the comment before opening the doors. "That's *exactly* why I would never jump out of a plane. Bring that up again, Moorfield, and maybe you'll find me up in that C-130 pushing you out with a big-ass grin."

They found Sergeant Holly waiting for them in the hall. She looked the soon-to-be graduates up and down and nodded. "I'd say you PV1s clean up nicely, but I can't lie to you on graduation day."

"Don't forget the Private First Class." Amber clapped Idina's shoulder and shook her a little. "Moorfield came into this better than the rest of us."

"Uh-huh." Holly chuckled. "Let's go."

"Better than the rest of you?" Idina muttered as the women followed their newest instructor rotated through Fort Leonard Wood. "I don't need you to make me look good."

Amber snickered. "I can't help it. You're about to fly off and get your little Airborne wings. I gotta give you shit somehow."

At least she's not bringing up the glowing green beer glass. I'll have to settle for getting a hard time about coming into the Army with a degree under my belt.

"Seriously," Idina added, leaning closer to her friend as they headed through the barracks to meet up with the men before they'd all enter the ceremony room. "What's a blood castle?"

"Trust me." Amber looked straight ahead, clearly fighting off a smile. "If you get one, you'll know."

"Kinda hard to ignore," Timbers added from behind. "Just don't cry."

"Ha. Great advice. Thanks."

The battalion commander, Lieutenant Colonel Elmscomb, was there to officiate and oversee the ceremony for Bravo Company's First Platoon. Idina stood at attention with the rest of her fellow soldiers soon to become official combat engineers. A handful of guests took up the back of the room—family members who'd come to see their sons, daughters, and siblings graduate from their first round of specialized training before leaving their home for the last six months and branching out with new orders for the next step in their careers.

Idina fought back a smile when she saw three men standing together in the back who were all-male versions of Amber Petrie. *Two brothers and her grandpa. Who's a general. No pressure or anything, Petrie.*

It only briefly occurred to her that she didn't have any family here to support her, as she hadn't when she'd graduated from basic.

I'm not the only one, though. It's not like any of the Moorfields are sitting around at the manor joining me in spirit and toasting my success. I don't need them anyway.

Lieutenant Colonel Elmscomb addressed those gathered to talk about the diligence, loyalty, respect, and successes of First Platoon during their AIT. What they'd been through, how they'd grown, how they exemplified the core values of the United States Army in everything they did and who they'd become.

Then he called up the soldiers of First Platoon to stand before the witnesses and receive their tabs.

At Staff Sergeant Remmington's commands, the soldiers moved toward the front of the room to receive their pins marking them as graduates and combat engineers.

"First Platoon, about-face!"

Everyone turned, standing perfectly at attention, and

Idina forced herself not to scan the faces of the family members at the back of the room.

Stop looking. Nobody's here. Nobody will ever be here where I am now. Because I left being a Moorfield behind me. The only thing my family gave me this time is a name.

"Private Thomas Bristol," Elmscomb read from the list of First Platoon's soldiers.

Remmington approached Brock first, who stood at the end of the line. While Elmscomb said a few words of personal recommendation about Brock and his performance during AIT, Remmington reached up to pin the Corps of Engineers tab on the soldier's uniform above the left breast pocket. They saluted each other, and Remmington moved on to the next soldier when Elmscomb called their name.

Idina drew a deep breath, listening to the impressive things being said about the rest of her platoon while the staff sergeant made his way down the line.

Not all of us made it. Those of us who did sure deserve a little recognition. At least they won't say anything about how my green lights make me an exemplary soldier who can see numbers and patterns and hear voices no one else can.

That almost made her laugh, but she held her stoic mask as firmly as she could and fixed her gaze on the doorframe at the back of the room.

Remmington moved down the line, finished pinning the tab on Private Finnegan McCoy's dress blues, then stood directly in front of Idina.

"Private First Class Idina Moorfield," Elmscomb called, "demonstrated outstanding dedication to her platoon and squad within numerous leadership roles, especially during high-stress exercises. Which we value in the Corps of Engineers."

Some of the soldiers' family members chuckled at this, and Idina caught a hint of a smile flickering across Remmington's lips as he raised a gold pin in his hand and slipped the sharp end out of the clasp.

"We are proud to have Private First Class Moorfield as a combat engineer."

Elmscomb had said the same thing after every other soldier's individualized commendation for their performance during AIT. Idina had expected the words with her name filling in the blank.

What she didn't expect was for Remmington to jab the gold tab through her uniform shirt the way he did. She definitely didn't expect the instant sting of the pin's sharp point digging into her flesh below her left collarbone before he quickly removed his hand to stand at attention facing her. Her instant reaction was to grunt in surprise, then clear her throat. Remmington smirked.

"Congratulations," he muttered.

"Thank you, Staff Sergeant." She saluted her platoon sergeant.

Remmington returned that salute, then nodded briskly and moved down the line to the next soldier of First Platoon who'd made it through AIT.

Idina gritted her teeth.

Blood castle. If I get one, I'll know, huh? Thanks for the heads up, Petrie.

While Elmscomb talked about Private Stevens' outstanding qualities, Idina briefly looked down at the castle-shaped gold pin on her uniform shirt. She had to lower her head quite a bit to get a good view, but at least there wasn't any blood staining through her dress blues.

That's a castle. The Corps of Engineers' seal, right? I'm wearing it in my damn shoulder with—

Before she could finish the thought, a surge of tingling heat raced through Idina's head and overwhelmed everything else. The battalion commander's voice disappeared. The hushed whisper and occasional cough of those watching the ceremony were gone too. The room and all the formal banners and plaques and flags around her vanished. The old musty scent of the ceremony room would've been a distant memory if Idina could focus enough to remember it.

She couldn't.

Because now she couldn't feel her body, wasn't aware of its previous existence. Everything was green.

The images flashed through her mind with rapid intensity. A stone castle built on an old hill without any trees. Green mist hovering over the damn ground and brown grasses. Handmade leather boots poked through that fog, which parted to reveal three people she didn't know standing in front of the castle.

Two men and one woman. All with black, curly hair. All standing proud and strong against some unseen force rising in front of them.

The men drew massive, heavy swords from sheaths at their hips. The woman lifted both hands in front of her, and her deep voice echoed across the land, unaffected by the thick fog swirling around all three of them.

"Rise, Warriors of the Moors! Rise for your people and the oath you swore to uphold! They cannot stand against us!"

A rumbling growl echoed across the open land around the castle. More figures materialized in the mist. The green light intensified, flashing and pulsing, and the woman drew an arrow from the quiver strapped to her back before nocking it in a gleaming red longbow embellished with swirling silver filigree.

The ground trembled. Another roar hurtled across the field, and all three figures so clear in their detail despite being green-washed open their mouths to let out blood-curdling battle cries.

Then it was over.

Idina was sucked back into her mind and body with a sharp, barely concealed gasp. She swayed slightly on her feet, blinking at the banners and flags decorating the graduation room. Beside her, Matthews glanced her way and raised his eyebrows in question.

Idina softly cleared her throat and looked straight ahead again. She knew he caught the tiniest shake of her head telling him everything was fine.

It wasn't.

What the hell was that? I get stuck with a pin and just... what? Leave my body? Shit, if I start hearing that creepy voice again like it's coming for me right here on base, I'm gonna lose it.

She waited diligently for Remmington to move down the rest of the line, pinning castle tabs on every soldier. Sweat quickly beaded at her hairline to trickle from beneath her dress cap. Her mouth ran dry. For the next ten minutes, she expected another full-blown episode to catch her right here, with all these people as witnesses.

They're paying attention this time. Everyone's watching. I can't rationalize more green lights with some bullshit about refracting light. Pull it together.

Idina didn't need to look down at her hands to know something weird was happening there. The familiar tingle of heat and cold that always accompanied the glittering specs of green rising around her hands told her it was already happening. She clenched her fists even tighter and stared straight ahead, forcing herself not to give anything away.

Suck it up, Moorfield. You made it this far. Don't ruin it now with your freakshow.

"Please join me once more in congratulating the U.S. Army's newest combat engineers," Elmscomb said.

The polite clapping and a few wayward whistles rising from the family members at the back of the room pulled Idina completely back into the present. She straightened her spine and accepted the applause meant for all of them, but now the urge to wipe the sweat off her cheeks and forehead was unbearable.

Of course, I can't simply stand here at a graduation ceremony to get my tab. It's been two months without a close call, and now I have to stand here getting visions *while all eyes are on me. Awesome.*

Her racing thoughts drowned out the last of Lieutenant Colonel Elmscomb wrapping up the end of the ceremony. All she could think about was what she'd seen.

Who were *those people? What were they fighting? What the hell does it have to do with me?*

CHAPTER FIVE

After the post-ceremony celebration that wasn't nearly so formal, Idina headed back to the woman's bay to change out of her dress blues and at least look at the damage done to her shoulder. She had to jerk the sharp point of the castle tab from her flesh before she removed her uniform shirt. It came as no surprise to find both her shoulder *and* the pin covered in blood, plus the inside of her shirt.

"Great," she muttered, grabbing a tissue to wipe her shoulder gingerly. She poured some water on the puncture wound to wash the rest of it, then kept staring at the puckered skin and red hole, waiting for something to happen.

My hand healed itself after NIC at Night. So what's taking so long?

"Take a picture, Moorfield." Amber stepped into the women's bay. "It'll last longer."

"No, it won't." Timbers snorted. "That's gonna scar for sure."

"What?" Idina turned to frown at them.

"No way. Don't tell me you have a problem with scars." Amber stripped off her uniform to change into civilian clothes. "Not with where *you're* going."

"I don't know..." Swiping at her shoulder again, Idina found herself getting a headache from ducking her chin to her chest to get a good view.

"Let's see it."

"You don't need to see where Remmington stuck me in the shoulder." She turned away, but Amber and Timbers were right beside her in a flash, spinning her around to take a look.

"Damn. That must've hurt like a bitch," Amber muttered.

"Technically, they're not *supposed* to do that still." Timbers folded her arms and looked Idina up and down. "Somebody's a fan of Moorfield's style."

"Yeah, okay. Now you got to see the blood castle. Carry on."

The other women laughed and returned to their bunks as Idina tugged on a plain black t-shirt and changed into a pair of jeans.

Listening to the other women talk about whatever after-hours celebration the rest of the platoon had planned for the night, Idina tried to ignore the ache in her shoulder. More than that, she tried to ignore the strange sense of doom creeping up on her as if she'd done something wrong.

So I hear voices at the end of basic and heal a gash on my palm with the green light. A pin gets jammed into my body, and that's not *gonna heal? Right, 'cause I got visions instead. What's going on here?*

"You coming, Moorfield?"

"Nah. You guys have fun." Idina sank onto the edge of her bunk and pulled out her phone. "I'm gonna chill for a bit."

"Yeah, recover from your *wounds*." With a soft laugh, Amber headed toward the bay doors and called over her shoulder, "Later, Private Super-Special."

When the bay was empty again, Idina couldn't help but continuously study the progress of the puncture in her shoulder. Her green lights didn't reappear. No glow and quick sealing over of broken flesh.

At least I'm not having another vision, though. Doesn't mean this isn't weird as shit.

She folded up her dress blues and almost didn't want to look at the gold tab with the Corps of Engineers insignia carved into it in the shape of a castle. She couldn't leave the pin lying around, so she forced herself to stick it back through the fabric of her uniform shirt before folding that up too.

This better not be the part where I'm seriously losing my mind and start having mental breakdowns every time I see a castle.

That made her snort, and she picked up her phone to open her emails. There was nothing new of any real importance, but she spent the next five minutes weighing the pros and cons of sending Reggie another email update.

Right. Hey, Reggie. I graduated from AIT, made it into jump school, and had a vision of creepy foggy castles and three random people who looked like they could do what I do, only better. And also in some kind of military.

"Please," she muttered, rolling her eyes. "If I talk about

this, I'll get thrown in a psych ward faster than I can say, 'Just kidding.'"

So she settled for watching a documentary about some of the world's greatest chess masters instead, propping her phone up on her pillow. *At least I get a little time alone to come down from all this. Whatever* this *is. I should've gone out to get some art supplies before everything closed down for the night.*

Idina spent the next few days celebrating with her fellow soldiers now that AIT was officially over—when they were off-duty, of course. One by one, they each received their next orders to report to either their company barracks or somewhere else. Or in Idina's case, to report to their next round of training. Of all the new soldiers from Bravo Company's First Platoon, Idina was the only one who'd wanted to go off to jump school immediately and had gotten a slot.

"That's the way things work, Moorfield," Remmington told her during their next meeting. "You got lucky."

"Really." She tried to hide a smile as they sat at a table together in the front reception area of the barracks. "You're trying to tell me *luck* has anything to do with this?"

He chuckled. "For the most part, it doesn't. Sometimes, things fall into place the way you want them to. You'll figure it out when you get there. Jump school isn't only for privates fresh out of AIT."

"What do you mean?"

Remmington shuffled through the papers on his desk. "I mean anyone who wants their wings gets in when there's an open slot. So you'll be training with NCOs and officers. Probably not only with the Army either. Air Force. Marines. This isn't the beginning of the road anymore, Moorfield. It's a hub. And you got in."

He slid the stack of papers across the table toward her. "You're a Twelve Bravo now, Moorfield. You'll be leaving here any day now. Wish I could tell you there's something awesome for you to do with your time, but it's pretty much a shitshow while we all wait for the next best thing to come along."

She grabbed the paperwork and smirked. "Thank you very much, Staff Sergeant."

"Uh-huh. See you on the other side. Maybe."

Her orders to report to Fort Benning in Georgia came two days later. Then it was Idina's turn to pack her things and get ready for another super cheap flight from one base to the other, courtesy of the Army's not-so-deep pockets when it came to covering airfare. Her friends who hadn't left yet shouted and slapped her back when she headed out of the barracks with all her gear and personal belongings.

"Don't die, Moorfield."

"Don't fall, either. I heard that's bad for a paratrooper."

"Hey, don't worry." DeLafor punched her in the shoulder, inadvertently nicking the still-sore area. "We'll think about you every time we blow something up."

She gave him a crooked smile and shook her head. "If that's the only time you think about me, maybe you should forget me altogether."

That brought a round of laughter, and DeLafor shoved her farther down the hall. "Can't get *everything* we want, can we?"

Idina headed out of the barracks, excited about the new adventure ahead of her and already a little nostalgic.

That's crazy. Nostalgic about basic? Nope. I'm not losing my mind. I'm delusional.

When she stopped at the van where the civilian contractor waited to take her to the airport, she turned for a final look at her friends. DeLafor spread his arms like he was still daring her to do something about the way he reacted to anything. Hughs raised a hand in farewell, and McCoy flapped his arms like a bird before the others smacked his arms down and shoved him around.

Nope. Definitely won't miss the basic barracks. But I'll miss the idiots who lived there with me for the last five months. Kinda like better versions of my brothers.

She didn't see Amber or Timbers, but that was fine.

They have my number. I have theirs. Not like we're planning to call each other every week or anything.

"You ready?" the driver asked.

"Yeah. Thank you." Idina lugged her gear into the back of the van, then got into the back passenger seat and prepared to take off from the first place she'd considered home since leaving her family's estate back in New Hampshire.

All part of being in the Army, right? Home is wherever you get sent, and you make it work. That's exactly what I plan to do.

This next part of her journey as a soldier was nothing like her first as a recruit into basic training. She didn't expect it to be the same, but it was still weird to conduct herself in a much more relaxed manner now, even after the slack the drill sergeants had given the entire platoon after basic was over.

The NCOs who picked her up at the airport were friendly and talkative, joking around about how much she enjoyed basic and AIT.

"So what was your favorite part, Moorfield?" asked the sergeant behind the wheel.

Idina looked up at him in the rearview mirror and raised an eyebrow. "Probably the fact that I don't have to talk about it or think about it ever again."

That made them both laugh, and she smirked out the window as they headed quickly down the dark highway toward Fort Benning.

The guard operating the security gate onto the base looked like he'd been up for twenty-four hours straight with at least that many cups of coffee to keep him going. He checked the driver's ID, then peered into the back at Idina. "You got the black-tie service tonight, huh?"

She grinned at him. "I'm just lucky."

He *hissed* a sigh and backed away from the vehicle. "Yeah, and you're pushing your luck with that shit-eating grin."

"Whoa!" The other NCO in the passenger seat—she thought his name was VanDolf but couldn't see his nametag to double-check—twisted and widened his eyes at her. "Looks like *you're* off to a good start."

She shrugged. "So far so good."

Chuckling, the driver pulled through the security gate and onto the base. "Staff Sergeant Erikson's had a bug up his ass since the first day I met him. Pretty sure nobody hates gate duty as much as he does, and that's probably why they still send him out there once a week."

"Doesn't sound that much different than Leonard Wood," Idina muttered.

"Ha. Yeah. You're gonna *love* it here."

The NCOs shared a knowing glance and snickered.

Pretty much exactly the same thing the officers said when we drove onto Fort Leonard Wood for basic. There's no way whatever's waiting for me here is anywhere near as bad as that.

This time, the in-processing for Idina's spot in jump school took all of thirty minutes before someone showed her to the women's bay in the barracks. "Grab a bunk. Settle in. The barracks commissary opens at seven if you need anything."

"Thank you."

The woman nodded and left without another word.

Idina opened the bay doors and found only one other woman sprawled out on a bunk. The rest were empty.

"Hey." Idina lugged her gear inside and claimed a bunk that was respectfully far enough away from the other woman but wouldn't force them to yell at each other if they wanted to have a conversation.

Slowly, the young woman lowered the book she was reading into her lap and looked up at Idina without any expression whatsoever. "Damn. Here I thought I'd have the whole bay to myself."

"Sorry to ruin it for you." Idina got to work making her bunk with the provided bedclothes. "Moorfield."

"Crimshaw. Renee." She looked Idina up and down and brushed her incredibly short auburn bangs out of her face, tossing her short hair as if she'd only recently cut it and had forgotten it wasn't long anymore. "Where'd you come from?"

"Fort Leonard Wood."

"Doing what?"

"Uh..." Idina huffed out a laugh. "Basic training and AIT."

Crimshaw jerked her chin up. "What's your MOS?"

Idina smoothed her hands across the made bunk, then opened the trunk beneath and looked over her shoulder again. "So this is my first official interrogation, huh?"

The other woman shrugged. "We'll probably never see each other again after we get our wings. I've been here by myself for two days. I'm still not convinced I'm not hallucinating you."

"Ha. Twelve Bravo. You?"

"Sixty-Eight Whiskey. Combat Medic."

Idina sat back on her heels and looked the other woman over from head to toe. "No kidding."

"I don't really do jokes. So..." Crimshaw never finished the sentence but instead lifted her open book again and continued reading.

Wow. Okay. I get one roommate for the whole women's bay, and she doesn't do jokes. This'll be a fun three weeks.

When Idina finished unpacking her things and locking the rest of her gear in the provided lockers along the bay wall, she returned to her bunk and flopped down on it with a sigh. "You *are* here for jump school, right?"

"Yep," Crimshaw replied blandly.

"I thought they filled the spots."

"Yep."

"So…what? We're the only women for this cycle?"

Crimshaw lowered her book, narrowed her eyes, and leaned forward. "That's a stupid question."

Idina couldn't help but snort, but she quickly covered it up when she realized her new friend in the bay was completely serious. "Right. Okay. You mind telling me why?"

"I do mind. But you're obviously clueless, and that's more likely to get you or someone else killed while we're training. And jumping."

Idina blinked and glanced around the bay. *Yep. Still empty.* She puffed out a sigh. "Okay…"

"There aren't a whole lot of privates here," Crimshaw finally continued. "It's mostly NCOs and bigwigs."

She said bigwigs. Like, important military personnel. Okay.

"They all get their fun, private rooms in other barracks." The woman went right back to her book without another word.

Idina waited a moment longer to see if her fellow enlisted soldier felt like explaining any further, but that was a no. "Cool. Thanks for the explanation—"

"I don't recommend letting yourself go now that you've finished AIT."

"Um... I don't plan on—"

"Things are a lot more relaxed in general now, but that doesn't mean this won't be a life-or-death situation for all of us once we get to jump week. I don't plan to die anytime soon."

"Right." Feeling completely out of her element with this woman—and her element had been a women's bay that wasn't empty and a platoon she could joke around with—Idina wasn't quite sure how to react. So she went with the kind of humor she'd picked up in basic. "So you're a hypochondriac medic then, right?"

Crimshaw's eyes widened in surprise, and she stared at Idina as if she'd been insulted. "And you're an engineer. I can't say this was a great talk because it wasn't, so I'd like to get back to my reading."

She didn't give Idina any time to reply, which was probably for the best.

Okay, then. Crimshaw's the most literal person I've ever met, and she's focused on her goal. I guess I can scratch making friends with anyone in the bay off the list. At least she's dedicated to her job. Which is the same as mine for the next three weeks.

Trying not to laugh, Idina set her alarm for 05:30 and checked her emails one last time—because she couldn't think of anything else to do in an empty bay when the rest of the barracks were probably already asleep, if not close to it.

Then she set her phone on the small table beside her bunk and crawled under the sheets. *I guess getting close to anyone when she expects to see a lot of dead and wounded soldiers in the field has a lot to do with all those walls she put up.*

Or maybe she doesn't like people. Honestly, it could go either way.

She entertained herself with imagining what it would be like to train with someone as literal and standoffish as Private Renee Crimshaw and the rest of the soldiers and officers admitted to jump school.

CHAPTER SIX

The training cycle didn't officially start for another two days, so Idina had plenty of time to explore the barracks at Fort Benning and get a feel for where everything was. Of course, she had to report to the doctor on base for her Airborne physical.

Fortunately, that visit with the civilian doctor contracted to double-check military personnel were fit for jumping out of the sky was a lot more personable than Idina's other medical exams thus far. The doctor took her time—making sure Idina's ears popped, checking her bone density and the strength of her reflexes, and spending quite a bit of time examining Idina's eyesight and depth perception. Finally, Idina didn't feel like another military number in a long line of soon-to-be soldiers pumped through initial exams and reception.

In her mid-fifties with short-cropped red hair and freckles coating her face, Dr. Moultrie tried to hold a conversation with her current patient, which Idina appreciated especially. "How do you feel generally?"

"Pumped for Airborne school." Idina smirked. "A little nervous."

Dr. Moultrie looked briefly up from her clipboard with Idina's records on it and chuckled. "I might be worried if you weren't. I've heard there's nothing quite like jumping out of one of those giant planes. Most people who get this far love it. Some don't."

"I'm confident in my instructors' ability to teach me everything I need to know first."

"Ah. Spoken like a true soldier." The woman flipped through the papers in her clipboard again. "Are you currently on any medication?"

"No, ma'am."

"Have you ever *been* on any medication in the past that might have at one point in time hindered your ability to think clearly or function normally during everyday tasks?"

"Um..." Idina frowned and shook her head. "Not that I know of."

That's a flat-out lie. I mean, technically my old meds didn't make it hard for me to function. Only for my green light episodes to give me hallucinations and self-healing.

"Great." Dr. Moultrie set her clipboard down and rolled back on her wheeled stool, gesturing for Idina to hop out of the exam chair. "Everything looks good. You're medically clear to jump, PFC Moorfield."

"Excellent. Thank you." Idina knew this was the part where she was supposed to leave the exam room and continue with her regular perusal of the barracks before she was to report to PT early the next morning. But she couldn't bring herself to leave. Not quite yet.

This doctor's given me way more time than any of the others. Maybe she'll *give me a straight answer.*

Dr. Moultrie smiled warmly and leaned forward. "Do you have any questions for me, Private?"

"Yes. Only one." Idina rolled her shoulders back and cleared her throat. "Have you heard of a medication called Anagracin?"

"Hmm. No, it doesn't sound familiar. What is it?"

"Something I heard about before I enlisted. That brings up another question if you don't mind."

The woman glanced at her watch. "I'm not expecting anyone else right now. Go ahead."

"Okay." Idina swallowed thickly and drew a deep breath. *I'm entering seriously uncharted territory here, and I have to make it casual. Unrelated to me. Or she'll write everything down on my chart and take back my medical clearance to jump.* "I read this thing a while ago about medical doses of Atropa belladonna. Deadly nightshade."

Dr. Moultrie didn't say a word.

"Is there any medical relevance for prescribing something like that?"

"Prescribing deadly nightshade." The woman raised an eyebrow. "PFC Moorfield—"

"I'm asking for my brother, actually," Idina added quickly. "I know that's probably not the way an Airborne exam works, but I don't have any other access to doctors right now. I'm worried about him, Doctor.

"He mentioned wanting to try this new prescription Anagracin. Something about it being suggested to help treat his depression. But it's deadly nightshade, so obviously I'm a little concerned. I thought maybe if I spoke to another medical professional and got a second opinion *for* him, I might be able to help."

Frowning now, Dr. Moultrie glanced around the exam room and tilted her head. "Well, it has anesthetic properties, as well as causing severe drowsiness. Small doses can produce hallucinations. I'm not entirely sure *deadly nightshade* would be a particularly effective way to treat depression."

Produce hallucinations? Great. And I'm the one freak who gets hallucinations after *I stopped taking that crap.*

"You said this was experimental?"

"That's what he told me, yeah." Idina nodded, and the woman reached for a plain pad of paper on the small table beside her. "I guess this second opinion is a hard no, right?"

"That's my first instinct. Now you've got me curious, and I'd like to take a closer look at this Anagracin medication. How do you spell that?"

"A-N-A-G-R-A-C-I-N." Biting her lip, Idina watched her scribble the word on the paper, which at least was unattached to her medical chart as a soldier. *I wasn't trying to get it written down anywhere at all. I'm no closer to figuring out what the hell's going on with my green lights now.*

"Thank you." Dr. Moultrie set down her paper and pen. "I'm always intrigued by new medications on the market. Experimental or otherwise. There's a lot of good modern medicine provides these days, even when it seems counterintuitive."

She huffed out a disbelieving laugh. "Like deadly nightshade. If I were you, I'd tell your brother to do as much research as he possibly can before making his decision. If a medical doctor who's overseeing his care prescribes it, I'd say it's safe to trust."

"Right." Idina stood from the exam chair and stuck out her hand. "Thank you."

"Don't mention it. Sorry I couldn't be more helpful."

They shook, and Idina's gut turned on itself while she tried to smile as normally as possible. "I appreciate the fact that you didn't look at me like I was insane for bringing it up."

The woman smiled faintly at that, then showed Idina out of the exam room before returning to her work.

That was pointless. Now one more doctor is researching Anagracin without any clue what it's for. But two military doctors saying they'd never heard of it? I'm not so sure Dr. Kruchek or *my family were telling me the whole truth about that stuff. So I have to deal with this on my own and hope I don't start having visions of screaming castle warriors while I'm trying to get my wings.*

For the next two days, Idina opted to take her meals in the barracks' mess hall, watching the much smaller number of soldiers here at Benning than what she was used to at Fort Leonard Wood. She chatted with some of them during meals and learned that Fort Benning was a hub base for training infantry, Rangers, and Airborne soldiers all in one place. She found it amusing that she was sitting with new privates at or below her E3 paygrade who'd moved up in their careers as quickly as she had.

She didn't see any of the so-called "bigwigs" Crimshaw had mentioned.

Because they get their private rooms in the officer barracks while they're here, and what officer would want to sit for a meal in the mess hall with all their subordinates?

She tried everything she could think of to take her mind off the weird vision she'd had during the graduation ceremony and her attempts to figure out why she'd seen it in the first place. Morning PT was the best outlet, and for the next two days, she went out to the PT yard to lift weights or run at least twice more during the day.

Her dress blues and the castle tab pinned on the left breast remained neatly folded in her trunk in the women's bay. Idina had questions, sure. Still, there was no one around to answer them, and she had to focus on being ready for an entirely new round of training *without* having another serious episode.

The morning of her first day of jump school, she went out for PT yet again and found the yard a lot fuller than it had been previously. The Rangers taking up most of the equipment in the shipping container where the barracks kept the free weights laughed and joked around, spotting each other and offering tips.

Idina listened to them as she worked through her sit-ups and tried not to laugh. *They're getting it all wrong. And nobody's here to tell them. Except for an engineer who can see their mistakes lighting up right in front of her.*

She tried not to look inside the container or around the entrance where other soldiers were pulling out weights and benches. Her green lights kept flashing in her peripheral vision, and it grew too annoying for her to stay silent.

So she finished her set, pushed herself to her feet, and headed toward the equipment as though she meant to pull out a set of weights for herself.

An incredibly muscular Ranger three inches shorter than Idina and only a few years older stood beside his PT buddy, barking at him almost like a basic drill sergeant. *Probably as encouragement. Only he's encouraging the guy to pull every muscle in his back with that stance.*

She grabbed a kettlebell and paused. The guy deadlifting five hundred pounds settled the bar back into place and grunted at the effort.

"Yeah, dude. Fuck yeah!" The short Ranger clapped his buddy on the shoulder. "That's what I'm talking about."

His friend rolled his shoulders back and shook his head. "That's gonna hurt tomorrow."

Idina couldn't help herself. "It won't if you shift your weight onto your heels."

Both men turned to look at her. So did the other soldiers who *weren't* part of the buddy system with these Rangers, though she had a feeling they were all here together for the same training.

The short guy folded his arms and smirked at her. "You think you could do it better?"

"I know I can't deadlift five hundred, that's for sure." Idina pointed at the taller Ranger's feet where her green lights had been flashing nonstop for the last fifteen minutes. "But *you* won't be able to for much longer either if you don't fix your stance."

With the snort, the short guy slapped his buddy's arm. "You're good, man. I was watching you the whole time."

"Put at least sixty percent more weight on your heels

until you're up," Idina added. "Hinge forward at your hips the whole time. It'll keep you from landing in the med bay with shredded nerve endings and torn muscles. Which *will* happen if you keep going the way you're going."

"Oh, yeah?" With a crooked smile, the guy getting free advice from an eighteen-year-old combat engineer turned back toward the weight bar and removed the hundred and fifty pounds in combined weights from each side. They *clinked* heavily back onto the racks. Then he gestured toward the bar. "You think you can show me with two hundred?"

"Dude, trust me," the short guy muttered. "You're good."

"I wanna see her try. Sounds like good advice."

"Well shit." After looking Idina up and down again, the muscled-out Ranger snickered and headed for the weight bar. "Then at least take off another fifty. I'm not getting ripped a new asshole because this chick thought she could handle—"

"Leave it there." Idina put back the kettlebell she hadn't planned on using and headed toward them. "I'll show you what I'm talking about."

"Very funny."

"No, I'm serious. Spot me?"

The guy pointed at himself and laughed in disbelief. "You want *me* to spot you with…what? Deadlifting your entire weight including your boots?"

She flashed him a grin. "I'd ask your buddy, but then he won't be able to see what I'm talking about."

"Fuck *me*." The short guy shook his head and headed behind the bar to take his place as her spotter. He even grabbed the bar from its rack and dropped it on the ground with a *clang* so she wouldn't have to. "Looks like *someone's* overcompensating."

"For lifting injuries none of us can afford? Yeah. I'm overcompensating." Still grinning at the guy, Idina took her place in front of the bar and paused to look up at the tall Ranger she was teaching how to do PT correctly. "Back on your heels. It's a squat with added weight."

"He knows what a fucking squat is, smartass."

"Dude." The tall guy shook his head at his friend. "Let her try."

Awesome. One guy's pissed that a girl's trying to show them how to improve, and the other one pities me because he doesn't think I can handle this. What am I supposed to do? Let them hurt themselves until they can't walk? Pretty sure that's as important for a Ranger as it is for a light sapper.

Idina cleared her throat and went through the motions of deadlifting without actually touching the bar. "This is what you were doing. See your center of gravity? Too forward on the toes. Hips tilted too far back and up. You gotta go legs, abs, arms, in that order, on your way up."

"This is bullshit," the short guy muttered.

"Hey, man." Idina turned toward him and shrugged. "Opinions are like assholes, right?"

The tall Ranger and the other soldiers around the equipment laughed, which only made the guy who'd agreed to spot her scowl that much deeper. "Says the brand-new E1 who thinks she's hot shit."

She didn't bother to correct him about her rank or paygrade, neither of which had anything to do with not breaking one's back in a deadlift. Instead, she bent to grab the weight and started her demonstration. It helped that her green lights and the burning hot and cold of her strange ability kept her posture in line. Everywhere Idina needed a split-second adjustment with a particular muscle group, she felt it lighting up like someone was standing right there tapping her with a stick.

With a grunt of effort, she lifted all two hundred pounds of weights to her shoulders, squatted slightly again, and pushed it all straight up before *clinking* the entire bar back down on the rack.

Someone in the yard let out a low whistle.

Idina turned to face the tall guy she was trying to help and shrugged. "Like I said. Get your posture right, and I bet you could add another hundred pounds to what you were already doing. Maybe."

The short man who hadn't wanted anything to do with her now stared at her and looked a little scared.

"What's your name?" his buddy asked.

"Moorfield."

"Damn, Moorfield. Thanks for the advice." He offered his hand. "I'm Willis."

She shook his hand and nodded. "Have fun with the rest of PT."

Willis laughed, and Idina turned to head away from the shipping container toward the empty yard beyond.

That was a bunch of unnecessary flexing, I know. I was trying to help. Guess I'll spend the rest of PT running to keep everybody from staring at me some more.

As she jogged out to the open yard where she planned to do a few laps, she noticed a man standing outside the barracks doors. His pitch-black hair was the same color as his mustache, and he stared at Idina through narrowed eyes with his hands clasped behind his back. She couldn't clearly see his pins from so far away, but he was a high-ranking officer.

Oh, good. I caught someone else's attention. That wasn't the plan. I guess I'm here with officers and soldiers of all ranks for the next three weeks. Whoever he is, I hope he's not one of my new instructors.

CHAPTER SEVEN

After PT and a quick shower, Idina dressed in her OCPs and headed out to the yard to report for her first day of jump school. She'd received all the information she needed to prepare for the new cycle, and while it stated work started at 09:30, she made sure she was out in the yard twenty minutes early.

So had most of the other trainees.

Idina found her place among the soldiers and officers gathering to receive their first instructions for the day. Two of the Rangers she'd seen at PT that morning were there, but Willis and his short friend weren't among them. The different uniforms of other military personnel standing around her made the attendees of jump school look like a quickly assembled hodgepodge—Marines, Air Force, and Army soldiers from multiple different corps.

Crimshaw was already there, front and center. Of course. Then Idina recognized the man with the black mustache she'd seen watching her almost two hours ago.

She glanced at his uniform shirt and found the insignia

a lot easier to read now that only two other soldiers stood between them.

Holy shit. I'm in jump school with an Army major. No wonder they told us not to salute outside on the training grounds. We'd never get through the end of it with all these high-ranking officers.

Two other sergeants stalked toward them in the yard, both of them wearing black hats with their uniform instead of the standard-issue caps with their OCPs.

Yep. My instructors are still sergeants. This definitely isn't basic.

"Good morning," the closest sergeant said. His voice echoed across the yard as he clasped his hands behind his back. "Welcome to jump school. My name is Sergeant Airborne. You can call me Sergeant Airborne."

He gestured at the man standing beside him, who had one of the biggest noses Idina had ever seen. It looked like he'd broken and had it reset at least five times. "This is Sergeant Airborne. You can call him Sergeant Airborne."

No one laughed or made light of the strange way the instructors introduced themselves, and Sergeant Airborne seemed particularly satisfied by that.

We're gonna have a hell of a time telling them apart. I guess that's the point. They're here to train us and lead us out of the plane. In three weeks.

"We're your jumpmasters for the duration of this cycle," the sergeant continued. "So let's get—" He stopped immediately at the *clack* of boots hurrying across the yard toward them. With dark eyes, the sergeant stared at the final soldier jogging toward the trainees. "What's your name, soldier?"

"Private Second Class Greenburg, Sergeant," the young man replied.

"You're not getting off to a good start, Greenburg." Sergeant Airborne glanced calmly at his watch. "You're five minutes late."

The private looked incredibly confused and swallowed thickly.

"Training starts at oh-nine-thirty. Which means you get here at oh-nine-fifteen. The next time you're late will be the last time you report to the training yard for jump school. Understand?"

"Yes, Sergeant."

Sergeant Airborne studied the faces of the trainees and nodded. "Let's get you geared up."

There were no barked orders, no diligent marches, no falling into formation the way Idina had known during basic and to a lesser degree for the two months of AIT. Instead, the trainees followed both Sergeants Airborne across the training yard toward an open door at the back of the barracks.

They're not gonna yell at anyone here or make a bunch of their superiors march after them. It's like night and day here. And probably a lot easier to screw up.

The second jumpmaster disappeared through the open door, and Sergeant Airborne stood outside beside it. "Everyone gets a helmet and a harness. This is your training gear. You're responsible for the helmet and harness for the duration of this cycle and will return them upon graduating. In the condition in which we issued them to you."

The trainees lined up beside the barracks and the

open door, where Jumpmaster Airborne doled out gear one at a time through the opening. Sergeant Airborne watched the gear changing hands and didn't say a word. Idina noticed that he did nod at the Army major who was here to get his wings in the same cycle as newly minted privates.

This is so weird.

Idina received her helmet and training harness and immediately wrinkled her nose in disgust. Jumpmaster Airborne smirked and nodded for her to step aside so the next soldier in line could get theirs.

"Aw, come on…"

She turned to see Private Greenburg behind her, grimacing at his helmet. "Smells like someone shoved a bunch of used PT uniforms in here between cycles."

"I'm pretty sure we will too once we get to jump week," she replied, smelling the years' worth of stinky sweat wafting from her gear.

"Except I'll be taking multiple showers before we get that far. Can't expect the Army to pay for new helmets. Or a good wash."

"If it ain't broke, soldier, don't fix it." A tall airman clapped Greenburg's shoulder and chuckled. "That's the Army's motto, right?"

"Yeah…" Greenburg grimaced at the airman rejoining his buddies with their gear. Then he leaned toward Idina and muttered, "They think they're so much better than us."

"Maybe." She shrugged. "They had to come to an Army base to get their wings like the rest of us."

"And their helmets don't smell any better than ours." He nodded at her, his nostrils flaring at the stink of their gear.

"I guess you heard Sergeant Airborne calling me out. I'm Greenburg."

"Moorfield."

He looked her up and down and narrowed his eyes above a knowing smile. "You were at the weights for PT this morning, weren't you?"

"Oh, so you've heard about me."

Greenburg *hissed* a laugh. "Man, Hapton wouldn't shut up about you until I left. Like it somehow blew his mind a chick could—Uh...sorry."

"That a chick could deadlift two hundred pounds and have some good advice?" She laughed. "Maybe it's a good thing I didn't tell him I'm here for jump school. He might not be able to handle that either."

Shaking his head, Greenburg kept shooting her amused glances as the last trainees got their gear and gathered to wait for their next instructions.

"All right," Sergeant Airborne called. "Week one focuses on getting to know your gear inside and out. It'll be another extension of you, like everything else you carry and operate in the field.

"The goal is to have you clipping and unclipping in your sleep. Unclipping from your chute at the right time when you land can mean the difference between coming to ground smoothly or getting caught in obstacles. Trees, barbed wire, bodies of water. Sergeant Airborne here will give you a demonstration."

The other jumpmaster proceeded to do that by strapping on another worn, decades-old harness that had been used and reused through jump school by countless other trainees and Sergeants Airborne before him. The motion was swift and easy like he was putting on a jacket instead of life-saving gear for jumping out of military aircraft.

The clips fastened, the straps were pulled taut around his middle, and he shoved his helmet onto his head and nodded.

"Any questions?" Sergeant Airborne asked. "No? Then listen up. Your helmet, which will be *your* helmet for the duration of your training, has a number on it." He looked over the trainees and nodded at the Army major who'd been watching Idina that morning. "Major Hines. What's your number?"

Hines smirked, his mustache twitching, and glanced down at the front of his helmet. "One-oh-four."

"The first number on your helmet is your chalk. That's your platoon for Airborne school. The numbers after that tell you where you place in your chalk. Since Major Hines is number four, he's the fourth man from the front in Chalk One.

"When we get to jump week, and you line up in that C-130, you'll line up with your chalk. In order. I want Chalk One over here with me. Chalk Two with Sergeant Airborne."

The trainees looked down at their helmets to figure out where their assignments. Idina frowned at hers. *105. Awesome. I get to be behind a major for everything I do. Better make a good first impression.*

The Black Hats split between chalks to instruct their groups, and Sergeant Airborne kept going. "Your gear buddy is the person right beside you in your chalk. One-oh-one and one-oh-two. One-oh-three and one-oh-four.

You get the idea. Find your gear buddy, and we'll run through quickly and efficiently strapping on your harness."

"I'm one-oh-six," Greenburg muttered as he turned his helmet around to show Idina. "You?"

"One-oh-five."

"Well, that was convenient." He shot her a crooked smile. "You know what you're doing with that harness?"

"Not a clue." As they waited for the rest of Chalk One to pair up by numbers, Idina scanned the other trainees and found Private Crimshaw paired up with Major Hines. The sight almost made her burst out laughing before Sergeant Airborne continued his instructions.

"Your gear buddy is here with you to make sure you do this right. No twisted straps. Nothing caught on your uniform. Nothing broken, damaged, or defective. *Not* looking for those things is how people die jumping out of aircraft. Helping someone else look for red flags is the best way to get to know your gear as intimately as you need to know it to get your wings."

The man demonstrated putting on his harness, then told them to practice with their gear buddies and clear them at all the checkpoints. Idina and Greenburg worked quickly, watching each other strap on their gear and double-checking that they cinched everything tightly and correctly.

"Jesus." Greenburg reached down to readjust one of the bottom straps wrapped around his leg, trying to be inconspicuous about it and failing. He shook his leg to the side, pulled at the crotch of his uniform pants, and grimaced. "Do they have to be this tight?"

Idina snorted. "If they're not tight now, they'll be a hell of a lot tighter when your chute deploys."

"Aw, shit…" He hiked his pants down and the leg strap up, then tried to forget about the whole thing and patted down the front buckles of his harness instead.

"You forgot to double back that one." She pointed at the cinching strap on his leg. "That could come undone if you don't slip it back through the buckle."

"Huh." Greenburg did as she'd instructed, then looked her up and down. "You sure you haven't done this before?"

"I'm pretty sure they don't let anyone *try again* if they don't get their wings the first time. I've been rock-climbing."

"What?"

She glanced at the other trainees helping each other with their harnesses, then pulled on the chest strap of hers. "It's basically the same thing with chest and shoulder straps."

"What are you, Moorfield? A Swiss Army knife?"

"Maybe. Or maybe I've done a lot of rock-climbing."

Greenburg laughed and shook his head.

Sergeant Airborne walked up and down the rows of paired gear buddies in Chalk One, checking their execution of strapping on their harnesses and keeping everything flush and tight the way it was supposed to be.

I might be a Swiss Army knife if that's a real thing. Not lying about the rock-climbing, though. Who would've thought four years of boarding school at White Mountain would give me an advantage in jump school?

CHAPTER EIGHT

That first week consisted of essentially the same drills over and over. Putting on a harness. Taking it off. Checking it for defects. Ensuring everything worked exactly the way it was supposed to. Clipping in the parachute lines and unclipping from the anchors at the harness' hip-support straps. No one clipped into a parachute or practiced landing from a jump, but Idina knew that would all come later.

The stark contrast between jump school and basic training took a while to get used to. At first, Idina didn't exactly know what to do with herself during her free time now that the rules, regulations, and responsibilities were a lot laxer.

Everyone at Fort Benning was here to train as paid military personnel, both active and reserve duty. There were no drill sergeants or strict schedules other than reporting to the training yard at 09:15 hours, again at 12:30 hours after lunch, and being dismissed at 17:00 hours.

Finally, she got to experience the autonomy of being a soldier on base. The rules here were pretty simple. Trainees had to stay around the barracks during the week and had the weekends off to do whatever they wanted, provided they stayed away from alcohol and out of the woods around the base.

Other than that, it was entirely up to her where she wanted to eat her meals, how she wanted to spend her evenings after work, and who she spent her time with when she wasn't practicing harness safety with her chalk.

It was a lot easier to get to know the other jump school trainees going through this cycle with her than it had been to learn the names and faces of all the soldiers in her platoon during basic. Mostly because they could speak to each other and didn't have to stand at attention constantly. There were also fewer people in the program. Other than Greenburg the first day, no one stood out above the other trainees for screwing up like a basic recruit and getting everyone smoked for that mistake.

There were four Air Force airmen in her chalk, three other privates besides Greenburg and Crimshaw, Major Hines, and a first lieutenant who constantly looked pissed to be there. Idina tried to ask him once when they were released for lunch why he'd chosen jump school, and the guy tightly clenched his eyes shut before walking away from her and muttering, "I fucking hate this."

She didn't try to ask him again.

That weekend, feeling well-rested and looking forward to the second week of jump school—which would be a lot more exciting than week one as they built up their skills to jump week—Idina knew how she wanted to spend her first Saturday.

After morning PT, she showered and headed off base in her civilian clothes to the art supply store in Columbus. Paying for an Uber to drive her out there wasn't anything new. Meeting that Uber driver outside the base's security gates and paying for it with her new Navy Federal Credit Union account synced to her phone was.

This is how it's gonna be for me from now on, isn't it? Budgeting my hard-earned cash for Uber rides and art supplies instead of having access to the Moorfield family accounts for whatever I want as long as it doesn't go over my "allowance."

She smirked as she stared out the back window of the Uber and watched the trees and traffic pass her.

Allowance. I can't even call it that when I had a five thousand dollar monthly cap while I was at boarding school. Not like I spent it all then anyway. What the hell could I possibly buy out here that would come anywhere close to that?

The satisfaction of walking into the art supply store, choosing the art supplies she hadn't bothered to bring with her from home, and paying for it with the money she'd made herself—from Army basic training, of all things—was also new. When she made it back onto base with a plastic bag of supplies dangling from her hand, she was grinning.

Despite all the different companies represented by the soldiers in the training barracks—mostly infantry, Rangers, and Airborne—it was a lot quieter during the weekend with everyone off-duty for the next two days.

I didn't expect to be walking around the post with a bag of art supplies and looking for the perfect spot to work on a few sketches. Still, this is probably the best thing I could be doing with my time right now.

Idina scanned the area at the end of the training barracks—a large patch of grass beyond the asphalt with two trees and a picnic table—and headed that way. For a Saturday at the beginning of February, the weather was incredible.

I have enough time to start something before lunch. Maybe even finish it, if I'm not interrupted—

"Hey, Moorfield!"

She stopped, turned toward the barracks, and found Greenburg and his other Ranger buddies sitting in the recessed stairwell leading up to the second floor. She recognized the short, muscular Hapton right away, as well as his taller friend she'd tried to help with the weight-lifting pointers. "Hey, what's up?"

"Killing the time, man." Greenburg lifted a brown paper bag in his hand toward her in a toast. "Wanna join us?"

Idina snorted and shook her head. "I'm good."

The rules include no drinking. Of course, there's always somebody who doesn't care about the rules on their days off.

Hapton clicked his tongue and stood from where he'd been sitting on the top step before pulling out a pack of cigarettes from his back pocket and lighting one up right there.

"Shit." The tall guy who now knew how to deadlift correctly looked Idina up and down. "I'm getting cold just looking at you. You know it's February, right?"

"I'm from New England," she called. "This feels like October."

The Rangers chuckled, and Greenburg waved her forward again. "Come grab a beer, huh? It's on Hapton."

"The hell it is." Hapton jerked his cigarette out of his mouth and pointed at the case of beers sitting in doubled-up plastic bags between the other Rangers. "This isn't freebie day, asshole."

Greenburg took a long pull of whatever was in his brown-bag bottle, then nudged the tall guy sitting beside him. "You hear that, Rorden? There's a *freebie day*. Who fucking knew?"

"Give her a beer, man," Rorden said. "She knows shit."

"She said she's good." Hapton took another drag of his cigarette and stared at Idina. "Wouldn't wanna mess with her perfect form, right?"

Jeeze. This guy really doesn't like women who know their way around weight training.

"Yeah, there's that." Idina headed past the stairwell and called over her shoulder. "Wouldn't wanna be even more of a pain in your ass if someone found out you were giving beer to a minor."

The beefy Ranger choked on his cigarette smoke, then fell into a fit of coughing before swallowing it with a huge chug of beer.

"No shit," Greenburg shouted after her. "You're not twenty-one?"

"Nope. Guess I won't be joining you for a while." Idina smiled as the Rangers' lowered conversation echoed out of the stairwell after her.

"Then how old is she?"

"Dude, fuck if I know. I don't go around asking everyone's age."

"Y'all're a bunch of morons. You know that?"

"Yeah, like Hapton with his squats." A burst of laughter followed that.

"I'm not the one asking a fucking minor to drink our beer."

"Don't let all that shit bottle up for too long, man," Greenburg added. "She's in my chalk. Hey, how much would that suck if you see her again down the road and she's a damn staff sergeant while you're still stuck here with the rest of us?"

"I'd probably kill myself."

More laughter followed, and Idina ignored the banter and whatever grudge Hapton already had against her.

None of my problem if he can't handle women in the military. Or around the weights. There's always gonna be an asshole somewhere, right?

She sat at the picnic table, set down her bag of art supplies, and pulled out a fresh pad of sketch paper and the new, perfectly sharpened charcoal stylus holder she'd bought.

They can drink and make fun of each other all day if they want. Hell, they can make fun of me for being "the baby" in jump school. I have this. I can't believe I've gone over five months without drawing anything.

It took her a few minutes to figure out what she wanted to create and what exactly the subject would be. When it finally hit her, she grinned and got to work, moving the charcoal over the paper in brisk, crisp strokes to outline the shapes.

She hardly noticed when her green lights returned to illuminate areas of the sketchpad where it would be best to place her next line, or where she needed to shade more, or what was perfect and therefore didn't bring up any glowing green specks in her vision. When she was drawing, Idina wasn't separate from her ability—only from the dangerous consequences of letting it go unchecked into a full-blown episode. The worry and concern that arose whenever her abilities affected her daily life, especially in the Army, didn't fill her when she worked.

She'd wanted to become an artist, after all. Instead, she was Private First Class Moorfield, a third of the way through earning her jump wings.

Time flew past her in a blur. Idina hadn't considered how long she'd been sitting at the picnic table with her charcoal flying across the sketchpad until someone cleared their throat behind her.

"What—" She jerked her drawing hand away from the page and spun on the bench. "Jesus, Greenburg. Were you *trying* to sneak up on me?"

"Not really." He laughed and turned to survey the barracks. Right now, they were the only two people in view. "You were really focused, though, huh?"

"Yeah." Idina glanced at her watch and widened her eyes. "Wow. So focused that I completely missed lunch. That hasn't happened in a while."

"Can I see?"

"What?"

With a small, sheepish smile, Greenburg shrugged. "The drawing."

"Oh."

"I mean, I figured it's not supposed to be a hundred percent private if you're out here in the cold where anyone could see…"

She chuckled, set down her charcoal, and slid the sketchpad across the table. "Compared to where I'm from, this kind of weather registers as *slightly cool.*"

"New England, right?"

"Yep."

"I've spent a few summers there. But I'm from Colorado." Greenburg sat beside her in front of the sketchpad and studied her newest drawing. "Holy shit. That's… You just drew this *today*?"

Idina shrugged. "Like I said. I was focused."

"This is insane." He pulled the sketchpad closer and studied the detailed lines. "Okay, don't hate me for saying this, but that looks like Crimshaw."

"It is. Or at least it was inspired by her. Obviously, it's a little more cartoony than the real thing, but I was feeling satirical."

"Damn." Looking up at her again, Greenburg grinned. "You could do those portraits at, like, the fair or whatever. You know, the ones where the artist always blows up the person's face and makes 'em look real weird."

"Oh, thanks." She snorted. "That's exactly what I was going for. Making her look *real weird.*"

"Naw, this is way better than those. I'm serious. You even got her weird expression right." He pointed at the areas of the drawing Idina had whipped up of the only other female private in jump school and coincidentally in the women's bay with her. "I haven't seen her with any other look on her face all week, but somehow, she still looks pissed off all the time."

"Not as pissed as First Lieutenant McCabe, though."

They both laughed. "Yeah, I don't know what his deal is. Or why you drew *Crimshaw* instead of anyone else."

"Oh, yeah?" Idina folded her arms and gave him a crooked smile. "Who else should I have drawn?"

Greenburg cleared his throat. "You could draw me."

"Nope."

"Why not? You think my face would break your pencils?"

She sprayed the drawing with a fixative, collected her supplies to stick them back in their packaging, and paused to lift one toward him. "Charcoal. Not pencils."

"Same difference."

Pressing her lips together, Idina fought back another laugh and finished putting her supplies away.

I don't need to sit here correcting a Ranger's misconception of drawing mediums. He's weirdly interested.

As she closed the sketchbook and put everything away in her plastic bags, she felt Greenburg's gaze on her and fought back the urge to shove him off the picnic bench so he'd back up out of her personal space. Apparently, the guy wanted to keep the conversation going.

"You know a lot about art and stuff, don't you?"

Idina laughed. "And stuff, yeah. My brother Bryan used to say the same thing."

"Does he do drawings?" The question was completely genuine, but Idina almost burst out laughing in Greenburg's face at the mention of Bryan Moorfield doing anything remotely creative.

"Nope. He's neck-deep in the family business. Investment banking."

"Ugh." Greenburg wrinkled his nose. "Sounds boring as shit."

"That pretty much sums it up." As they sat at the picnic table under the two trees in the makeshift courtyard beside the barracks, Idina looked around for signs of anyone else. *So now we're sitting here alone, and there's an awkward silence, and I don't want to assume anything about why he's still sitting here...* "What happened to your Ranger buddies?" she finally asked.

He clicked his tongue and shrugged. "Fuck if I know. They got bored sitting on the stairs, and I got bored listening to them talk about absolutely nothing. Once you get past the fact that Hapton's a complete asshole, he's not a bad dude."

"Ha. I'll take your word for it. I'm guessing you all showed up here together already knowing each other."

"Yeah." Greenburg rubbed the back of his neck and studied the picnic table's peeling surface. "I'm the only one here for jump school."

"How did that happen?"

"Lucky break, I guess. What about you?"

Idina busied herself with tying the handles of her plastic shopping bags together in a loose knot. "Pretty much the same. One of my COs at basic recommended me for a slot, and it all kinda fell together at the right time."

His mouth popped open, and he stared at her with renewed interest and a little amusement. "You came from basic."

"Well, after AIT, but yeah."

"Shit. Okay, now I gotta ask. How old are you really?"

She met his gaze, fully expecting to be made fun of for her age despite most recruits in basic not being much older than nineteen or twenty. "I turned eighteen in Red Phase."

"No shit." He looked around the courtyard and gestured vaguely toward the barracks. "So you thought, 'Fuck it, I'll join the Army'?"

Idina barked out a laugh and shook her head. "Trust me. This wasn't my first choice. It wasn't at the bottom of my list either. So far, it's working out better than I expected."

"That's good. I think." Greenburg propped a forearm on the edge of the table and turned a little more to face her. "What was your first choice?"

She nodded toward the bag of her new supplies. "Art school. That was the plan, anyway."

"Pretty big leap from art school to Army."

"Yeah, you're telling *me*."

"So...what? You didn't make it in?"

Idina wrinkled her nose, gave him one more glance, then grabbed her supplies and stood from the picnic table. "I made it in. Ended up here instead."

Who knows whether or not my green lights and all the weird-ass visions would've shown up at Dartmouth like they showed up here. Greenburg's asking too many questions.

"Hey, whoa." He stood and moved to head after her but stopped himself. "Sorry, Moorfield. Didn't know you were so sensitive about it."

His observation wasn't intended with malice or to give her a hard time, and Idina sighed before turning around to face him. "No problem. Just trying to keep an old dream alive, I guess." She lifted the bag of art supplies and tilted her head. "Why are *you* here?"

Greenburg let out a self-conscious chuckle and sniffed. "I took a long, winding road that didn't look like it was going anywhere until I ended up here. Didn't hit college first either."

"Then I guess we're in the right place." She turned to head back to the barracks, and this time, her newest art admirer followed her.

"I'm serious, though. Your drawings are really good."

"Thanks."

"Hey, if I paid you for one, would you take a commission?"

That made Idina stop and stare at him. "Commissioned sketches?"

"Yeah."

"Maybe. Depends on what you want."

Greenburg glanced at the barracks and wiggled his head back and forth. "I gotta think on it. And you think on a fee."

"I'm not gonna charge you for—"

"The fuck you won't. That's what you'd be doing if you went to art school anyway, right?" He waved her off and headed toward the staircase to the barracks' second floor. "And you ended up *here* instead. Swiss fucking Army knife."

Idina smiled as she watched him walk up the stairs.

I guess there aren't a lot of artists in the Army. Or maybe there are, and they all keep it a secret because they don't want other soldiers commissioning custom sketches.

CHAPTER NINE

Two days later, Idina began her second week of jump school, which was worlds more exciting, amusing, and challenging than week one.

The trainees gathered in the yard at 09:10 hours to wait for the Black Hats to join them, everyone already strapped into their harnesses with their helmets tucked under their arms. Sergeant Airborne—whom Idina had discovered was Sergeant Birch—looked everyone over and might've nodded at Greenburg when he saw the soldier hadn't made the same mistake twice of showing up late to being early. "Now that you all know how to gear up properly and could do a gear check with your eyes closed, you get to learn how to use it. Let's go."

The trainees fell in line to briskly follow Sergeant Birch across the yard toward a separate outbuilding behind the training barracks. Sergeant Hutchinson—the other jump-master for this cycle—sidled up to one of the airmen from the Air Force for a muttered conversation when the man had questions.

With her stinky helmet nestled in the crook of one arm, Idina leaned toward Greenburg and muttered, "So how many times have you been through specialized training with other branches of the military?"

He shot her a surprised look. "Just now. Why?"

"I don't know. Part of me feels like I took someone else's spot."

Behind her, someone else cleared his throat. "If you made it into this rotation, Private, you're supposed to be here."

Idina looked over her shoulder and found Major Hines behind her. His dark eyes glittered in the morning light, and his black mustache twitched when he smiled.

"Thank you, sir." She nodded.

I should keep my mouth shut from here on out. This isn't basic with a bunch of new recruits together in the trenches. The officers are here too, and apparently, they're listening to everything.

"It's refreshing to see enlisted soldiers taking on jump school right away," Hines continued. "I've waited years for an opening to line up in my schedule."

"Then I guess we're supposed to be here at the same time."

The major raised his eyebrows and quickened his pace to step up alongside her. "That applies to pretty much every aspect of the job." He glanced at her last name on the right breast and rank insignia on the right arm of her OCP shirt and nodded. "Good to have you here, Private First Class Moorfield."

"Thank you, sir."

Sergeants Birch and Hutchinson stopped at an open-air building that looked more like a long shed with the walls and ceiling removed. All that remained in their place were thick metal poles supporting the frame, and where the ceiling would've been were metal beams spanning the length of the structure. From the beams hung rows of straps and cables.

"When you're in the air," Birch began, "it's not about cruising on the wind and letting your chute carry you wherever it damn well pleases. Whether during jump week or out in the field, you *will* come across obstacles before you hit the ground. When you have control of your parachute and the direction of your descent, you have an additional advantage over unknown variables. Trees. Power lines. Thermals at a thousand feet."

Sergeant Hutchinson snorted. "Those are fun."

"Slipping at any angle allows you to avoid those obstacles and extract yourself from them if you're one of the lucky few who jump right on top of all the fun. Sergeant Airborne will give you a demonstration. Then it's your turn to practice."

Wearing his harness, Hutchinson clipped himself into the lines simulating parachute risers. He grabbed a nylon strap from its anchor on his harness and tugged on it. "When we do this for real, these risers will be attached to your parachute. Pulling a slip allows you to maneuver in the air with some semblance of control. It's not great, but it's better than nothing." Then Hutchinson jammed on his helmet, fastened the strap beneath his chin, and nodded. "Okay!"

"Green light. Go!" Birch shouted.

With his grip on the risers, Hutchinson sat back in his harness and drew both bent knees up and off the ground.

"Slip right!" Birch shouted.

The other jumpmaster pulled the rear right riser, and both his harness and his body tilted slightly to the left.

Idina watched intently and narrowed her eyes. *If he were in the air, the chute would tug down to the right, and he'd be going right. Looks like he's rocking around for no reason up there, though.*

"Slip left!"

Hutchinson pulled the rear left riser and swung in the opposite direction.

"Hard right!"

This time, the jumpmaster dangling from the metal beams pulled both right risers and launched himself to the left again at an incredibly steep angle. Some of the trainees chuckled at his legs dangling at almost a forty-five-degree angle before he released the risers and swung back to center again.

"The front risers slow your momentum to allow for sharp turns," Birch added, turning to address the chalks. "If we had state-of-the-art gear, those turns would be a hell of a lot sharper than they are. Most of the time, you won't need to bank hard in either direction during a jump, but there will be a need for it. Pulling too hard on the front risers for too long—or both at the same time—will pitch you forward in your chute. That means you come in hot face-first, which nobody wants. Any questions?"

No one said a thing.

"Then line up for slips." Birch gestured toward all the risers and straps hanging from the beams. "Chalk One, line up in jump order the same way you found your gear buddies. Sergeant Airborne will help you tie in with the risers. Then you wait for the command."

The trainees lined up beside each other as instructed, already familiar with their jump order after practicing the lineup only a few times the week before. Idina tried not to stare at the soldiers strapping in across from her.

On her right, Greenburg leaned forward toward her shoulder and muttered, "At least we get to leave the ground today. Sort of."

"I wonder when we get to fall."

Major Hines on her left clicked his tongue but didn't say anything.

Was that in amusement or disapproval? Training with officers is way too weird. But it's not like making a few comments while standing in line counts as screwing up enough to get booted from the cycle. Right?

The trainees took to sitting back in their harnesses and slipping on command as quickly as anyone could expect from trained military personnel. True to form, Crimshaw didn't make a sound when Sergeant Birch ordered them to "jump." The woman was even smaller than Idina, her light weight barely rocking her at all when she lifted her legs and gripped the risers on either side of her harness.

Birch barked out the series of slip commands—left, right, hard right, hard left—mixing them up every time so there wasn't any kind of pattern. What Crimshaw hadn't expected was for the jumpmaster to call out in quick order multiple sharp turns where both risers of one side were involved. As the combat medic tried to carry out the commands successfully, the urgency and repetition got to her.

Idina watched it happen as if it were playing in slow motion. Birch shouted, "Hard right!" Crimshaw slipped hard right. "Hard left! Hard right!"

Everyone else responded well enough. Crimshaw's hand on the wrong front riser lit up in Idina's vision with a glittering green light because that was the mistake that needed to be corrected. Crimshaw wasn't fast enough, and she ended up pulling both front risers.

Idina grimaced and sucked in a sharp breath before the risers reacted to the other woman's hard pull.

Crimshaw grunted and jerked forward in her harness. If she'd been dropping from the sky with a real parachute, she very well could have pitched all the way forward to end up dangling upside-down. Instead, she dangled there at fifty degrees forward until the risers slipped from her gloved hands.

"That's what I'm talking about," Birch said as he headed toward her to help tilt her upright again. "Both rear risers won't get you anywhere at the same time. Both front risers will cut five seconds off your descent if you're not careful."

Crimshaw cursed under her breath. "I'd like to try again, Sergeant."

The Black Hats shared an amused glance, and Birch nodded. "Trust me. This isn't a one-and-done kinda deal. We're not done with slips."

The woman looked furious with herself as she readjusted the straps of her harness to get back into position.

Idina tried to meet her gaze and give the only other woman in jump school a reassuring smile, but Crimshaw wouldn't look at her.

If she's as literal about her training as she is about questions and no jokes in the bay, she's beating herself up right now. Which won't help when she's so pissed she can't concentrate the next time.

Major Hines took to the beams and the risers with ease, making the other trainees and even the Black Hats chuckle when he cursed at his first hard-right slip.

"Takes a little getting used to, Major," Hutchinson said as he helped the man down.

"You can say that again." But his face lit up with a new excitement Idina hadn't seen on him this far.

He loves this. Makes sense if he's waited this long to get a slot in jump school. Now I'm up.

As for Idina, she was completely consumed by the quick series of slip commands when they lifted their legs and drilled again. Sergeant Birch shouted directions, and she wanted to be perfectly sure that no one else saw her green lights flaring into action. They lit up in her vision one right after the other around one or two of the risers at a time—at the exact instant Sergeant Birch called the directions. Her hands worked even faster, releasing one riser, grabbing two, releasing and grabbing and jerking left and right.

"Good start, PFC Moorfield," he finally shouted as he walked toward her to take a closer look at her grip on the risers. "That was impressive. Kinda."

"Thank you, Sergeant." Slightly out of breath, Idina lowered her legs briefly to give her core muscles a quick break. "Not so bad after all."

He raised an eyebrow. "Your hands always do that?"

"What?" The rush of excitement that had fueled her through finally learning how to maneuver a simulated chute seeped out of her in an instant, only to be replaced by a tight knot in her gut as she wiped her gloves on her uniform pants. *There's no way anyone saw my green lights. No way. There wasn't any fog. I don't have a viable explanation for whatever the hell happens when other people see—*

"Move so quickly," Birch clarified. "If I didn't know better, I'd say you'd done this before."

"Oh." Idina huffed out a laugh—mostly of massive relief—and shifted in her harness. "Just good hand-eye coordination, Sergeant. No, I haven't done this before."

He looked her up and down with a small smile, then nodded at the other trainees. "We're going again."

Swallowing thickly, she lifted her legs with everyone else. Something happened to Greenburg's clipped-in lines that made him start wobbling and twisting before he made a sound halfway between a shriek and a croak. Soldiers burst out laughing as the Ranger dangled from his harness and had to try several times to get a good grip on the risers.

Birch called the slip directions over and over.

At least Greenburg didn't pull a hard stop and flip himself forward. Idina watched the Ranger who might have been her first friend at Fort Benning and couldn't help but laugh with the others.

"I said *left*, Private!" Birch shouted.

"Left, Sergeant Airborne! I know, I know. It's—" Greenburg made another weird sound when he yanked on the correct riser and jerked to the side.

Look at that. A Ranger who doesn't know left from right

when he's in the air.

Idina glanced at Major Hines on her other side and briefly caught his eye. The man was chuckling with the rest of the trainees. He nodded at her before focusing on his harness and straps.

Nod of approval? Or that we can laugh at Greenburg dangling like a piece of meat? Either way, it's not like I have to impress the major. Only the Black Hats, and I'm pretty sure that already happened. Maybe.

The slip drills they ran for the rest of the morning and that afternoon were more exhausting than Idina had expected. Even the hour-long break for lunch and all the time spent standing in line wasn't enough to make up for the physical effect of gripping and yanking on the risers as many times as they did. When 17:00 rolled around, and the Black Hats dismissed the chalks for the day, Idina's hands were stiff and sore and hardly responded to her intentions to move them.

"Damn." She stripped off her field gloves and slowly flexed her fingers. "That's gonna hurt tomorrow."

Greenburg chuckled as he walked past her. "You mean you aren't used to pulling your body weight by a few little straps over and over?"

She playfully rolled her eyes and tried clenching her fists again.

It's not like I'm not used to sharp pain by now. Something tells me this isn't even the worst of it coming up in the next two weeks.

CHAPTER TEN

Idina quickly grew accustomed to having free time at the end of the workday to do whatever she wanted. She would've sat to work on a few more sketches in the bay, but her hand shook merely trying to hold the charcoal stylus, and she gave up trying until whenever her hands got used to the abuse.

Fortunately, the next day of training didn't have much to do with using her hands at all. Only everything else.

When the chalks gathered in the yard before 09:15 hours, Sergeants Birch and Hutchinson were waiting for them. This time, they'd brought a three-foot platform with them that didn't have any stairs.

Huh. Idina tilted her head and studied what was nothing more than a wooden box. *Feels like we're going backward from ten feet to only three.*

"Today, we're focusing on Paratrooper Landing Form," Birch started. "You'll have this drilled into you by the end of the week because a correct PLF is what keeps you from breaking every bone in your body when you hit the ground. In a nutshell, you wanna land like a limp noodle."

Some of the trainees chuckled.

"Sergeant Airborne?" Birch gestured toward Hutchinson beside him, who slightly bent his legs and lifted both hands beside his shoulders like he was reaching for the risers on his chute. "Always be thinking about how you're going to land. That starts when you're still in the air. Which way are you going to roll?"

"On my left side, Sergeant Airborne," Hutchinson replied flatly.

"Once you decide on a direction and side of your body, slip in that direction with the riser against your chest. Lean into the slip. Your focus should be on rolling that way and relaxing every muscle. Legs, torso, arms. Everything. You want to make these five points of contact every time. With your arms up by your face to protect yourself."

Hutchinson hopped up onto the three-foot platform with a *thump*. With a nod from Birch, he jumped down and paused.

"Balls of your feet."

The other jumpmaster lowered into a slow, deliberately fake roll on the ground while Birch called every contact point.

"Calf. Thigh. Buttocks. And your pullup muscle right here." Birch reached across his chest to slap the muscle of his upper back beneath his opposite shoulder.

Hutchinson rolled halfway onto his back and stopped.

"The likelihood of injury is incredibly low when you hit all five points of contact. PLF done right."

The other jumpmaster slapped a hand against the shoulder strap of his harness before standing.

"After that, you pull your release rings. Doesn't matter if you think something's broken, if you don't quite feel your body yet, or if you can't see a damn thing around you. Always release your chute first. Otherwise, you'll be ending a jump from twelve hundred fifty feet with being dragged across the landing zone for dozens of yards and getting tangled up in the lines. I've seen it happen to Sergeant Airborne here a time or two."

Hutchinson folded his arms. "It sucks."

"Before anyone gets up on this platform, we're drilling how to fall. Limp noodles, trainees. That's what I want to see all over this yard."

Idina bit her lip to hold back a laugh when the chalks lined up with four feet between each soldier and practiced falling and rolling onto their sides like pillows tossed off a bed. Their area of the yard filled with grunts and groans, *thumps*, curses, and the occasional bit of advice given from either their gear buddy or one of the Black Hats.

Falling wasn't exactly in Idina's repertoire, but keeping her body loose and pliant was. *I can thank Master Rocha and his sparring forms for that.*

When the jumpmasters were satisfied, the chalks lined up again in jump order to climb up onto the three-foot platform and hop down again to execute their PLF. Half of the trainees took to it as naturally as Idina did, while the other half struggled with *not* landing on their feet. And the Black Hats had comments for every single one of them.

"You broke your knees, Lieutenant."

"You think you rolled your ankle *now*? Try breaking it

at a ninety-degree angle when you land like that on a live jump."

"Arms up by your head, Private. Yeah, I know it feels wrong, but you'll land a jump without a face at all if you don't figure out how to protect it."

By the time they broke for lunch, dust and dirt covered the trainees' uniforms, and grit rained down from their hair after rolling over and over again on the ground.

Idina brushed as much debris as she could from her hair as she headed toward the barracks. Her legs and hips were sore from the landing but not as painful as they would've been if she hadn't caught on to proper PLF as quickly as she had.

"Moorfield. Wait up." Greenburg jogged to catch up with her, and she slowed a little until he'd made it to her side. "Never thought I'd be drilling how to play dead out of the sky."

She laughed. "It's better than actually *being* dead."

"What? No way. Hey, where are you going for chow?"

"The dining facilities are open. I'm grabbing something there."

"Mind if I come with you?"

Idina glanced at him sidelong, leaned away a little, and couldn't help a small frown. "Are you gonna spend the whole hour asking me for tips about how to fall like a dead person?"

"Uh..." Greenburg rubbed the back of his neck and gazed all around the yard. "No. But you couldn't kick me out of the dining facility even if I said that's exactly what I planned to do."

"It's a free country, Greenburg."

"Ha. Yeah. Thanks to us."

She laughed and kept walking toward the barracks entrance.

Looks like I have a new Ranger friend. As long as he doesn't start asking all the wrong personal questions again, I guess I'll let him stick around.

After lunch, they spent another hour drilling PLF in another area of the yard with two more three-foot platforms set so the trainees could get enough practice without wasting too much time standing in line. Beside them was a bare-bones plywood structure with a curved arch cut into one side and a one foot drop from the platform behind the simulated "door" to the ground.

"We covered the basics of Paratrooper Landing Form. Now you need the basics of jumping out of an aircraft. Commands. Form. Handling your reserve."

"Speaking of reserves," Hutchinson added with a crooked smile. He stepped up beside Sergeant Birch and lifted both hands in front of him. "You'll receive those soon, but you're not touching any other gear until you know how to handle it properly.

"Your reserve is your backup lifeline if your chute malfunctions during a jump. Before you step onto that platform line and off the aircraft, your hands go to your reserve. Hold it like a hamburger. Fingers spread wide, and hands clamped around both sides."

He jerked his hands in toward his chest with about ten inches of space between them. "At your chest, 'cause if you're trying to eat the damn thing, you shouldn't be here."

Birch raised an eyebrow at his fellow jumpmaster and cleared his throat. Then he gestured at the wooden "plane."

"On the gravel pit is your C-130. When your jumpmaster gives you the green light, your only job is to jump. Correctly. Eighteen inches out. Six inches up. Feet together like you're jumping off a diving board and trying not to make a splash. Knees slightly bent, and your head tucked *down* toward the..." Pausing in his demonstration of proper jumping form, he turned to raise an eyebrow at Hutchinson. "...hamburger reserve."

The other Black Hat shrugged.

"Your chute has six seconds to deploy fully," Birch continued. "That's when you look up to make sure it did. If not, your reserve comes in pretty damn handy."

Without being told, Hutchinson headed toward the plywood cutout of an aircraft door and ducked beneath the supporting beam to step up inside. With his hands clamped around a nonexistent reserve parachute at his chest, he bent his knees and looked straight ahead through the curved opening.

"Green light, go!" Birch shouted.

The other Black Hat jumped and landed with both feet firmly planted in the gravel before hopping forward. "One thousand! Two thousand! Three thousand!" With each second he counted aloud, Hutchinson jumped forward again to clear the jump space behind him.

Idina looked around at the rest of her chalk. As she expected, a few other trainees tried not to smile at the sight of a decorated jumpmaster hopping around in the gravel.

Hold the reserve like a hamburger. Jump away from the plane like an elementary-school potato sack race. At least they're metaphors we won't forget.

"Six thousand!" Hutchinson looked up and slightly behind him, then stepped out of his bunny-hopping and returned to Sergeant Birch's side.

"We're running this 'til I see everybody executing the proper form and counting. Don't forget to check your chute. Or it could be the last thing you ever forget. Chalk One, line up behind the aircraft. You're jumping four at a time, two seconds between each jumper. I wanna hear everybody counting."

Chalk One lined up behind the prop aircraft, and the first four climbed inside. At Sergeant Birch's command, Stone leapt out first with his hands "hamburgered" in front of his chest and started hopping and counting.

It was hard not to laugh at two Marines, Crimshaw, and Major Hines bouncing around in the gravel like little kids and counting out their six seconds in terse shouts as they cleared the front of the simulated plane door. Still, no one did.

Because this teaches us how not to die once we're falling from over twelve hundred feet of elevation. I'm gonna have this image branded in my head for a long time.

Pretty soon, their section of the training yard filled with shouting voices of both Black Hats and trainees cycling between the PLF platforms and the jump door.

"PLF!"

"Green light, go!"

"Three thousand! Four thousand!"

"Riser to your chest, soldier!"

"I counted four points of contact, Private. Where's your fifth?"

"One thousand! Two thousand!"

"You dropped your reserve, Marine."

The shouting and jumping seemed to go on for an eternity before Sergeant Birch blew sharply on his whistle and nodded toward a different area of the yard. "All right, let's kick this up a notch."

He led the chalks to another station with a taller platform and a zipline.

We can't call this a formation anymore, can we? Nobody's standing at attention for drills. I guess it still counts as an orderly fashion if we're all lined up in our chalk's jump order.

"Since you've all gotten a handle on a three-foot jump, it's time to get your PLF down at six feet. Sergeant Airborne will clip you into the zipline. I want to see perfect form for every landing by the end of the day. You only have three more days this week to learn and integrate all the other skills and training needed for a successful jump. And nobody gets a do-over with unsuccessful jumps."

Some of the trainees chuckled at that, and Idina was surprised to see a smile flickering across Major Hines' face as well. Then she realized all the soldiers and airmen and the two Marines who'd found Birch's last comment amusing were NCOs or high-ranking officers who were also combat veterans.

Because military humor is a special brand, isn't it? Laughing in the face of death. It's better than the alternative.

Crimshaw, however, didn't look remotely amused by the macabre joke. The woman was scowling at anyone and everyone around her who'd chuckled or so much as smirked.

Of course, she doesn't think it's funny. Her MOS literally handles life and death.

When Sergeant Hutchinson finished positioning the wooden platform beneath the zipline and nodded, Birch scanned the faces of his trainees and cleared his throat. "Chalk One. Get up there. Chalk Two and Chalk Three, get in line."

Clipping their harnesses to the zipline with Sergeant Hutchinson's help was the fastest part of this new upgrade to their previous drill for the day. The young Marine private named Stone was the lucky one to boast the number 101 on his helmet. He was and would continue to be the first among them to do everything, including jumping through that door when the time came.

Idina didn't envy the guy's status as numero uno, but today, Stone didn't resent his randomly assigned number. The guy stepped up onto the platform with a huge grin, smacked his helmet, and nodded at Hutchinson.

"Jump."

Stone leapt forward off the platform, gaining almost a foot of air above the wooden surface before his harness caught him and he sailed across the zipline. The decline wasn't steep enough to make him pick up any real speed. The biggest surprise came when Sergeant Hutchinson revealed he'd been holding one of the zipline anchors through a rope ratchet attached to the pole where the zipline started.

Without warning, Hutchinson released his hold on the rope.

"PLF!" Birch shouted.

Stone grunted as he dropped just under six feet, trying to utilize their training from earlier in the day. He slapped a hand to his chest before hitting the ground, but only one of his arms came up beside his head to protect his face. And he was two seconds too slow in loosening his muscles so he could drop into a roll. Instead, he staggered sideways with one ankle buckling beneath him and crashed to his knees in the dirt.

"Good thing this isn't your last practice run, Private," Sergeant Birch called. "Riser to chest until the second your boots hit the ground. Then both arms up. Roll. Trust me, not trying to control it hurts a lot less. Next."

The next soldier in Chalk One gave Stone a questioning glance, and the Marine dusted himself off with a shrug before heading back to the end of the line. The entire time, he didn't stop grinning.

At least he's enjoying himself. I'd bet everything in my shiny new bank account I know exactly who's going to love this and who's gonna get pissed when they're not perfect on the first try.

Idina leaned slightly to the side to peer past Major Hines standing in front of her so she could get a good look at Crimshaw. The other woman stood stiffly at ease as the trainee in front of her got up onto the platform to clip into the zipline, and she barely moved.

Yep. I bet she hates how chill our training is now.

The soldier on the zipline dangled there for a moment longer, pretending to grab nonexistent risers while Sergeant Birch barked out directional slip orders.

"Crimshaw," Idina muttered.

Frowning, the young woman slowly turned to meet

Idina's gaze and stared at her as if she'd grown an extra head.

"Keep your elbows in." Idina lifted both arms beside her head to demonstrate. "You'll roll easier that way."

Crimshaw's eyes widened even farther. "Sergeant Airborne already gave us those instructions."

Wow. Probably should've realized she doesn't understand friendly reminders along with all the jokes she'll never get.

Idina shrugged. "I noticed you were doing that earlier. Thought it might be—"

"Whoa!" The soldier on the zipline dropped from where he'd been practice-slipping and forgot to do anything with his arms as he rolled. They got pinned to his sides, blocked from protecting his head. Fortunately, his issued training helmet was there to save him from what could've been a concussion when his head slammed against the ground after the rest of him.

A collective inhale of discomfort rose from the trainees before some of them shouted encouragement or jokes about the soldier's head or both.

"—helpful," Idina muttered, wincing a little as she watched the soldier on the ground clap a hand to his helmet and shake his head.

Crimshaw was the only trainee who hadn't immediately diverted her attention to watch the guy in front of her. She kept staring at Idina. "I suggest focusing on your form, PFC Moorfield. What *I* do with *my* elbows won't keep you from injuring yourself."

"Keep it moving," Birch called, but the woman was already walking briskly to the platform to climb up and clip herself in.

Idina exaggerated a long blink in the medic's direction and shook her head.

Why did I think she'd react differently to a quick suggestion than to anything else I've said to her in the last week? Can't help everyone, Moorfield. Deal with it.

Major Hines stepped sideways to look at Idina over his shoulder, and she immediately straightened, trying to look focused on the task at hand as she kept her gaze forward on Crimshaw jumping off the platform. The major raised an eyebrow. "Have any tips for the guy in front of you, PFC Moorfield?"

She blinked and met his gaze. "Sir?"

Hines tipped his head in what was probably his version of a shrug. "Not all of us have a problem with good advice. Assuming your observation of PLF is as accurate as your observation of improper deadlifting form."

An airy laugh escaped her. "Oh."

I knew he was watching me when I pissed off that Ranger during PT. Now he's bringing it up a week later?

Clearing her throat, Idina looked the major up and down. She'd only half-expected her green lights to flare up in her vision now that he'd asked her to offer her opinion, but that was exactly what happened.

The slightly off-center angle of his hips. The top of his left shoulder was slightly higher than his right. One of his feet rested half an inch in front of the other despite the fact that when viewed as a whole, the man seemed to be standing perfectly centered.

Each variable of the man's body composition and the barely visible strain on his right side glowed green one right after the other. It was over in two seconds, and Idina nodded. "Yes, sir. I would tell you to lean right and roll right every time you land. If possible."

"Really?" Hines' lips twitched, and he glanced down at his uniform. "What makes you say that?"

"An observation, sir. From where I'm standing, your right side looks more capable of relaxing enough to take the fall."

"Hmm. I've been trying to even that out for years. I take it you have some kind of background in medicine."

"No, sir." Swallowing, Idina clasped her hands behind her back and glanced at the zipline. "Finance."

Hutchinson released the rope, and Crimshaw dropped silently to the dirt with a *thump*. Her body leaned and rolled sideways. As Idina had tried to help her avoid, the woman's elbow sticking too far out away from her body *cracked* into the ground and ended Crimshaw's roll like a bully's foot stomping on a runaway kickball.

"Elbows in, Crimshaw," Birch shouted as the woman grimaced and pushed herself to her feet. "Tight at your ribs. Work on that, and you're golden."

Crimshaw nodded and stalked tensely across the dirt to take her place at the end of the line.

Not the place or the time for 'I told you so.' Or the person. If she didn't hate me already, she does now.

"Right side," Hines muttered as he stepped up to the platform to clip in.

Idina watched him intently.

An Army major asked me *for advice, and I told him I have experience in finance? What the hell's wrong with me?*

Greenburg muttered over her shoulder, "So, what? You wanted to be a *financial* artist?"

She jerked sideways and snorted. "You're an idiot."

"I'm just trying to figure it out, Moorfield. Which one is it?"

"None of your business." When he didn't say anything else, she playfully rolled her eyes and turned her head slightly over her shoulder to add, "Both."

Greenburg snickered and shook his head. "I have no fucking clue why you're here."

"Does it matter?"

"Nope. Which makes your whole Swiss Army knife thing that much weirder."

With her gaze still focused on Major Hines now dangling from the zipline, Idina shrugged. "Don't worry, Greenburg. I don't have any tips for *you*."

He laughed right as Major Hines dropped from the zipline and rolled onto his right side with a grunt of effort and surprise.

"That's it, Major," Birch shouted. "Now you get to do it fifty more times before dinner chow."

Hines chuckled as he stood and quickly dusted off his pants.

Idina headed for the platform for her turn to drop and roll from six feet instead of only three. She glanced at the major and found him already watching her on his way to the end of the line. A brief smile flashed across his face, and he raised his eyebrows at her before disappearing behind the rest of the line.

That looked like a thank you. Now I have a high-ranking officer watching me *because I couldn't keep my mouth shut.*

She leapt up onto the platform and clipped her harness into the zipline.

So if I have another episode or more visions or some stupid burst of glowing green fog at the wrong time, he'll be the first to see it. Not the kind of attention I was looking for when I joined the Army.

"Jump," Hutchinson told her.

Idina leapt up and forward off the platform and barely felt the jolt of her harness catching on the taut cable. She swung from side to side as she descended the gentle slope.

"Slip left!" Birch shouted.

Her left hand shot up to grasp the nonexistent risers and pull.

"Hard left!"

Miming the pull of both forward and rear risers, Idina glanced at the ground rising slowly to meet her as she zipped closer toward the end of the line.

Then she was weightless.

Her stomach lurched into her throat, and the rest of her body moved on autopilot—which was a setting she didn't know she had for dropping unexpectedly from three feet or six feet or any other height.

The searing, icy-hot tingle of her abilities raced down her right arm, which she clamped forcefully across her chest and harness straps. She hardly felt her boots touching the ground before she practically crumpled and rolled, both forearms braced around her lowered head and elbows tucked tightly against her ribs. The training helmet intensified the sound of her body toppling into the dirt and her heavy breathing as she rolled over and over. When she stopped, she still couldn't feel much of anything at all.

She couldn't hear anything, either.

Shit. I did something wrong. Why can't I feel my—

"Moorfield," Birch shouted. "If your PLF looks like that every time you jump, there's no way in hell you have a reason to be lying there for so long. On your feet."

Idina opened her eyes and pushed herself to her feet, realizing that every part of her body did in fact work exactly the way it was supposed to. The freezing tingle in her limbs returned then instantly faded again, replaced by the slightly throbbing pressure at various points in her arms, legs, and right shoulder.

She looked at Birch and found the jumpmaster flashing her a quick smile and a nod before he called up the next trainee.

Okay. So I either completely lost my cool... Or my green lights turned into a giant numbing agent so I wouldn't brace against my fall? Jesus, I even sound *insane just thinking this.*

Several other trainees standing in line nodded at her or smiled or muttered, "Way to fall," as she passed.

When she made it to the end of the line, Major Hines looked at her over his shoulder again, his black mustache twitching as he tried to hold back a laugh. "Did you say *finance?*"

Idina brushed dirt and loose strands of winter-dried grass off her uniform and nodded. "Yes, sir, I did."

"Very funny." The man faced forward again and folded his arms to watch the next soldier hopping up to practice stop, drop out of the sky, and roll.

He doesn't believe me. Because that's not the kind of Moorfield I am. Whatever that is when I can see the way things work and heal myself from cuts but not a blood castle scar. Nobody would believe that shit either.

CHAPTER ELEVEN

By the time 17:00 rolled around and they were dismissed from training, Idina felt like she had when she'd first started training with Master Rocha when she was eight. Her limbs were stiff from tucking and dropping and rolling, her body bruised from so many unexpected falls.

I've only been out of basic for ten weeks. There's no way I softened up this *much since then.*

She wasn't the only trainee who was feeling the PLF drills, though. Even Major Hines rubbed his shoulder as he headed toward the officer barracks.

"Aw, shit." Greenburg staggered toward her, rubbing the back of his neck and rolling it from side to side. "Nobody mentioned three weeks of being a punching bag for the damn ground."

Idina laced her fingers behind her back and pulled to stretch out her shoulders. "It beats not knowing how to jump when we get to next week."

"Don't remind me."

They headed toward the training barracks, and Idina

glanced at him sidelong. "Any idea what The Swing is supposed to be?"

Greenburg snorted. "They're not taking us out to the playground tomorrow. I can tell you that."

"Aw..." She clicked her tongue and exaggerated a grimace. "Bummer."

"Whatever it is, Sergeant Birch and Sergeant Hutchinson looked like a couple of mad scientists when they said that was next."

Stone appeared on the other side of Greenburg and clapped the guy's shoulder. "Don't hurt yourself thinking too hard, Greenburg. Use your imagination."

"Huh?"

"Come on. We're at an Army base. You guys have something here called The Swing. What else could it be?"

Greenburg shrugged from under the guy's hand with a confused frown. "You lost me."

Another Marine in their training cycle snickered as he caught up to them and spread his arms. "Sex swing, soldier. What, they didn't break you in with that thing when you got here? You *are* in the Army, right?"

The Marines snickered, and Greenburg shoved Stone away from him with a crooked smile. "Yeah, Jennings. That's all we do here."

"I *knew* it."

Idina smirked, familiar by now with the crude humor between enlisted personnel and the occasional officer. *I'm going through jump school with a bunch of thirteen-year-old boys trained and cleared to carry automatic weapons. Fun.*

"So get excited, Greenburg." Jennings shot him the guns

with both hands and winked. "I bet you can show the rest of us how we do it, right?"

"Stone's the one who gets to break it in first for the rest of us." Idina fought to keep a straight face as she shrugged. "I bet he'll have a shitload of great tips for you afterward."

All three men paused and turned to look at her, then Jennings burst out laughing. "Damn, Stone. She got you there."

Stone blinked in dumbstruck surprise. "Well, fuck *me*, right?"

Idina shrugged. "Hey, man. Whatever you do on your time is none of my business."

"Don't bring it to The Swing." Greenburg smirked.

The Marines snickered and flipped them both off before stalking away toward whatever they'd be doing for their off-duty hours.

"Marines." Greenburg watched them leave and belatedly raised a middle finger in the direction of their backs. "They're almost as bad as the Air Force."

"Right. Because the Army's the only branch that doesn't have any self-esteem issues."

"Whoa. I wouldn't have pegged you for a shit-talker, Moorfield."

"Oh, yeah? Was it the lipstick and heels that threw you off?"

He broke into a wide grin and shook his head. "I can't figure you out."

"Well, the shit-talking comes from having three brothers." She scrunched up her nose and looked across the yard. "Probably."

"And the rest?"

"Come on, Greenburg. You think I'm gonna tell you my whole life's story because you complimented me?"

"Huh." The guy couldn't settle on an appropriate response. His face kept morphing in and out between a goofy grin and embarrassed confusion. "You're welcome?"

"Yeah, okay." Idina continued walking across the yard, the growling of her stomach masked by all the other conversations of off-duty personnel leaving the training yard.

"Okay, hold on." Greenburg jogged to catch up with her again. "You're not offended, right?"

"By what?"

"I don't know. For some people, it doesn't take a whole hell of a lot. I mean, I'm not saying you're like everybody else. Obviously. You just have this...weird *thing* going on, and I don't really know how to handle it."

Idina stopped dead in her tracks and turned toward him with wide eyes. That was all he needed to stop smiling, and now the guy looked like he'd gotten something stuck in his throat. "Weird thing?"

He took a step back and blinked quickly. "What?"

"You said I have a weird thing going on."

"I did?" Greenburg let out a nervous chuckle and glanced around the yard. "Not *weird*-weird."

He doesn't know anything about me or what I can do. Green lights or otherwise. That's not what he's talking about. Now I'm making him even more curious. So fix it, Moorfield.

"What does that even mean?" She tried to lighten the mood with another laugh that sounded strangled.

He gaped at her, his gaze darting all over the place, and shrugged. "Uh...you burned a bunch of Marines at jump school, impressed Major Hines with personalized PLF tips, and started our first week by basically telling Hapton he has no idea what he's doing with the PT weights. Plus, you're *here* instead of at...finance-art school where you really wanted to be."

Idina lifted a finger to stop him. "You're kinda mixing up the—"

"You seem totally cool with it. Maybe even happy. Not like First Lieutenant Fuck It over there." Greenburg gestured at McCabe, who happened to be walking past them.

McCabe looked up at them, realized they were using him as an example, and groaned. "You gotta be fucking kidding me." Then he stalked across the yard as if he'd received orders to scrub the barracks toilets with a toothbrush.

Idina and Greenburg stared mutely at the officer. Then she hummed in disagreement. "I'm pretty sure everyone on this base is happier to be here than him."

"Fair point." He rubbed the sore spot on the back of his neck again and sighed. "All I'm saying is you're...different. As a soldier. Obviously."

She nodded and pressed her lips together so she wouldn't laugh in his face. *I could've told him* that. *At least he's not trying to say I'm different than other women in the military, or I'd think he's trying to hit on me.*

"We're all in the same boat, Greenburg," she told him. "We're all here."

"Uh-huh. Which only makes it stand out when somebody like you shows up as a Private First Class getting her jump wings."

Oh, good. Somebody else telling me I've got too much potential to start from the bottom and work up.

"Honestly?" Idina dropped her gaze to the asphalt as they approached the barracks' back doors. "I was kind of on a time crunch."

"To drag yourself through basic and kick off your career with a bunch of idiots?"

"Ha." She opened the door and paused. "Something like that. I'm gonna hit the showers now, so..."

"Yeah. Yep." Greenburg punched his opposite hand and sucked on his bottom lip, looking like he'd just now realized they were standing behind the barracks with the door open in her hand. "Cool."

Idina watched him with an amused frown, waiting for him to spit out whatever he wanted to get off his chest.

I can't stand here forever and make this any less *awkward.*

"Greenburg."

"Yeah."

"Just say it."

"Nah, it's all good." He waved off her invitation to say his piece and punched his hand again. "Hey, you're not still going to the dining facility for chow, right?"

"The food's decent."

"Yeah, sure. But it's, like, not really—"

"Greenburg!"

They both turned to see the group of his Ranger buddies heading across the yard, all of them already changed into civilian clothing to head off base for the night.

Rorden spread his arms. "You comin' or what?"

Greenburg snorted. "You think I'd let you idiots leave without me?"

"Don't see you trying to stop us."

"Well, fucking wait." He flashed Idina a self-conscious smile and walked backward away from the door. "I gotta go. Someone's gotta make sure they don't tear this town apart. See you tomorrow."

"Yep."

Then he turned and jogged toward his friends, spreading his arms and muttering something she couldn't hear.

Whatever it was, Hapton didn't seem all that excited about hearing it. He shot Greenburg a dirty look, then fixed his gaze intently on Idina and glared at her.

He's still holding a grudge, huh? For no reason other than I kept his buddy from ripping open his back. And for not having a Y chromosome. All types in the Army, right?

It probably would've made things easier if she'd ignored the muscular Ranger's glare and pretended he didn't exist. But she couldn't help herself.

Plastering a massive, cheesy grin onto her face, she jerked her chin up at Hapton and thrust a fist in the air. He wrinkled his nose like she'd done something vulgar enough to offend another soldier, then quickly returned his attention to his buddies turning back toward their side of the training barracks so Greenburg could change out of his uniform.

He can hold a stupid grudge all he wants. Doesn't mean I can't enjoy screwing with him.

Chuckling, Idina stepped inside and let the heavy metal door swing shut behind her as she headed for the showers.

CHAPTER TWELVE

Greenburg didn't bring up their conversation about Idina "being different" after that, and she didn't mention him being strangely awkward at the barracks door, either. Mostly, that was because they didn't have the time.

Now that they'd reached the middle of their second week of jump school, the training intensified drastically. So did the expectation that every trainee in this cycle could handle the abuse of what both jumpmasters so fondly called The Swing.

Sergeant Birch stood at the base of a fifteen-foot wooden structure and spread his arms.

"Welcome to The Swing." His lips flickered in and out of a smile as he folded his arms and studied the trainees' faces. "This is where it gets real fun."

Idina looked up at the platform on the top of the tower, where the multiple attached cables looked like they only stretched about halfway between the platform and the ground. *It's just cables without anyone strapped into it.* We're *supposed to be the swing.*

"We're simulating the last few seconds of your jump." Birch gestured toward the tower. "You can see the ground below. You know it's coming. But those last few seconds are impossible to predict. Barring any malfunction with your chute, the need to deploy your reserve, or avoiding any other airborne obstacles, those last few seconds are the most vital. So you better make sure you get your PLF right before you leave the ground next week."

That was all the explanation he gave them before Hutchinson called Chalk One up to the platform while the others waited in line—which also gave them a perfect view of the painful hilarity that ensued until it was their turn to try it out for themselves.

Idina had barely finished climbing the stairs to the tower's top platform when she heard Sergeant Birch shout from the ground, "Green light, go!"

As the first trainee to hit every drill, Stone sprang from the edge in perfect form. The cables *clinked* and *twanged* as they drew taut, quickly followed by groaning as they swayed between their anchors in the wooden ceiling that covered the tower and the wood chips lining the ground in front of it.

Stone whooped as he swung far forward. His back-swing nearly sent him beneath the top of the platform before he swooped forward again.

Idina looked up to see Sergeant Hutchinson standing at the platform's edge in front of the next trainees in line. Before the green lights flashed in her vision and lit up his hand and the series of connected wires and pulleys leading to the cables swinging Stone back and forth, she knew what it was all for.

Okay, now I get it. They should call this The Broken Swing.

Some of the trainees on the ground chuckled or pointed at Stone as he kept his hands firmly clamped around the cables simulating his chute risers.

He grinned back at them. "You know what? I think I kinda like it up—"

Hutchinson tugged on the handle connected to The Swing's mechanism, releasing Stone from the cables in the middle of his forward swing. The Marine let out half a shout in surprise before his ass hit the wood chips and he skidded slightly forward across them.

The trainees watching from the ground backed up and couldn't contain their laughter after that.

"Somebody wasn't paying attention." Birch folded his arms. "On your feet, Marine. Unless you're a fan of getting dropped on by another two hundred pounds of trainee."

With a groan, Stone pushed himself to his feet and scrambled out of the way as Hutchinson finished drawing back The Swing's cables to hook up the next trainee in line.

"Five points of contact," Birch reiterated. "Balls of your feet. Calf. Thigh. Buttocks. Pullup muscle."

"Hey, you hear that?" someone called from the line of Chalk Two. "You hit one out of five."

"Any idea which one it was?"

The trainees laughed and clapped Stone on the back as he passed them with gritted teeth.

Idina smirked and continued studying the mechanism Hutchinson used to drop trainees whenever he damn well pleased.

"*Oh*, yeah," Greenburg muttered behind her. "He has a real handle on the Army Swing, all right."

She snorted and focused on the second man in her chalk clipping in with Sergeant Hutchinson's help.

That's how we get this drilled into our heads, right? No pain, no gain. If we're surprised by how much it hurts after falling twelve hundred feet from a C-130, we're doing something wrong here.

Her green lights flashed, and her body surged with the icy-hot tingle of her ability highlighting which parts of her body to use, but there wasn't a weird genetic add-on ability to cover the element of surprise. That day reminded Idina all over again how important muscle memory and rote learning were when it came to new physical skills. The training she'd had with Master Rocha most of her life had come in particularly handy in basic, but jump school was the only thing that could prepare a person for jump school.

Soldiers, Airmen, and Marines dropped out of The Swing at Hutchinson's mercy, and none of them were particularly graceful with their landing that day.

One guy from Chalk Two ended up with a mouthful of wood chips when he smacked the ground face-first. Another dropped and started to roll in one direction before his body betrayed him and sent him sprawling onto his back. Idina wasn't an exception, but every time she launched herself off that platform and was released with no warning, she came closer to nailing a correct PLF.

They all did. Which was the point of spending an entire day getting battered, bruised, and jolted.

The chalks split up to drill other aspects of their prep

for jump week, now only five days away. While Sergeant Hutchinson yanked the release cord on unsuspecting trainees dangling from The Swing's cables, Sergeant Birch instructed the others on the prep commands for their first jump and every jump after that.

They went over the proper positioning for sitting and standing in the aircraft and how to correctly clip their parachute's static line to the line cable. That included how clipping in or turning the wrong way when they jumped could end up ripping their arms or heads from their bodies before they'd even left the plane.

Birch also handed out their reserve parachutes. They were as stained and worn as the training harnesses and helmets and became mandatory gear to carry while actively working and in uniform. Idina and her fellow trainees now had another thing to pay attention to while gleaning all the knowledge, wisdom, and safety techniques they could from the jumpmasters.

The importance of being aware of everything around them at all times and where their gear sat relative to everything else got a perfect demonstration at the end of the day when Birch dismissed them at 17:00 on the dot.

"Get ready to do it again tomorrow, people," he called after them. "And again on Friday, if we have to."

A group of guys from Chalk Three laughed and joked around as they headed across the yard toward the barracks. Idina sighed and looked down at the bulky covering of her reserve chute strapped to the front of her harness.

"It's a good look for you, Moorfield."

She smirked at Greenburg and thumped her reserve. "You too. Goes with your eyes."

"Really? I was thinking more like it matched the bruises in my soul after today. Hey, Stone!"

The Marine had been heading toward the laughing group of soldiers in Chalk Three but now turned to walk backward and jerked his chin up at Greenburg. "What do you want, dipshit?"

"I can't figure it out. Did you nail that swing, or did it nail you?"

With a laugh, Stone flipped him the bird and turned to hurry toward the rest of his buddies. He didn't see the overhanging tree branch at the edge of the yard, right at chest level. Nor did he see Lieutenant McCabe walking in front of him until it was too late.

The tree branch snagged through the emergency pull on Stone's newly assigned reserve chute. The jerk of the reserve deploying made him stumble backward before the entire chute puffed out in front of him with an airy *thump*. Right into McCabe's back.

The first lieutenant staggered forward, then spun and slapped furiously at the billowing parachute fluttering in the breeze. "Goddamn shit motherfucking ass with your fucking shit!"

Soldiers burst out laughing all around them, and Stone stepped back with wide eyes, trying to gather up his chute as McCabe delivered the longest sentence anyone had heard from him since training began. "Sorry, sir. My bad."

McCabe grimaced as his face darkened to a boiling red and clenched his fists. With a growl, he turned and stalked back toward the barracks, his head tilted back so he could glare at the darkening sky.

"Always aware, Private Stone," Birch called amid the

laughter. "That reserve's your lifeline. Can't just give it up to every tree and first lieutenant you see."

Stone wrinkled his nose and tried to bunch the reserve chute back into its deployment bag before Hutchinson finally approached to help him repack it correctly.

Greenburg's hands rose slowly to either side of his reserve strapped to his chest, and he gripped it like a little kid afraid of the school bully snatching away his lunchbox.

Idina laughed. "You think he blames *you* for that?"

"Definitely. Never turn your back on a Marine, Moorfield. Look at him."

She gazed across the yard to see Stone's reserve chute packed away again. Glaring at them, he pointed at his eyes with two fingers, then pointed right at Greenburg.

"See?" Greenburg snorted and turned to head across the yard.

Idina followed him, unable to keep down another laugh. "So you're turning your back on a Marine."

"I didn't mean literally. Just that you can't let your guard down. Now I'm prepared."

Jokes and more jokes. Nobody's pulling a chute on purpose. I'm pretty sure that falls under things not *to do if you wanna make it to jump week.*

The next day, they drilled PLFs on The Swing over and over until Idina wondered how she was still standing. Still, the proper technique was finally starting to sink in. Even the soldier who'd consistently and unintentionally landed squarely on both feet over and over—to laughter from the other trainees and exasperated eye-rolls from Sergeant Birch—figured out how to drop and roll with five points of contact. Idina was sure she could execute PLF in her sleep, which was what the jumpmasters were going for.

She wasn't anywhere near as exhausted at the end of an eight-hour workday as she'd been during basic training, but the bruises were a lot more frequent.

When Friday morning—the last day of week two—arrived, she hit her morning PT with a renewed energy she hadn't expected. Hapton was out there in the shipping container with the weight equipment and wouldn't stop scowling at her as she approached.

Screw that. It's not like we're in a bodybuilding competition. I'll skip the weights.

So she settled for warming up with sit-ups, pushups, and crunches instead, leaving plenty of space between her and Crimshaw, whom she hadn't seen touch the weights since the beginning of their training.

Maybe Crimshaw has the right idea. Especially when that Ranger's playing King of the PT Mountain.

Idina finished her final set and sat up, puffing out a quick breath as she draped her forearms over her knees. "Crimshaw."

The other woman was already standing again with one foot pulled up behind her for a quad stretch. She met Idina's gaze with wide eyes and didn't say a word before grabbing her other foot to stretch that side too.

"You going for a run this morning?"

Crimshaw blinked. "Why wouldn't I?"

"No reason. I was thinking about doing a few laps this

morning instead of weights. So if you want a running buddy—"

"I don't care what you do for PT, Moorfield." The woman jogged in place, looking straight ahead, then took off across the yard at a steady pace to begin her usual route.

Idina laughed and jumped to her feet before calling after the medic, "Good talk!"

Fine. Private Literal doesn't want *a running buddy. If she cared, she would've said that instead.*

So she jogged after the petite combat medic joining her in jump school and quickly caught up to the woman. They ran in silence together, Idina sticking close to Crimshaw's side and taking the other woman's non-verbal cues as to where exactly her running route led.

This isn't bad either. Running's good for endurance. I don't care if Crimshaw doesn't want to say a damn word while we—

"He's a prick."

Idina almost laughed at the words so unexpectedly leaving the mouth of her running partner. Trying to keep a straight face as her breath moved to the rhythm of their footsteps, she asked, "Who?"

"Greenburg's Ranger buddy. The beefcake." Crimshaw didn't look anywhere but straight ahead at the rest of her regular morning PT route, her expression unchanged from its constant blankness.

"Yeah." Idina wiped a sheen of sweat off her forehead and nodded. "I figured that out a while ago."

"If we were anywhere else *not* two-thirds of the way through jump school, I'd tell you to kick his ass."

"Whoa. Slow down, there, Crimshaw…"

The medic did exactly that, and Idina noticed her mistake in using a well-known figure of speech with someone so incredibly literal. She jogged right past Crimshaw, paused, then doubled back.

"I didn't mean literally," she said with a crooked smile.

Crimshaw jogged in place, then sped up again at her normal speed. "Then what did you mean?"

"It was supposed to be a joke, which I know you're not into. Sorry. Force of habit."

"I don't see how that's supposed to be funny."

Idina cleared her throat as they turned at the edge of the yard to run around the far perimeter. "I'm surprised you'd suggest something like that. If we were anywhere else and *not* in jump school, of course."

"Anything could get us kicked out if we're not careful," Crimshaw replied flatly. "Honestly, the same should apply to over-pumped, brooding misogynists who can't get over women in the Army or any branch of the military."

"Can't argue with you there." Idina glanced at the shipping container where the Rangers—including Hapton—were still pumping iron as they did every morning. "Has he been giving *you* a hard time?"

"It's not hard for me. More than anything else, it's distracting him from *his* work, not to mention everyone else around him who apparently can't gather enough courage to tell him off about it." Crimshaw looked at the shipping container too, then glanced at Idina. "I wanted you to know I don't appreciate his attempts to intimidate you out of doing *your* job. If you want to run with me for PT, that's fine. If you want to use the equipment, that's your right."

"Thanks." Her heart beat steadily at an increased rate and her breath matched. Idina swallowed in a dry mouth and let out a weak chuckle. "I'm not *intimidated* out of anything. I figured I'd switch it up a little today. It's good to have that invitation for the future."

They finished the run in silence after that until Crimshaw slowed behind the barracks, signaling the end of her route. Then she grabbed her water bottle and towel from where she'd left them against the wall and wiped her sweaty face and neck. "I don't offer this to everyone, but if he does anything beyond glaring at you and making all the wrong comments, I've got your back."

Idina wiped her forehead with a forearm and nodded. "Thanks. Same here."

The other woman nodded, looked Idina up and down, then quickly headed for the back door of the barracks to finish getting ready for the day.

Wow. Solidarity from the other woman in jump school who said she wasn't interested in making friends. Definitely didn't expect that. *Still, if people like Hapton bothered me that much, I wouldn't have made it as far as I have.*

With a surprised chuckle, Idina headed back into the barracks as well for a hot shower and to grab morning chow from one of the dining facilities. Now she had one more friend where she'd least expected to find one—however reclusive, literal, and socially odd Crimshaw was.

CHAPTER THIRTEEN

When everyone gathered that morning in the yard for their last day of week two, Sergeant Birch looked the trainees over with a smirk, his eyes glistening in expectation.

"Today, we see who's ready and willing to make the jump. Literally. We have one more simulation, and no, it's not from twelve hundred feet. It *is* the highest jump you've made this week. It'll help you prepare for the real thing. After today, there's no going back. So let's get it done."

The Black Hats led everyone on a short trek out of the training yard and out into a massive field on base, where the trainees' next obstacle stood out like a sore thumb. The thirty-foot tower looked suspiciously like the Warrior's Tower in basic. Only this one wasn't for rappelling with a harness fashioned from climbing rope.

At the top of the tower was a large platform with curved walls rising all around it, cut to much more accurately mimic the size and shape of a C-130. The only way up was to climb the incredibly tall, narrow ladder to the inside of the "plane."

At multiple angles around the tower's top platform were four thick zipline cables, each of which stretched down to the landing pads at the end of the lines. Two came from the rear loading ramp and one each extended from side doors on the right and left sides of the structure.

"This is your last hurdle before the real deal," Birch told them. "There's nothing to catch you at the end of the ziplines, so utilize PLF and unclip yourself once you land. We have NCOs waiting at the bottom if anything should happen, but you're doing all this on your own."

He pointed at the top of the platform. "That's the C-130. The dimensions of that hull on top of the tower are exact. That's what the inside of your aircraft looks like. You'll hook up to the static line anchor like you will next week for your required jumps. Sergeant Airborne and I will give the commands when we're up there. Then you jump.

"This is as close as it gets to being prepared for the real thing. And I'd be lying if I said this is anything like what you're about to do on Monday. Line up."

Already equipped with their harnesses, jump helmets, and reserve chutes, the trainees lined up at the tower's base and headed up the ladder after Sergeant Birch. Somehow, climbing this particular ladder felt a lot longer than when Idina had scaled the Warrior's Tower in basic.

As close as we can get to the real thing. No kidding this doesn't prepare us enough. It's a tower, not a plane. A zipline is a hell of a lot more reassuring than jumping out with literally nothing but a chute to catch us.

Despite the fluttering nerves in her belly at the thought, Idina climbed purposefully behind Major Hines, the rest of her chalk behind her and Chalks Two and Three behind them. Everyone was silent, dutifully awaiting the moment they'd jump from "as close to a C-130" as they were going to get.

She was the fifth soldier to make it to the platform on top. Waiting for the rest of the trainees to finish their climb and take their places in the simulated aircraft felt like it took forever. Finally, Sergeant Hutchinson brought up the rear, and the jumpmasters looked around to double-check that each chalk had lined up in correct order and position along the walls of the aircraft.

"This is where you'll hook your static line." Hutchinson tugged on the cable running the length of the interior walls. "You're jumping four at a time, six seconds apart. When you receive your T-11 on Monday and jump out for real, you won't wait for the four in front of you to land before it's your turn. Six seconds is way too long."

"Time to move." Birch nodded at the first four trainees of Chalk One standing closest to the rounded doorframe cut into the aircraft's fuselage. "Hook up!"

"Hook up!" The four trainees in front of Idina echoed the command as trained. Major Hines grabbed the zipline clip to attach it to his harness, and the other three in front of him did the same, moving forward one at a time toward the opening.

It'll be a little different next week when we're hooking static lines to the cable and not ziplines to our harnesses.

Idina watched intently as Birch quickly inspected the zipline clips, then he nodded. "Green light, go!"

Stone sucked in a sharp breath and launched himself off the tower. The thin *whir* of the attachment racing down the zipline filled the air, joined by his shouts of counting down to six seconds. The sound quickly faded, then the next soldier behind him jumped. Crimshaw and Major Hines went next, and Birch looked particularly pleased to see the first four soldiers in Chalk One eagerly launching themselves off the platform as their countdowns echoed up to the tower.

There were no windows in the walls built to simulate the C-130. The jumpmaster by the ramp was the only one with access to the view below and how the first four trainees had done. "Next four!"

Idina quickly stepped toward the door and ran through the rest of the commands with the three soldiers behind her.

"Green light, go!"

She didn't hesitate. With her hands clamped around her reserve chute, she jumped the way she'd been taught over the last week and let herself go. Time seemed suspended as she sailed up and out, then down. When the zipline caught her, the ensuing jolt of tension on her harness briefly made her breath catch in her throat. Then she counted. "One thousand! Two thousand! Three thousand!"

Once she got to six, she looked up over her shoulder and back. Of course, there was no parachute, and she didn't expect to see one deploying.

She also didn't expect to see the sky above her illuminating with the glowing green outline of what *looked* like a parachute deploying above her.

What the hell?

For a moment, she forgot all about being on the zipline and what was expected of her as she neared the end. Her green lights glittered behind her, billowing out in the massive balloon shape of a parachute that didn't exist and wasn't supposed to be there at all.

"PLF!" an NCO shouted from the base of the zipline, tearing Idina out of her confusion just in time.

She looked straight ahead again and found the landing platform racing up to meet her. Clamping a hand down over her reserve—where she'd pull her chute's riser when it existed—Idina leaned forward into her right side. Her feet touched down, and she jerked her arms up beside her head before rolling beneath the zipline at the bottom stop-catch. Immediately, she lifted a hand to her chest, moving through muscle memory of drilling the action over and over despite the parachute's release clip not being there on her harness today.

"Good work, Private," the NCO muttered as he stepped toward her and helped her off the zipline attachment. "Though you might wanna spend more time looking ahead of you instead of behind, huh?"

"Yes." She pushed herself to her feet, absently dusted off her uniform pants, and turned to look up at the tower. Her green lights in the sparkling outline of a parachute were gone. Greenburg shouted out his countdown as he raced down the zipline toward her.

What am I supposed to do with a warning from my lights like that, *huh? Yeah, I know I'm supposed to have a parachute while falling out of the sky. That's not what this is. So...what? The lights are malfunctioning now?*

"Step aside," the NCO muttered. "Soldier coming in hot."

Idina removed herself from the landing platform. She

tried to smile when Greenburg nailed his PLF, unclipped, and shot to his feet with a grin.

"That's how it's *done,* Moorfield! You see that?"

"Yeah, good work."

He paused as he headed toward her, his smiling fading. "Well, shit. You landed yours too. What's wrong?"

"Huh?" Blinking quickly, she shook her head and headed toward the tower's base where the other soldiers who'd jumped before her had gathered, waiting for orders to either climb back into the plane or head somewhere else. "Nothing's wrong."

"You nervous or something?" Greenburg took her lack of rebuttal or any reply at all as confirmation. "Ha! You *are* nervous."

"No, I'm not. I just...have a few things on my mind."

"Uh-huh. Like how nervous you are." He playfully punched her in the shoulder and picked up the pace toward the tower. "Don't worry about it, Swiss Army. TGIF, right? Trust me. I'll slap the nerves right out of you. Just let me handle everything."

"Dude, I don't need—"

"Bup-bup-bup." He lifted his open palm in front of her face to stop her, then pointed at her. "I'm your gear buddy. And I'm the coolest dude in Chalk One. If anyone can get you to loosen up a little before we jump for real, I can."

Idina playfully wrinkled her nose. "That's not as reassuring as you think it is."

"What?" He scoffed and waved off the comment. "Nothing *too* weird. You need a break. And to get off base at least once."

"I've already gone off base."

"I don't care how good you are at art stuff, Moorfield. This is different. Let that settle in and percolate a little. Gives you something to look forward to." Greenburg waggled his eyebrows, then they joined the other soldiers at the tower, most of whom kept busy by watching the other trainees launching off the platform overhead and zipping down the line as they shouted their six-second countdown.

Idina would've folded her arms, but her bulky reserve chute was strapped to her chest and made it impossible. As Greenburg and Stone ramped each other up about what it would be like getting up in the C-130 for real, Idina couldn't help but smile.

Maybe I do *need a little R&R. Or something fun that doesn't include being by myself all the time and making new sketches that won't go anywhere. Especially into a portfolio for art school. As long as that wasn't Greenburg asking me out on a date, I guess it's something to take my mind off all this weird crap with my lights.*

She scanned the faces of the trainees who'd already jumped—their numbers quickly growing as those who'd landed returned to join them—and saw Major Hines and Crimshaw deep in conversation a few feet away. The major nodded at something Crimshaw said, raised his eyebrows, then turned and immediately locked eyes with Idina.

That's...weird.

Crimshaw looked at her too, then quickly looked away and walked around the other side of the tower's base to get a better view of the jumping soldiers.

No way they're talking about me. Yeah, we had a chat about Hapton and his issues during PT this morning, but she's not going through the proper chain of command by saying anything about it to Major Hines. Unless they're talking about something else... Like seeing the shape of a weirdly green parachute flickering out behind me on a zipline.

She'd had enough close calls with her lights during basic and AIT—with Brock's rope harness and again at the pizza place with her friends the night she'd told them about going to jump school. The last thing Idina needed now was to cause any more suspicion here at Fort Benning, especially when she'd already caught the attention of an Army major getting his wings right alongside her.

Let it go. Until anybody says something about it, I'll keep pretending to be clueless. Because I have no idea what else is about to happen with this stupid ability that keeps freaking out all over the place.

After another round of jumps off the C-130 zipline tower —and two other trainees getting their reserve chutes caught on unseen obstacles to deploy them unwittingly on the ground—the jumpmasters drilled them again on everything they'd learned. Birch ended the day by explaining more of what jump week entailed and giving them a quick rundown of the process they could expect come Monday morning.

"You need five successful jumps to earn your jump wings," he told them. "At least one needs to fall in each of these categories. Hollywood jump, combat jump, and night jump. The rest could be a combination of any, but five's your magic number.

"Don't ask when you'll jump or which type they'll be. Sergeant Airborne and I don't find that out until right before we tell you it's happening. We want you out in the yard at five hundred hours Monday. Obviously, no morning PT. I suggest you skip any morning snacks too."

Sergeant Hutchinson snickered.

"That's it, everybody. Have a good weekend."

The mood among all the chalks was mostly excitement with an undertone of nervous energy. Everyone headed back toward the training yard behind the barracks amid conversations of what jump week would be like when they got to it.

Idina was grateful for the weekend ahead to relax and focus on something besides the upcoming jumps and the strange way her ability had been acting out over the last two-and-a-half months.

As long as I don't keep having visions of random castle warriors or keep hearing monster voices in my head, I'll be fine. Jumping out of a plane can't be nearly as bad as going through the worst of basic, right?

CHAPTER FOURTEEN

She'd expected Greenburg to find her after dinner and hound her about whatever his plans were to help her "relax." Her new Ranger friend wasn't anywhere to be found, which was a relief that night. Idina wanted to relax, and with Crimshaw out doing her thing, she had the entire women's bay to herself.

It would've been a nice, quiet night with nothing to distract her from not thinking about any of the issues she faced in the immediate future—namely what the hell was going on with her green lights.

When she opened her email inbox on her phone and found an incoming email from Reggie, she couldn't help but smile.

Here's a good distraction. Thanks, Reg.

Miss Idina,

I hope this finds you well. After your last email, Mrs. Yardly and I took it upon ourselves to inves-

tigate in more detail the structure and requirements of your current enrollment in jump school. At least, in as much detail as two civilians past their prime and with a rudimentary knowledge of scouring the Internet can achieve. Mrs. Yardly and I surprised ourselves when we eventually unearthed a description of what your current training entails.

Of course, we did already suspect the rigors of jump school would be overshadowed by what you endured and succeeded over in basic training. This time, I imagine the qualifying tests for graduation are the more noteworthy aspect here. Specifically, jumping from a military aircraft at over twelve hundred feet.

Mrs. Yardly nearly fainted when she read that part, and I must admit I felt rather queasy myself. Rest assured, we have the utmost faith in your ability to overcome all obstacles laid before you, including successfully jumping out of said aircraft and surviving. Five times.

Idina chuckled and grabbed her full water bottle off the bedside table beside her bunk. "Good thing you and Mrs. Yardly aren't making the jumps, then, huh?" she muttered before continuing to read.

All lightheartedness aside—Mrs. Yardly has corrected me several times on my apparent

misconception that anyone of sound mind, military personnel included, is permitted to jest about such life-threatening training—I must again broach a topic I'm already well aware you might find displeasing.

I'm also fully aware that not once have you brought up such issues in the otherwise detailed and meticulous accounts of your exploits as an Army soldier. Be that as it may, this remains of the highest importance, Idina. So take the following information as you will, no matter your experiences over the last six months.

She had to stop reading again and drew a deep breath. Pulling her gaze away from her phone, she studied the empty woman's bay and exhaled slowly and heavily. *Come on, Reggie. You made a joke in an email, and I was excited about this. Why'd you have to ruin it with a precursor like that?*

Still, though she had a very clear idea of this "topic" he was about to broach in his email, Idina couldn't bring herself to close her inbox and leave it at that. She had to keep reading.

I bring this up because, while you were at the tender age of nine when it occurred and might not fully remember the sequence of events, I'm practically the same age now as I was the day your Uncle Richard left the manor for good. Comparatively speaking, at any rate.

I cannot speak for what you've already experienced during your time thus far in the Army, but I *can* speak for what Richard experienced. Or, at the very least, the way I perceived it and what little he shared with me.

Many small events, one after the other, led to the "manifestation" of your uncle's unique talents. The common thread throughout them was a high level of physical, mental, and emotional stress. Not necessarily always in a negative light, but it might be difficult to distinguish positive from negative should you experience these same episodes. Believe me when I tell you, Idina, that the instances I refer to in this email are nothing close to what we've been calling your episodes for the past eight years.

Your uncle shared only brief accounts with me over the years when we were still in contact. It's not my place to divulge the details of those accounts, but do not misplace my intentions in this. I imagine you might discover why maintaining the privacy of those details is my only real choice in this endeavor.

However, I can offer some advice that might aid you should a strengthening of your episodes come to fruition, if they haven't already. At least, that's my hope. I believe Richard would say the same, were he in contact with either of us.

Whatever you might see, Idina, whatever you might hear, rest assured it is not a product of some mental breakdown or a deficiency on your part. It is not the call of insanity, nor is it a consequence of any wrongdoing on your part.

It is *all real.*

Whatever reveals itself to you during your training or at any point in your career, you will most certainly be the only one with an awareness of its existence. I cannot tell you what to expect, but I *will* tell you to face it head-on the way Richard faced it when the time came.

The majority of your family would indeed prefer that I not write this email in the first place, let alone send it. You deserve a much better explanation than the pitiful attempt I can offer, but my wish for you now is that you're at least somewhat prepared. In part, I blame myself for your uncle's disappearance from all our lives because I didn't share with him what little knowledge I had, passed down through generations of the Moorfield family line.

In many ways, Idina, you're already breaking free of the patterns that have trapped your family for hundreds of years. Perhaps this is my way of breaking free from the same.

—R.

P.S. Please send word after the end of jump week so I can inform Mrs. Yardly with all confidence that you've survived the end of your training. We're all rooting for you.

That was the end.

"Shit." Idina tossed her phone beside her on her bunk and stared blankly across the bay.

Is he serious right now? Sending me an email like that before I'm about to put my life at risk by jumping out of a plane in three days?

Her mind reeled with the revelations contained in that email. If anyone else had sent her a combined confession and warning like that, she would've laughed in their face and called them crazy. This was Reggie Archibald. Ever serious and stoic, dedicated to his job and the responsibilities that came with being head of staff for the prestigious Moorfield family.

This man was more like a grandfather to Idina than Harold Senior had ever been. He'd probably been more of a father to Richard too, but she couldn't confirm that one way or the other.

Reggie knew way more than he'd let on for the last ten years since Idina's ability had first entered her life with a flickering burst of green and nothing but fear and distaste from her family. She couldn't think of any circumstance under which the man would lie to her. Not about this.

It's all real.

She cleared her throat and shook her head, trying to get

rid of yet another bout of lightheadedness sweeping through her.

The green lights and occasional burst of glittering fog when a situation got particularly heated were one thing. Her reaction time. Her ability to see strategic moves to the end, five steps in front of her opponent. Her skill with any drawing medium.

Even the strands of light in the air and all the numbers, statistics, and impossible data that had floated through her head toward the end of basic—she could handle all that. None of it had seemed all that far-fetched because she'd already been dealing with it in one form or another for over half her life.

Sure, spontaneously healing myself from a barbed wire cut was new. Even that somehow makes sense. But the rest? That voice calling me Warrior. The ground shaking. The vision of those people *when I got my engineering castle. A goddamn invisible ghost-parachute on a zipline?* That's *all real?*

Trying to incorporate that new knowledge into what she already knew about herself felt like jamming a square peg into a round hole.

How am I supposed to deal with this right now? I don't have my medication. I can't keep it down. Holy shit, I've been keeping it down*!*

The heat of rage flared through her—the kind she'd only experienced three times that she could remember, the last of which had sent actual green lights blazing from her palms and smashing the floor of the bay in the training barracks while her drill sergeants smoked the entire company to hell and back. She gritted her teeth and clenched her eyes shut.

If it's all real, my family had to know. They were pumping me full of Anagracin from the very beginning. It's probably not a real prescription. What if Dr. Kruchek isn't a real doctor? Is anything *before I joined the Army more than one giant lie they kept feeding me? I was stupid enough to believe them the whole time...*

"Fuck!" All the rage, confusion, and doubt that had only needed a good ten minutes to boil up inside her exploded with that single shout. Pulses of searing heat and icy cold rippled through Idina's limbs, up and down her back, and into her head where they rattled around and made thinking of anything else nearly impossible.

Her eyes flew open to a green light surrounding her that emanated from her clenched fists. There was no haze of glittering fog this time or small, wisping tendrils of an ability she couldn't explain.

Everything was green—a thick, dark, glowing green rising around her like a full-body halo.

"Holy shit..."

Idina whipped her head up toward the bay doors, which had fortunately closed again. The green light around her snuffed out instantly, but not before she glimpsed Crimshaw standing inside the entrance, her arms hanging limply at her sides, staring right at Idina in the middle of the lead-up to a full-fledged episode.

The women stared at each other in mute shock, then Idina snatched her phone off the bunk and held it up with a shaky, unconvincing chuckle. "Hey."

"What..." Crimshaw turned slowly to look over her shoulder, still completely expressionless and now apparently at a loss for words. "What did I see?"

"What do you mean?" Idina glanced at her phone again and pretended to scroll through something a lot more important than acting like this wasn't the worst situation to find herself in.

"That *light*." The medic took two steps forward, then stopped and looked Idina up and down. "You were green."

"Oh. Right." Idina waggled her phone at Crimshaw and shrugged. "You know, I upgraded to my phone's newest version right before I went to basic. The screens on this thing... Super bright. Vivid colors."

Crimshaw blinked heavily, then slowly tilted her head. "So you were...watching a green screen."

"Looking at some artwork. Someone else's. Not mine." Swallowing thickly, Idina tossed her phone onto the nightstand and turned on her bunk to face the other woman slowly walking across the bay. "Shades of Green or something like that."

Yep, I sound totally insane. If anyone but Crimshaw had walked in on that, a dumbass explanation like 'looking at artwork' wouldn't have cut it. She's the last person to believe I've been sitting here glowing through my skin...

"What are *you* doing?" She rushed to change the subject.

Crimshaw gave her a condescending frown as she approached her bunk. "Going to bed."

"Right now? It's a little early, Crimshaw. Even for you. No early wakeup tomo—"

"It's after twenty-three hundred hours." The other woman stared at Idina in disbelief.

At least Idina assumed it was disbelief. It was hard to tell with Crimshaw, who never really showed any emotion at all. Except for now. The problem was knowing if that disbelief came from a mention of jokes or from walking into the women's bay and seeing a fellow soldier glowing green.

Idina snickered. "Funny."

Crimshaw tilted her head again. "I thought we already covered the fact that I'm not a fan of *funny*."

"Well, yeah. But there's no way it's that late. I'm not an idiot." Idina snatched up her phone again to prove her point and froze.

Holy shit. She's not *kidding. How is it almost midnight?*

She nearly choked on her surprise and lowered her phone into her lap. "Oh."

"Are you getting sick or something?" Crimshaw grabbed her pajamas from her trunk and frowned. "Because if you are, you can forget running with me during morning PT. I'm not interested in going through jump week with a head cold. Especially not one as bad as whatever you've got."

"What? No." Idina shook her head and took three long, desperate gulps from her water bottle before saying anything else. It did nothing for her dry mouth. "No, I'm not sick. Really. I feel fine."

"Uh-huh."

"You know what? Maybe it's nerves." The lie tasted so wrong in her mouth. Nerves had never been an issue for Idina Moorfield. She didn't get stage fright or cold feet. She didn't back out of a decision once she'd made it.

I guess lying about what's going on with me is worth it if it keeps her from asking any more questions.

"Nerves." Crimshaw whipped off her civilian t-shirt and immediately replaced it with her pajama top. "You make terrible jokes and have a knack for pissing off he-man Army Rangers, but you don't seem like the kind of person to lose track of time because of *nerves*."

Idina stared at her. *What is* up *with this chick? Can she read my mind or something?*

"Well...I guess we're all full of surprises, huh?"

Crimshaw finished changing into her pajama pants and blinked across the bay before returning her gaze to the only other woman in there. "As long as you don't pull out any of those surprises when we're in the sky. I jump before you, obviously, but you'll still be holding up an entire aircraft and three chalks if you can't pull it together before then."

Without another word, the woman turned down the bedclothes of her bunk and slipped quietly under them before rolling onto her side with her back facing Idina.

That was probably the best thing she could've done at the moment. Idina didn't have to see the doubt and suspicion and a little pity on Crimshaw's face, and Crimshaw didn't have to look at the stunned expression Idina couldn't seem to erase.

Great advice, Medic. Don't fuck it up for everyone else because I'm going through a little something weird on my own. Jeeze, that was close. It looks like she bought the lie.

Idina sighed, set the alarm on her phone for 0600, then changed into a tank top and cotton shorts before heading across the bay to turn out the overhead lights for them both. When she returned to her bed, she couldn't stop thinking about Reggie's email and the look on Crimshaw's face when she'd stepped into the bay and found Idina...glowing.

I didn't have enough time to process what he said in that email. I mean, apparently, I did. *How did I let four hours slip away from me like that? How long were my lights freaking out? What the hell am I supposed to do with being told all the weird visions, voices, and crazy stuff my ability's been doing is all* real?

For a moment, she considered pulling out her dress blues to take another look at the engineering castle pin still snugly affixed to the right breast above her name. Still, that would only keep her awake longer.

I don't need to sit here with my uniform, having another vision of that woman screaming for the "Warriors to rise" while Crimshaw's sleeping right there.

Clenching her eyes shut, Idina focused on her breathing and attempted to clear her mind. The last four hours had passed in the blink of an eye, but the fifteen minutes it took her to fall asleep felt like eons.

CHAPTER FIFTEEN

It only took twenty seconds when Idina woke the next morning for Reggie's email to rush back to her all at once. The knot in her gut returned with it, tightening even more when she got out of bed and rifled through her civilian clothes to pick an outfit for the day. She didn't look at Crimshaw's bunk until she was fully dressed and ready to leave the bay for breakfast. When she did, the other woman's bunk was empty, crisply made, and the bay was empty.

Right. Dumb of me to assume she'd give herself a break on the weekends when we don't technically have to be anywhere. At least we don't have to wade through the awkwardness after last night. Unless she went off to talk to Major Hines or some other officer about what she saw...

Idina shook her head, stuffed her feet into her sneakers, and grabbed her jacket. "Not gonna happen, Moorfield. Brush it off. Move on with your day."

The new affirmation knocked her a little more out of her uncertainty, and she walked briskly across the bay to start her weekend of not training and not freaking out about her abilities. At least, that was the plan.

By the time she'd finished breakfast in the dining facility and had decided she'd spend the day working on a few new sketches to clear her mind, she'd forgotten all about Greenburg's overeager promise to "loosen her up" for jump week.

He hadn't.

"Moorfield!"

Idina spun in the hallway to see him striding toward her with a wide grin and his arms spread.

"Where are *you* going, huh?"

"Back to the bay..."

"Nice try. I told you we were gonna do something fun, and *I* keep my promises."

Shit. He's serious about this.

"I'm good, Greenburg." Idina shook her head and started to turn back down the hall toward the women's bay. "I think I'm gonna—"

"What?" He skirted around her and blocked her from going anywhere else. "Gonna sit around and pretend you don't need to cut loose a little? Come on. That's bullshit, and you know it."

"It's not." Despite being caught off-guard like this and physically blocked from going where she wanted, she snorted. "I appreciate the effort, though."

"Good." Greenburg cocked his head and looked her up and down. "It's a hell of a lot more effort than I thought I'd need to get you to come with me. And I don't put in an effort for free."

"Um..."

"I mean you're coming with me." Just then realizing how close he stood in front of her, he took two steps back and glanced behind her down the hall. "That's the only payment. Plus the price of entry."

"To what?"

"That's part of the effort, Moorfield. Now shut up, turn around, and have fun, dammit!"

Idina laughed and pointed in the direction she wanted to go. "Thanks, Drill Sergeant. But I have a date with my—"

"Paper and charcoal?" Greenburg smirked. "Yeah, I pay attention. No, your date's off. The stylus is gonna have to suck it, 'cause you're coming with me. Let's go."

"Dude, I'm not—"

"*Move,* Private!"

"Jesus..." Playfully rolling her eyes, Idina turned and scanned the mostly empty hallway leading toward the front of the barracks. "You're not gonna let me off the hook, are you?"

"No chance in hell. Unless, uh... I mean, you need to grab a purse or anything—"

"Fuck off, Greenburg. I don't have a *purse.*" The sheepish grimace on his face was enough to bring a genuine laugh from Idina, and she lifted her jacket slung over her arm to signal she had everything she needed, wallet included. Then she gestured down the hall. "If I'm not getting out of this, you better make it good."

His grin returned, and he bumped his shoulder against hers as he passed to lead the way. "Trust me. It's all taken care of. Minus the—"

"Price of entry. Yeah. I heard you the first time."

She followed him down the hall and tried not to hold on to at least *looking* resentful a little longer.

No one knows exactly what I'm going through right now. It needs to stay that way. But I have a super serious, intensely literal medic friend—kinda—with a knack for bashing hard truths into my head. And this goofy-ass Ranger intent on forcing me to have fun. Maybe that's all that counts right now.

Half an hour later, they pulled up in Greenburg's black Honda Civic to the front of the strip mall not far off base. He parked, turned off the engine, and raised an eyebrow at her. "Get ready, Moorfield. It's on."

"Whatever *it* is, it sounds like you got a faulty training helmet before hitting your head one too many times off The Swing."

He scoffed and opened the driver's side door. "Get the fuck out of the car."

Their doors *thumped* shut behind them, and Idina held back more laughter as she followed him through the parking lot toward the sidewalk in front of the strip mall. "Seriously. What are we doing here?"

"You'll love it. If you don't, you're doing it anyway."

"Okay, if you think taking a girl with you to go shopping will make you feel better, you picked the wrong girl."

Greenburg scrunched up his face and forced a sarcastic guffaw. "You're hilarious. Why the fuck would I take you shopping?"

"Well, you're being a dick by not telling me why we're *here*."

The friendly banter was something she'd gotten used to after the first month of basic, standard in the Army and across pretty much every military branch when they weren't on duty and standing at attention. Still, an image of Idina's mother flashed through her mind—Annette Moorfield's flared nostrils and pinched lips whenever foul language made the mistake of reaching her ears.

Idina snorted. *The whole family would have a stroke if they saw me out here on Saturday with Greenburg, driving in a Honda Civic, talking like this. Doesn't matter. They didn't recognize me when I was living right under their noses. They sure as hell wouldn't recognize me now.*

She almost ran into Greenburg before she realized he'd stopped at a storefront, then backtracked to put more space between them.

He chuckled and looked her up and down. "You look distracted."

"Maybe I'm too busy trying to figure out why the hell you drove me to a dumpy strip mall."

Greenburg slowly swept his arm toward the glass door in front of him and gave her a pert smile, clearly impressed with himself. "Well, now you can stop trying so hard before you hurt yourself."

She looked at the door with the company's logo on a decal plastered across the glass and blinked. "Laser tag."

"Laser tag."

"Seriously?"

"Seriously. You need to let loose, Moorfield. We don't have clearance to use the firing range on base, so we're going with the next best thing."

Pressing her lips together in a failed attempt to keep a

straight face, she shrugged. "I would've picked the demo range anyway."

"Ha. Yeah, of course, you would. Fucking sapper." With a snort, Greenburg slammed a hand against the door and stepped inside.

Idina followed, gazing around at the dark front room and the black lights illuminating the multi-colored murals of stars and moons and comets all over the walls. *This is the last place I would've expected to be two days before I jump out of a plane. Or ever. If he asks, this is* not *my first time playing laser tag.*

The guy behind the counter looked incredibly bored to be there, but Greenburg flashed him a massive grin anyway and pulled out his wallet. "We're ready to go, man. Don't forget that military discount, huh?"

"I just need to see some ID."

Idina reached into her back pocket for her wallet and flashed the man her Eagle Card. He looked back and forth between the picture and her face, then shrugged. "That'll be five dollars for each of you."

"That's it?"

Greenburg elbowed her in the ribs and muttered, "Don't fight it, Moorfield. Perks of the job."

With a snort, she handed over her card to cover the price of being an Army soldier at a damn laser tag arena. When that was finished, the man stepped out from behind the counter and headed toward the double doors on the right-hand wall. The sign above them was lit up with blacklight too, marking it as "The Laser Zone."

"You guys ever done this before?"

"Come on, man." Greenburg chuckled. "We're not amateurs."

"Just have to ask. Even if you say yes, I have to give you the rundown anyway." The employee droned on in a tiresomely monotone voice as he relayed all the rules and regulations of the game, how to strap on their vest, how to use the laser guns, and what each little sound meant when they heard it emanating from their gear. "Any questions?"

"Nope." Idina shook her head. "That was very thorough."

Greenburg snorted.

"Great." Blinking heavily, the employee gestured toward the doors. "You'll pick your gear in The Laser Zone. Have fun." Then he turned and shuffled back toward the desk to spend the rest of his shift in an empty lobby doing absolutely nothing.

"Cheery guy," Idina muttered.

"You would be too if you got to spend all day in an awesome place like this." Greenburg yanked on the door handle and held the door open for her.

I can't believe I'm doing this right now. But hey. Maybe it's the kind of blowing-off-steam I need to deal with all this—

"Jesus Christ," someone said in the mostly dark room. "Took you fucking forever. Next time you gotta take a shit, hold it 'til we're—"

Idina's vision adjusted quickly to the semi-darkness lit only by the neon lights of the gear racks lining the walls. So she saw the two other people standing in the room, and apparently, the light was enough to illuminate her face too.

The door closed again behind Greenburg, and Hapton

glared at the guy as he folded his arms. "What the fuck are you doing, Greenburg?"

"Playing a little laser tag, genius."

"I mean what the fuck are you doing bringing *her* here?" Hapton flicked his hand at Idina, and the only thing she could think of in response was to laugh.

"Good to see you too."

Rorden—the tall Ranger she'd helped with his deadlifting form—widened his eyes above a slowly growing grin and stared directly at her.

Hapton looked up at the guy standing over a foot taller than him and rolled his eyes—the white illuminated by the blacklights. "Yeah, I bet." Then he turned to face Greenburg, who walked along the walls to a rack with vests in his size, labeled with more blacklight paint. "Dude. We set the thing up for three-man play."

"Sure did." Greenburg strapped on a vest without looking at his buddy. "I switched it to two-on-two."

"You couldn't have asked Hawkins or Acker to come down here instead?"

"Hawkins and Acker are dipshits." Greenburg met Idina's gaze and nodded at the gear racks. "Grab a vest, Moorfield."

"Smalls are over there," Rorden muttered, pointing toward the correct rack.

"Thanks." Idina turned to sift through the laser tag vests, and Hapton apparently couldn't keep it together.

He was practically shrieking at Greenburg now. "Don't you fucking put her on my team, man. You brought her. You can deal with her dragging you down."

"She's my first pick." Greenburg lowered his laser gun

in one fist at his side and shrugged. "At least over the two of you."

Hapton seethed at him, the giant muscles of his shoulders and back bunching as he clenched his fists. "You ruined the game, asshole."

Idina grabbed the gun attached to her vest and leveled it at Hapton's back. "If I didn't know better, I'd say you're scared to get your ass kicked by a woman."

He spun and stared at the plastic barrel of the gun in no way similar to any of the models the Army soldiers were used to handling. Rorden chuckled and shook his head. Greenburg watched the whole thing in silence now, and while Idina felt his gaze on her face, she didn't look away from the Ranger with a seriously outdated view of what certain people were capable of.

Hapton's nostrils flared in the semi-darkness. "You know better."

She shrugged. "Then you shouldn't have anything to worry about, right?"

"Man, just suck it up so we can play," Rorden added. "*I'm* the one who has to be on your team now." He clapped Hapton's shoulder and pulled him toward the door leading into the actual laser zone and not the gear closet.

"We're gonna bash 'em into the ground," Hapton muttered, letting himself be led away into the arena.

Greenburg and Idina looked at each other. He flashed her a crooked smile. "Didn't wanna ruin the surprise."

"Oh, yeah. Good thinking." They both headed toward the arena's entrance together, and she paused just past the open doors. "Okay, fine. You were right about a few things."

"Like what?"

"I mean..." Lifting the laser gun to give it a brief once-over, she shrugged. "It's not a real bullet, but I'm really gonna enjoy shooting him."

Greenburg laughed, then a whooping siren and a red flashing light over the doors between The Laser Zone and the arena blared to life. An announcer's voice rang through the speaker system over the loud electronic music.

"You're in The Laser Zone*! Players, take your places. Don't forget to reload at the laser ports in each zone. Three direct hits without a reload means* Game Over*!"*

The insane reverb at the end made Idina laugh as she navigated around the large cylindrical obstacles covered in thick mats. *That has to be a recording. I'm pretty sure our friendly laser tag employee couldn't drum up that much enthusiasm if they quadrupled his hourly wage.*

"On your marks," the announcer declared, followed by a short, high-pitched *beep*.

"We wanna work out some kinda strategy here?" Greenburg asked as he leaned toward her.

"Get set!"

"Naw." Idina shook her head. "That defeats the whole purpose of *letting loose*, right?"

He snickered.

"Laser tag!"

"Laser tag? That means *go*, right?"

Greenburg raised his gun at his shoulder and nodded. "Yeah, go fucking nuts."

Then he stalked out from behind the cylinder, which Idina noted had a slot for "reloading" their laser guns when they needed a virtual healing-reload combo.

Wouldn't that be great if those things existed in real life?

The thought made her pause briefly, and she blinked away a frown before choking back a laugh.

Holy shit. They do *exist. For me. At least the healing part. And nobody has a clue.*

Idina slinked from behind the cylinder to the next bit of cover. It was hard to see what the obstacle was in the darkness and with all the flashing lights, but it looked kind of like a playhouse without a roof. A narrow bridge rose from the other side of the matted structure toward a catwalk on the arena's upper level.

She headed that way, scanning the darkness for shadowed movement. With all the flashing lights, pinning movement to an actual opponent was nearly impossible. So was listening for enemy approaches. The music pounded through her head, most likely meant to disorient the players and get them pumped up for the next round.

Crouching beside the wall of the weird playhouse, Idina slowed her breathing and scanned the other obstacles around the arena. The one light that didn't flit all over the place with the others burst in her vision brighter than anything else. Of course, it was green...Idina's ability drew her attention to her opponent's vest blinking bright red in the darkness.

That's Hapton, all right. Rorden's chest probably wouldn't get that close to the ground even if he was on his knees.

The red light bobbed slightly with slow footsteps, the music pounded, and either Rorden or Greenburg shouted something on the other side of the arena. Idina didn't pay attention to any of it.

Once he turns his back, I'll get him. Then—what?

The blinking light on his vest disappeared behind yet another blackened obstacle Idina hadn't seen against the backdrop of even more black.

This is stupid. Running around like fifth graders pretending to know how to use a weapon or ambush an enemy. I can't see a damn...

Blinking quickly, Idina briefly rubbed one eye, her other hand occupied by not dropping the laser gun and giving herself away with an accidental *crash* and *burble* from the play weapon's microphone. Because she *could* see.

Hapton had disappeared behind a long, thick wall covered in mats, and there was no sign of the red blinking light on his vest. She saw him anyway. His silhouette, illuminated in pulsing, glittering green light, moved slowly down the side of the obstacle. She even saw him pause, turn to look up at the second level, and raise his gun in both hands.

From the other side of the wall.

I have X-ray vision now? What the hell is going on?

Idina quickly glanced down at her hands to be sure they weren't glowing the way Crimshaw had found her last night. All good there.

She sighed, tightened her grip on the plastic gun, and discovered she was bobbing her head to the music.

Screw it. No point in tossing my advantage aside, right? He still thinks I don't have any.

She grinned and darted out from behind the small house-like structure, heading right for Hapton's glowing green outline on the other side of the wall. He never saw her coming.

Rorden snorted and barely managed to swallow his mouthful of soda to keep it from spraying all over the table. "Dude, you should've seen your face!"

"I know what my face looks like, asshole. Thanks."

"Aw, man. Priceless."

"You realize we lost, right?"

"Hell yeah, we lost. It was *worth* it to watch you hit the ground like there was live ammo in the room. Ha! I thought you were gonna shit your pants." Laughing, Rorden tapped his temple before reaching down for the gigantic burger on his plate. "I'll keep that image right up here for a long time. A *long* time."

Hapton dropped the French fry he was about to eat back into the basket and glared across the table at Idina and Greenburg. "Fine. If the dick on my team has to rub it in so much, I bet you guys are dying to rub it in some more. Go ahead. Let it out."

Idina slipped the straw of her iced tea into her mouth and widened her eyes as she drank. Greenburg didn't say a word, and the fact that neither of the laser tag victors wanted to gloat about their win only got under Hapton's skin that much more.

"Seriously. Get it over with already. I'm giving you a free shot here."

"Really?" Greenburg glanced sidelong at Idina, then shook his head. "Nah, I'm good. Kicking your ass was satisfying enough."

Hapton glared solely at Idina after that and spread his arms. "If you wanna gloat, now's the time."

She stopped drinking her tea and smiled sweetly at him. "We both know who won. I'm not the bragging type."

"Jesus fucking Christ." He plopped his hands down onto the table, making the silverware rattle. "So I gotta sit here looking at both your smug faces, and we can't move past it?"

She shrugged. "I mean, I could remind you that you got shot out of the first round ten minutes in. And the second. And third..."

"Great. Now you're done. Shut up."

"But honestly," she added, "socking you in the face would make me a *lot* happier."

For a moment, their table at the diner was completely silent. Then Greenburg burst into uproarious laughter. Rorden had been halfway through swallowing more of his soda and couldn't contain himself this time. He lurched sideways out of his chair, snorting and spraying fizzy bubbles right out his nose before whisking his napkin off the table and clamping it to his face.

Hapton gave the guy a scathing glance and leaned away. "Are you kidding me?"

"You just..." Rorden wiped his mouth, widened his eyes at the burn of carbonation through his nasal cavity, and hissed out another laugh. "I'd give her what she wants, man. Otherwise, she'll keep coming for you."

"Bullshit." Hapton turned his glare on Greenburg, who hadn't stopped laughing and now repeatedly stomped one foot. "Is that what you want, Moorfield?"

Idina kept smiling as she held his gaze and leaned toward him over the table. "Oh, yeah."

That set the other Rangers into snorting bursts of

laughter all over again. Hapton's nostrils flared, one side of his nose twitching up in indignation.

He wants a staring contest? Okay. He spent the last two weeks making things weird for me. I'm happy to return the favor.

Then the guy's sneer cracked. Hapton scoffed, leaned back against his chair, and let out a sharp, barking laugh that made the other conversation in the diner momentarily pause. Several other patrons glanced at their table before returning to their lunches.

"Damn, Moorfield." He shook his head. "You don't break easy, do you?"

"Nope. But I did expect you to last a little longer in that arena."

With another chuckle, he flipped her the bird and leaned forward. "You know what? You're all right."

She picked up one of her breaded chicken fingers and grinned. "I'm flattered."

"No, you're not. Don't think this makes us best friends or some fucking shit like that."

"Well, then there really *would* be something wrong with me." Idina tore a huge bite of chicken finger off between her teeth and stared right back at him as she chewed.

The other two Rangers kept laughing before Greenburg finally lifted a hand in front of him and caught his breath enough to talk. "Okay, okay. Everyone's good now. We get it."

"Totally." Rorden wiped a tear from the corner of his eyes with the back of a hand and sighed. "Point made. Hapton's a sore fucking loser, and Moorfield's funny as shit—"

"We're moving on, asshole." Hapton punched him in the

shoulder, then reached across his plate to snatch a handful of fries off Rorden's plate.

"What the hell?"

"You gotta pay me somehow for putting up with your shit." Hapton crammed the fries into his mouth, then nodded at Idina. "You gotta be nuts for going into jump school. Especially with that clown."

Greenburg spread his arms and bowed over the table. "It's an honor."

Idina watched all three of them badgering each other with jokes and getting bites of food in between laughter.

Look at that. All it took to get Hapton out of the Stone Age was for me to be an equal jerk to his face.

"Seriously," Hapton added when the laughter and ribbing had settled down. "Why'd you go for getting your wings? I mean, Greenburg's doing it 'cause it's a requirement for us. Plus, he's psychotic."

"Professionally," Greenburg added with a grin.

"No way you're *that* level of crazy."

"I don't know." Idina dipped another chicken finger into the cup of dressing on her plate and shrugged. "My platoon leader at basic recommended it and asked if I wanted to go. So I'm here."

"Wait, basic?" Rorden swallowed his food and squinted at her. "As in that's where you came from?"

"Yep. Finished AIT and shipped out to Benning."

"As an E3?" Greenburg turned to look at her, clearly having a hard time putting two and two together.

"I mean, I went *into* basic as an E3—"

"Goddamnit!" Hapton dropped his next handful of fries back on his plate and slumped back in his chair. "Fuck me."

Idina laughed. "Sorry. Did I burst your bubble?"

"He's just pissed he got his assed kicked by a newb," Rorden explained, fighting to push the words out through bubbling laughter. "Who outranks him."

Hapton thrust a hand across the table toward her. "What is this shit, huh? She can't even fucking drink."

"I *can...*"

"Huh?" They all stared at her, and Idina pulled her drink closer for another sip.

"Unless it takes more skill than drinking iced tea."

Greenburg dropped his chin to his chest and snorted.

"You hear this?" Hapton looked back and forth between his buddies. "Fucking standup comedian over here."

"I already said she was funny," Rorden muttered.

"Yeah. Swiss Army smartass." Hapton rolled his eyes. "Drink your iced tea, Private *First Class*. I'm not buying you booze, and you're not better than the rest of us."

She looked up from her drink and glanced around the table, faking confusion. "You mean when we're not talking about laser tag, right?"

The guys burst out laughing again, even Hapton. Idina couldn't help but join them.

Looks like I turned the one pain in my ass into a friend. Or at least someone who doesn't hate my guts. One less thing to worry about before jump week. I'll take it.

CHAPTER SIXTEEN

After a Saturday of laser tag and lunch, Idina was grateful for the time she spent alone on Sunday. Thanks to Greenburg's master plan to get her off Fort Benning and out for a little unexpected fun, she did feel better. She also had their first jump to look forward to, all while her latest email from Reggie echoed in her mind.

Several times that day, she opened her email on her phone and tried to draft a response to the man that didn't sound either incredibly petty or desperate for answers. Idina wasn't ready to talk to anyone about the things she'd seen and the strange effects of her abilities after six months away from Moorfield Manor and off her "medication." Not yet.

The kind of questions she wanted to ask would only reveal that she *had* experienced much stranger pseudo-episodes. She doubted Reggie would have the answers she was looking for anyway. What she really wanted was to figure out where Richard Moorfield had gone into apparent hiding and how she could contact *him*.

That was impossible right now. Plus, Idina had more immediately important things to focus on.

Such as getting ready to meet the rest of the training cycle at 05:00 the next morning for their first jump out of a real C-130—from over twelve hundred feet in the air, with T-11 parachutes.

No one, even Idina, could truly anticipate precisely what that first day would be like.

At 05:30 on the first day of jump week, Sergeants Birch and Hutchinson brought the chalks out to the green ramp of the airport on Fort Benning, looking as dedicated and alert this early in the morning as they did when starting work four hours later. Every trainee wore their active duty uniforms like every other day, plus their helmets and harnesses. They'd returned the reserve chutes they'd practiced with during the last week.

Birch didn't waste any time dishing out instructions. "Down the edge of the tarmac and into that building, soldiers. Grab your T-11 and your reserve, then get back out here stat. Let's go."

The chalks moved swiftly down the edge of the tarmac, breaking into a jog to carry out their orders as quickly as possible. Inside the outbuilding that looked like a much smaller version of a hangar, another Black Hat Idina hadn't met stood beside the rows of T-11s and reserve chutes. He waved the soldiers forward and gestured toward the gear. "Move, move, move. Grab your gear and head out."

Idina grabbed the next available chutes off the racks

and tucked one under each arm like everyone else before turning and running back in line to where Birch and Hutchinson waited for them. Her breath misted in the morning air, and when she slowed behind Major Hines, Birch called their next instructions.

"You have a gear buddy for a reason. Rig up!"

Those who'd returned first paired off with their gear buddies to help each other rig the parachutes to their harnesses. When Idina turned to get to work with Greenburg, he grinned at her as he set his chutes on the ground and reached for hers.

"You ready for this, Moorfield?"

"As ready as you are." Smirking, she turned so he could strap the T-11 to the back of her harness. The weight of it hanging from her back felt almost twice as heavy as slinging the thing under her arm and running around with it unattached.

Of course, it feels heavy. This is the thing that'll save my life after I jump out of that plane. Pretty big responsibility to be carrying around on my back.

While Greenburg finished with her T-11, Idina strapped her reserve onto the front of her harness the way they'd trained, then she and her gear buddy switched positions so she could help him rig up his chute.

The rest of the chalks hustled back from the gear hangar to do the same. The tarmac filled with the rustle, *thump, clink,* and *zip* of chutes hitting backs, straps tightening, clips attaching, and soldiers giving their gear buddies reassuring pats on the shoulder or back once their gear was on.

"Lemme check you out," Greenburg muttered. He didn't

wait for Idina to reply before he touched all the safety points on her harness, front and back, and nodded. "Looking good."

"Turn around." Idina performed the same generic inspection on his gear as well. If there were any problems with any part of the chutes that weren't visible outside the deployment pack, the riggers on base would've already found them when packing the canopies. This inspection was to check for external issues.

As Idina motioned for Greenburg to slowly pivot so she could double-check every strap, riser anchor, and the static line on his right shoulder, she found what every soldier in jump school hoped to find before they ever left ground.

She would've seen the issue without her green lights flashing in her vision at one very specific spot on his gear. "Shit. Hold on."

"What?" Greenburg turned toward her with wide eyes, but she spun him back around before finding the base of his yellow static line and carefully lifting it away from the shoulder of his harness.

"It's ripped."

"Jesus."

"Your static line. Just a little bit of fraying, but that's not gonna fly."

Greenburg snorted and flashed her a sarcastic glare. "Cute, Moorfield. I won't be flying either with a defective chute."

She clapped his shoulder and turned to find the jump-masters watching the chalks rig each other up. "Sergeant Airborne! Possible defective chute over here!"

Hutchinson searched for her, found her raised hand,

and nodded before walking swiftly down the line of trainees toward them. "What's going on?"

"His static line looks frayed, Sergeant." Idina offered the jumpmaster the end of the line in question and watched him inspect it. "A little at the edge right there."

"Rigger!" Hutchinson shouted.

The closest of several riggers who'd joined them for just such an inspection jogged toward Idina and Greenburg and didn't wait for anyone to tell him what was wrong before he inspected Greenburg's chute himself. "Static line's compromised. That's a defective chute."

Greenburg puffed out a heavy sigh through loose lips, his eyes incredibly wide as the rigger quickly unhooked the bad gear.

"Grab another chute," Hutchinson told him.

The Ranger turned swiftly and followed the rigger toward the gear hangar to pull another T-11 off the rack, and Hutchinson nodded at Idina. "Good eye, Moorfield."

"Thank you, Sergeant."

"Look him over again when he's back with another chute." He walked away down the line of other trainees also diligently checking over their gear buddies for signs of defective equipment.

Idina rolled her shoulders back, already feeling the ache of the T-11's added weight on her back and the reserve on her chest. In under a minute, Greenburg ran back down the edge of the tarmac with a new chute tucked under one arm and the rigger slowly walking out after him.

"You saved my fucking life, you know that?" he panted before handing over the new parachute.

Idina took it and waited for him to turn around. "Part of the job, man."

"Ha. Yeah. So are these suicide jumps."

They both laughed as she worked to strap on his new gear.

He's scared stiff. I can't exactly say I'm a hundred percent confident, either. Joking about it is a hell of a lot better than the alternative.

No green lights flared up in Idina's sight for new defects. No visions popped up to fill her head at the absolute worst time, and no glowing green mist sparkled around her hands under the stress of getting ready for this very real upcoming jump. She gave Greenburg the okay on his new gear and waited with the rest of the trainees for the next step.

"JPMI!" Sergeant Birch shouted. Hutchinson and two other Black Hats who'd come to see the trainees off hurried down the line of trainees along the edge of the tarmac. They stopped at the far end of the trainees.

Birch continued, "This is your jumpmaster inspection, soldiers. Your gear buddies looked over your harness, helmet, T-11, and reserve. But your gear buddy isn't responsible for you as a soldier of any U.S. military branch.

"Whatever happens to you on this jump or any other in your future career falls on the shoulders of your jumpmasters. We train you. We guide you. We make sure we've mentally and physically prepared you for a successful jump. Line up."

The chalks had already made a relatively straight line for their buddy checks. Now every trainee turned away from their buddy to face forward and wait for the final inspection from their jumpmasters. The other Black Hat who'd stayed at this end of the line with Sergeant Birch pulled a black Sharpie from his side pocket and handed it to Birch before they started with Stone at the end of the line. Hutchinson and his jumpmaster second started with the last soldier at the end of Chalk Three and worked their way up the line to eventually meet in the middle.

Idina wasn't the only one who couldn't help but watch Stone's JPMI as Birch looked him over from head to toe, tugging on harness straps and clips, scrutinizing every aspect of both the T-11 and reserve. The process seemed to take forever, but the jumpmasters had to be intensely thorough.

There isn't room for mistakes with this. If they fail to find an issue with our gear before we have to use it, a soldier dies. End of story.

Breathing slowly and evenly, Idina rolled her shoulders back again and shifted her weight to the balls of her feet to more comfortably redistribute the weight of her gear until it wore down on her again.

When Birch finished his inspection of Stone, his jumpmaster second handed over a thick pad of what looked like stationary paper. Until Sergeant Birch peeled a shiny square sticker off the pad, slapped it to the side of Stone's helmet, and scribbled something on the sticker in black Sharpie.

Stone frowned and risked a glance at their jumpmaster. "What's that for, Sergeant?"

Birch raised his eyebrows and nodded. "To pinpoint who was responsible if we recover this helmet without you in it." Then he moved down the line to begin inspecting Jennings' gear.

Stone's gulp was audible over the *thump* and rustle of the jumpmaster tugging and handling every piece of the next soldier's gear as well.

Idina and Greenburg shared a glance, and she knew he was thinking the same thing.

Damn. Of course, they're not taking this lightly. We stopped Greenburg from jumping with a defective chute and kept Sergeant Birch from taking the fall for it. The Black Hats aren't only instructors teaching us how to jump. They're responsible for our lives. I don't envy them this part.

Standing at attention with what felt like a hundred pounds of gear weighing them down made JPMI for every single soldier in all three chalks feel like it lasted forever. Still, no one complained about the last vital step to ensure every trainee would make it through their first successful jump intact and alive. It wasn't nearly as rigorous or debilitating as what any of these soldiers had endured during basic training, Army or otherwise.

The jumpmasters called out three more defective chutes, the riggers confirmed them, and the individuals replaced them, only too grateful to jog down the edge of the tarmac one more time for another T-11 or reserve.

No one berated their gear buddies for not finding the defects. Their training covered how to jump, how to handle their gear, and how to perform a successful PLF to complete that jump. As the final checkpoint, the Black Hats and riggers were the only ones with extensive training in recognizing any gear that needed replacing. They did their jobs with all the precision and attention to detail required by being responsible for dozens of lives per cycle.

Finally, the jumpmasters met in the middle of the line and conferred briefly with each other in hushed tones. Birch addressed the trainees. "Now we wait for the bird."

They led the trainees away from the gear hangar across the tarmac. Every soldier held their silence in expectation, and the only sound rising around them was the steady *clomp* of combat boots against the tarmac and an occasional cough. The sun had already risen enough to light up the sky with vivid oranges, pinks, and yellows, but it did nothing to warm the mid-February chill in the air.

Idina glanced at her field watch—07:34 hours.

Feels like we've been out here a lot longer than that. Doesn't matter how long the prep and gear check takes before we're in the air. That's the most important part.

When the jumpmasters finally led them into the hangar and stopped, the trainees stood in front of an incredibly long row of specialized benches against the wall. The backs were concave in the relative shape of a parachute's deployment bag with a small shelf beneath to remove at least a little of the weight from the soldiers' backs before they were ready to board the aircraft.

"Everybody sit," Hutchinson called and gestured at the benches. "Nobody moves until our ride pulls up."

The chalks walked quickly down the row of benches, and every soldier sat. Idina carefully leaned back, intending to rest most of her chute on the small ledge for that purpose. It hardly removed any weight and made sitting slightly backward at such an odd angle surprisingly uncomfortable. So she leaned slightly forward instead and took the full weight of her gear on her shoulders again.

Beside her, Greenburg fidgeted in the paratrooper-shaped bench seat, grunting and sighing every time he moved a part of his body to get comfortable. "What the fuck were they thinking when they built these things?"

Idina smirked at him. "It's gonna suck no matter how you sit."

"Nah. I'll find the right position. Just takes a little maneuvering."

She didn't say anything else, opting instead to let him figure it out on his own. He would eventually.

It's not supposed to be comfortable. Getting comfortable leads to complacency. It's the same thing as in basic. They want us alert, aware, and on our toes. Plus, jumping from a plane during real-world combat situations doesn't come with a cushion, a full belly, and warm-fuzzy comfort. They're still simulating combat conditions because we're still training.

Birch walked down the row of benches again, glancing at every trainee in turn. "Your only job now is to settle in and get comfy, soldiers. In your seats, no exceptions. We'll be here a while. I'm not screwing around when I say if you get off that bench, if you touch anything, you'll finish this cycle early without any jumps at all. Understood?"

"Yes, Sergeant Airborne!" the chalks shouted in response.

"Feel free to enjoy a little recruiting video while we wait. It's good stuff." Smirking, Birch gestured toward one of the other Black Hats who'd joined him and Hutchinson.

The rumble and rhythmic *squeak* of a metal cart on wheels preceded the other NCO. An old, clunky television set rested on that cart, its screen black and reflecting the lights mounted on the wall above the jump benches.

The Black Hat pulled the cart out in front of the soldiers. A long black extension cord and several smaller cables trailed behind him. Then he stooped in front of the TV to turn it on, fiddled with the VHS player, and lovingly patted the top of the TV before rejoining the other jumpmasters.

Idina frowned at the insanely outdated piece of technology. "VHS, huh?"

On her left, Major Hines chuckled. "You know what a VHS is? I thought your generation lost that knowledge."

"One of my brothers collects old tech. I've seen an 8-track too, sir."

Greenburg huffed out a wry laugh and shook his head. "If it ain't broke, don't buy a new one, right? With a dinosaur like that, I wonder how old the video is."

Pressing her lips together, Idina leaned back against the bench to rest her chute for a moment and shrugged. "I'm guessing prehistoric."

Their laughter was tense and shallow beneath the expectant pressure of waiting for their aircraft to arrive. It probably wouldn't have lasted much longer even if the ancient TV on the metal cart hadn't let out a loud, clunking *click* before the screen crackled with static and wavered into the fuzzy opening shot of the so-called recruiting video.

A man's harsh, wannabe hardass voice boomed from the overhead speakers that had been plugged into the TV, though the age and quality of the VHS tape made the audio crackle as the tone warbled through highs and lows. *"Airborne. Three weeks of mind and muscle pushed to the limit."*

The screen filled with silent shots of soldiers running during PT, drilling on The Swing, and crashing to the ground. A noir-sounding bass meant to create an air of epic importance blared from the speakers at inconsistent volumes.

"If you don't think you can cut it, don't even try."

"This is bullshit," Greenburg muttered. "What's the point of a recruiting video when we're already sitting here ready to go?"

Idina shrugged. "Morale-building?"

"Yeah, right. Building my morale to get the fuck off this bench."

For the most part, he was joking. As the recruiting video played all the way through, it became more and more apparent how accurate Greenburg's statement had been. Especially when the video ended and the other support jumpmaster who'd joined them strolled out to the TV cart.

He pressed rewind on the VHS player and waited with a hand on the cart while the machine inside *whirred* and *clicked*. The whole time, he scanned the rigged-up soldiers sitting on the benches with a patient, closed-lipped smile until the VHS player let out another loud *click*. Then he pressed "Play," turned toward the other Black Hats sitting behind a fold-up table at the end of the jump benches, and raised two fingers in the air. "Two!"

"What the fuck?" Greenburg leaned slightly forward to watch the Black Hat return to the others, then gaped at the TV crackling to life with the video's opening shot. "For real?"

"Hey, maybe there'll be a pop-quiz afterward," Idina suggested.

Major Hines barked a laugh and immediately covered it up with a forced cough.

With another heavy sigh, Greenburg leaned back against the bench at the extraordinarily awkward angle and closed his eyes. "Wake me when it's over."

There's no way he can sleep here like this. None of us can. I'd probably take a quick nap over watching that crappy video a second time. At least we'll be in the air soon.

CHAPTER SEVENTEEN

The VHS player *clicked,* and one of the support jumpmasters strolled back out toward the cart. The entire row of trainees held a collective breath, hoping he'd press the power button this time. Instead, his finger hit rewind, and the machine's whirring was lost beneath a combined groan rising from every sore, stiff, anxiety-ridden trainee on the benches.

"You've gotta be kidding me." Idina tipped her head back to rest it against the back of the bench, but the crick in her neck made it an instantly terrible idea. She jerked her head back up, blinked heavily, and glared at the jump-master waiting for the video to rewind.

"I think I'm gonna puke," Greenburg muttered.

Jennings leaned forward toward the end of the line with a grunt and gave Greenburg a thin smile. "Head between your legs, soldier."

"Head out of your ass, Marine."

By now, none of them were in any mood to laugh at a

few jokes. The comments weren't exactly jokes at this point, either.

The VHS player *clicked* again, the jumpmaster pressed "Play," and the video started all over again. "Fifteen!"

"Nice round number, huh?" Sergeant Hutchinson called happily as the support jumpmaster rejoined the others.

The bench beneath Idina wobbled and reverberated with the shifting weight of so many trainees trying to get comfortable—or at the very least alleviate the aches and pains of having sat here for this long.

Greenburg's knee had been pumping up and down for the last fifteen minutes. He leaned as far forward as he could with the reserve chute on his chest, trying to prop himself up with his forearms on his thighs for a new position. "I can't feel my legs."

"I'm feeling shit in places I didn't even know I had," someone else replied from farther down the line.

Idina tried to massage her quad above the knee, but that only made the stiffness feel worse.

"Run, man," the video narrator continued for the fifteenth time. *"Run 'til your legs get tough. So when you hit, it's the ground that hurts."*

Greenburg looked at his field watch and groaned. "Fucking shit."

"Six hours and counting," Idina muttered, her voice stripped of whatever inflection it once had to resemble a toneless, emotionless robot.

"It's not coming," Jennings added. "I get it now. The plane's never showing up, and we're gonna sit here all fucking day with that goddamn video playing over and over until we drop."

"This is hell." Greenburg swiped a hand across his mouth and slowly shook his head. "We're all dead, and *this* is the fucking afterlife."

"I gotta piss so bad," Stone said.

Between Jennings and Major Hines, Crimshaw leaned forward to look at the Marine at the head of the chalk and shook her head before speaking for the first time in the six hours they'd been here. "Don't even think about it."

"Oh, sure. That's right." Stone rolled his eyes. "Let's talk about the fucking pink elephant on the tarmac and ignore it at the same time. I can't *not* think about it."

"If you get off this bench, you're done," she continued.

"You don't think I know that?"

Crimshaw shrugged. "You wouldn't be the first soldier to experience incontinence during jump week. Definitely not the first Marine."

The trainees who could hear Crimshaw's words over the static repetition of the recruiting video broke into weak, uncertain laughter.

"Isn't it so fucking great to have a medic in the chalk?" Stone grimaced and tightly gripped both thighs, his legs wiggling back and forth as he tried to keep his bladder in check.

Two hours ago, Idina had given up trying to find the least uncomfortable position sitting on the bench. Her shoulders, neck, upper and lower back, and legs were practically on fire with stiffness and the weight of her gear growing heavier by the second. The leg straps of her harness felt like they were cutting off the circulation in her thighs, but she couldn't stand to readjust them for at least a little relief. None of them could.

"I'm *this* close to calling it," Greenburg muttered, holding up his thumb and index finger a few centimeters apart. "*This* fucking close. It's not worth it—"

"Shut up," Idina told him. "You're fine."

He snorted and glanced at her sidelong, his grimace as close to a smirk as any of them could get right now. "You're a real fucking ray of sunshine, Moorfield."

"Yeah, you too."

A round of laughter rose from the table where the jumpmasters sat comfortably in their chairs. They were free from the weight of full jump gear and could stand and walk around whenever they wanted. Idina gritted her teeth at the sound of them enjoying themselves so much.

It's all part of the process. They've been through the gauntlet to get to where they are. Now it's our turn. Would've been nice if they'd told us we'd be stuck in a time loop for six hours, losing all the feeling in our limbs. And the rest of our sanity.

The recruiting video droned on and on. Then a new sound filled the air around them.

Greenburg whipped his head up and looked around. "What's that?"

A low whine was barely audible over the video through the speakers, but it quickly and steadily grew louder and higher in volume. The rumble that followed reverberated through Idina's chest. All the disheartened exhaustion that filled her from the last six hours of waiting and doing nothing now disappeared beneath an acute awareness rushing through her senses.

"That's the plane," she muttered.

"Fuck." Greenburg gaped at nothing in front of them.

His face turned ghostly white between the straps of his helmet.

At the same time, loud groans came from the jumpmasters at their table. "Aw, come on. I almost had this one!"

"You bet on sixteen, Sergeant Airborne. Didn't quite get there. So pay up."

"You didn't even guess a number."

"You were wrong, so I win. You can write me an IOU after you turn it off."

Idina blinked, briefly wondering if she'd misheard the conversation.

Seriously? They've been betting on how many times they could replay the damn video while we wait?

Greenburg slowly turned his head toward her, his face still drained of color and his eyebrows creased in pitiful concern. "Did you hear that too, or am I hallucinating?"

"I heard it."

Major Hines rubbed his palms along his thighs and inhaled deeply through his nose. He didn't say a word.

He's been through high-stress situations before. You don't get to major without it. Still, it's his first jump too. Idina swallowed and tried not to look at anyone else so she wouldn't see her anxiety reflected in her fellow trainees' eyes. *We're finally doing this. Shit.*

After hours of sitting, half her body numb and the other half tingling with pins and needles from lack of movement and partially constricted blood flow, she almost didn't recognize the burning, icy-hot sting racing down her forearms and into her hands. She automatically opened her hands to flex her fingers and caught a hint of flickering green in her peripheral vision, rising from her lap.

Shit. No, no, no.

She subtly tried to shove her hands beneath the outsides of her thighs. Doing so was difficult and painful when she scraped the backs of her hands on the bench's metal surface where the seat contoured to support a body. Gritting her teeth and fully expecting bruises later, Idina glanced down at her thighs and found no sign of her lights acting up.

I get it. High-stress situations. Thanks a lot for the heads-up, Reg, but nothing *you told me in that email helps me when this shit flares up.*

Her breath quickened as the roar of the C-130's engines reached their peak whine and rumbled down the tarmac outside, heading steadily toward them. From their position, none of the trainees could see a thing through the windows or the hangar door meant for personnel.

Sergeant Hutchinson walked straight out toward the TV cart and cut off the video mid-sentence. Some of the trainees let out weak cheers or clapped unenthusiastically. The jumpmaster ignored them all before wheeling the cart back toward the wall.

Greenburg looked down at Idina's hands crushed beneath her thighs and the metal bench and wrinkled his nose. "You good?"

"Nope." She shot him a weak smile. "Trying to find *some* body part that isn't completely numb."

"Right. Kinda makes it hard to stand when you can't feel your—"

The C-130's roaring engines finally grew loud enough to drown out the rest of his statement and any other conversation between the trainees. The massive aircraft taxied toward the chalks on their benches and finally stopped.

Sergeant Birch stepped out in front of them and gestured for everyone to stand. "Jump time! On your feet!" His shout was drowned out by the engines too, but no one had any misconceptions about what he meant.

The trainees struggled to their feet, using the backs of the benches as support to rise onto their aching, stiff legs and offering helping hands to their neighbors.

"Let's go!" Birch accompanied the order with a non-verbal command before pointing at the hangar's open door. Stone led the line as the first in Chalk One to climb up into the plane.

This is totally insane. We're all insane. And we're all still doing this.

Hutchinson waited for them inside the hull, gesturing toward the aircraft's starboard side where Chalk One would strap into their seats. The trainees had already drilled this plenty of times the week before. They knew where to go and what to do once they were there. Chalk One took their seats and strapped themselves in as Chalk Two entered, and finally Chalk Three.

The rows of jump seats were incredibly close, meaning each soldier was practically sitting on top of the other by the time everyone boarded, and the ramp closed with a rumble and a *hiss*. The C-130's engines weren't nearly as loud inside as they were out on the tarmac, but it still took a tremendous amount of effort to be heard over the craft's constant roar. The trainees didn't try.

When everyone was strapped in and jammed against each other like sweaty, stinky, white-faced sardines, Hutchinson and Birch took their seats along the starboard fuselage between the cockpit and the side door.

The doors that would open at twelve hundred feet and spew out first-time jumpers one right after the other.

Idina closed her eyes and tried to focus on anything but the nerves writhing in her stomach.

It's not like I'm about to do something that no one else has done before. The Black Hats know what they're doing. So do we. We wouldn't be here if we didn't.

She looked down at her hands on her thighs, relieved to see they weren't glowing and terrified that they would at any point during this first jump.

Keep it together long enough to get out that door. That's it. Because you don't have the room to hide your hands.

They didn't have room to move at all, and the cloying stink of so many highly stressed soldiers packed so closely together didn't make it easier to relax.

They could've sat there for five minutes or half an hour before the aircraft lurched beneath them and slowly taxied across the tarmac away from the hangar. Idina's gut lurched too. The soldiers around her exhaled heavy breaths, closed their eyes, or stared across the hull at those jammed into seats across from them. Everyone bounced in their jump seats. Static line clips jingled against harness straps. Knees bounced up and down. Someone in the front row on the other side of the plane groaned and leaned forward.

Please don't puke. Idina closed her eyes and forced

herself not to watch the guy. *Not here. Not in this stuffy can. We'll all lose it.*

Fortunately, the pale soldier in question managed not to unload his stomach contents before the C-130 left the ground. Probably because he'd listened to Sergeant Birch's suggestion *not* to eat anything before the jump. Apparently, so had everyone else.

Even if the engines hadn't been too loud for conversation, no one would've said a thing as the aircraft picked up speed, raced down the tarmac, then tilted slightly before finally being airborne. Idina was sure she felt her internal organs shifting up into her throat and down into her toes as they lifted off and began the steady ascent from the Fort Benning airport toward the jump zone. Eventually, though, they settled back into place. Mostly.

We spent six hours waiting for this moment, and now it's here. It's happening. This is all real.

Realizing she thought the same words Reggie had included in his email about her abilities brought a new round of nausea creeping up all over again. Then again, that could've been from the acrid stink coming from dozens of geared soldiers and their anxious sweating soaking through uniforms and harness straps and the padding of their helmets.

She gripped the straps of her harness and leaned slightly forward to look up the line at the jumpmasters in their seats. Birch and Hutchinson scanned the faces of their trainees as the aircraft climbed higher and higher. They briefly leaned toward each other to share some comment nobody could hear, and Idina closed her eyes again.

Blank mind. That's what you need. Don't think about anything but being in this seat right here, right now. It'll be over before you know. Successful jump. Nothing else.

Now that they were so close, though, that was easier said than done.

CHAPTER EIGHTEEN

It was impossible to tell how long the C-130 moved through the sky before they reached the jump zone on base. Idina had promised herself she wouldn't check her field watch, knowing it would most likely become a compulsion harder and harder to stave off the more time passed. There was no warning before Birch—with his harness affixed to a safety line against the bulkhead—stood from his seat and walked steadily toward the jump door. The metal handle *clinked* into position, and he opened the hatch.

A gust of cold air and the roar it brought with it filled the aircraft's hull. Even with the chilly temperatures at this elevation in February, the temperature change was a small but welcome reprieve to the stuffy heat. The change in pressure wasn't nearly as bad as Idina had expected, but they weren't at commercial flight altitude. Still, sweat soaked her OCPs like everyone else's, and the cool air didn't do a damn thing for her body's temperature steadily rising with the adrenaline flooding through her.

Sergeant Birch remained beside the door, watching everyone's reactions. So far, nobody had freaked out. Hopefully, that wouldn't change.

Idina tried to draw deep breaths and didn't meet anyone else's gaze. Instead, she watched her jumpmaster's face and caught on to the pride she thought she saw there.

Everybody's handling this like pros. Because we are. All part of the job.

A few minutes later, Sergeant Birch confirmed it was almost time when he shouted, "Ten-minute countdown!"

"Ten-minute countdown!" the trainees replied. A few muted groans rose after that, but now everyone focused intently on their jumpmaster and his next commands.

"Stand up!"

"Stand up!"

Idina struggled to her feet with everyone else who'd repeated the shouted order. She had to grip the straps of her jump seat to steady herself against the constant wobbling of the cargo deck beneath her, but she managed to stay upright.

"Hook up!" Birch shouted.

The members of every chalk echoed in unison, "Hook up!"

Hands went directly to static lines on the right shoulder of their harnesses. One by one, each trainee clipped in as ordered. No one fumbled with their static line. No one faltered. Idina waited for the sound of Greenburg's clip and his gentle nudge against her shoulder before she clipped herself in and nudged Major Hines in turn.

"Check static line!" Birch shouted.

"Check static line!" Everyone looked down at their

yellow lines to make sure the straps were flush against their shoulders, that nothing was twisted or caught up in a different strap. Then they checked the static line of the person who'd be jumping in front of them.

When Greenburg ran his hand along her static line from clip to harness and nodded, Idina turned toward Major Hines and did the same. She had to stop to untwist the bottom of the line where it had caught briefly against his harness' shoulder strap, but it was a quick and easy fix. The major met her gaze with a deep, determined frown and nodded before turning toward Crimshaw.

Holy shit, we're almost there.

Idina swallowed thickly and steadied herself with a hand against the wall.

After Sergeant Birch finished checking Stone's static line, he slapped the soldier on the arm and hollered, "Sound off for equipment check!"

The last trainee in the last row looked over the guy in front of him and slapped him on the back. "Okay!"

"Okay!"

"Okay!"

One by one, the trainees thumped each other and gave the proper response that everyone had been looked over and was safe to jump, their left hands extended to the side to signal they'd done their equipment check. Idina was surprised to find herself smiling a little when Greenburg's hand came down on her back before she did the same to Major Hines and shouted above the roar.

Finally, Stone barked at the Black Hat standing right in front of him, "All okay, Jumpmaster!"

Birch grinned and slapped the Marine's extended hand,

giving him a curt nod. Then he walked around the lined up chalks, slapping every other extended hand to ramp up morale and remind the soldiers of how far they'd come. With a matching grin, Hutchinson walked down the hull to stand beside his fellow jumpmaster, his eyes wide as he met every trainee's gaze and gave them the same nod.

They're as psyched about us making it this far as we are. Okay, maybe not in the same way. But that sure as hell looks like pride.

There wasn't anything else to do or say until Birch turned toward the cockpit to either check the equipment there or receive a signal from the pilot nobody else could see. Then it was Sergeant Hutchinson's turn to shout the next command. "One minute!"

"One minute!" The automatic response drilled into them rose from every soldier's throat before the full weight of what they'd just shouted truly sank in. Trainees groaned, drew massive breaths, or bowed their heads to try collecting themselves.

"Fuck, fuck, fuck, fuck…" Greenburg muttered.

There was nothing Idina could do or say that would prepare him for what came next. He had to find it in himself to make this jump, just like every other soldier on the aircraft. It was almost time.

For a second, she thought *she'd* be the first one to puke in the hull. Then the green lights above the back wall of the cockpit and right above the cargo ramp flicked on and turned bright green.

A strange but somewhat-familiar calm washed over her, accompanied by a fading tingle in her forearms and fingers. Time seemed to slow. The roaring engines faded slightly. The backward and forward motion of the soldiers swaying in front of her made her think of seaweed in an ocean current. Sergeant Birch's mouth moved without sound, but then it all came crashing back to her. Including her breath.

"Green light, go!"

Stone bent his knees and jumped.

The rest of the soldiers did what they'd trained to do, pushing themselves forward with the courage and determination they'd cultivated as armed forces members. Jennings was out. Two seconds later, Crimshaw disappeared. Major Hines looked like he was about to hesitate, but his feet left the deck, and he was gone.

Idina approached the open door, handed her static line to Sergeant Birch, and thought she saw him smile before her body seemingly moved of its own accord. She only glimpsed the blue-white expanse stretching out beyond the opening in all directions, but she didn't need to *see* what lay in front of her to know what came next. Her hands went to either side of her reserve, her knees bent, and she sprang off the platform the way she'd drilled.

If it hadn't been for the hot, whipping gusts of the C-130's propeller wash catching her the second she left the aircraft, she would've questioned whether she'd jumped at all. At first, it didn't feel like she was moving, let alone falling in a dead drop from the plane. Air whipped around her head, *crackling* and *thumping* in her ears with a deafening roar.

"One thousand! Two thousand! Three thousand!" She couldn't hear her countdown, and the vibration in her chest could've been from either her hoarse voice croaking out during free fall or from the constant shake and rattle of everything all around her. Her fingers clenched tightly around her reserve, but she wasn't thinking about having to use the backup chute. Not yet.

"Six thousand!"

Idina craned her neck up behind her to check for her chute, her gut churning with adrenaline-fueled apprehension. She'd remembered her training, and the static line had deployed her chute perfectly.

At first, she didn't recognize the ballooned shape above her, but her rational mind kicked in two seconds later. She brought her hands up to the risers above both shoulders and let out a shrieking, breathless laugh.

Below her, the other four soldiers in her chalk were all descending with their chutes deployed. The wind carried her wherever it would, and she looked up to search for the plane. It seemed incredibly far away, but not nearly as far as the ground steadily rising toward her.

The ground.

Idina returned her attention below and viewed the expanse of the jump zone stretching out before her—a few hills rising in the distance, a thin forest, the cresting dip of the land where she'd touch down in about fifteen seconds.

Those fifteen seconds felt like an eternity as she breathlessly scanned the world around her. The serene silence would've been complete if it weren't for the C-130's steady hum overhead, but even that was soft. Gentle.

This can't be real. It looks like I'm in a movie. Feels like a dream.

The overwhelming flood of surreal, blissful perfection surging through her could've been the rush of adrenaline or the pride in finally having jumped—or both. Either way, Idina didn't care where the most phenomenal sensation she could remember came from. She was here.

Then she looked at the ground again.

Shit. I'm at two hundred feet.

She grabbed her right forward riser and slipped away from the treetops rising in front of her. At first, tugging on the riser didn't do a damn thing until she yanked both right risers as hard as she possibly could. The chute only slipped slightly to the right after she'd pulled for a hard turn, and she thought she felt the top of a tree graze against the bottom of her boot. Then she was free of the tree line and coming in hot.

PLF, PLF, PLF.

Idina clapped the right front riser to her chest and twisted her body to the right, bringing both legs together. Her boots touched the brown grass, and she jerked her hand away from the riser to bring both arms up beside her head, then she crumpled to the ground.

The landing wasn't anything like what they'd practiced even on The Swing. It was impossible to tell if she'd hit all five contact points, but a blaze of pain shot through her right hip before she was lying on her side and watching her chute billow out above her before racing forward overhead.

It fluttered with heavy *whumps,* and before she remembered to unclip, the wind caught it again and hauled her a good fifteen feet across the grass. Her release rings on each shoulder pulsed with green light in her vision. Hissing as she tried to keep herself from being rolled off her back and eating shit in the dirt, Idina slapped the rings with both hands and fumbled for another two seconds with the release clips before it was finally free.

The chute flapped in front of her another few yards. She stopped sliding and *thumped* onto the ground, rolling onto her back now because that was her body's automatic response. As she lay there blinking up at the sky and the specks of other jumpers parachuting down into the jump zone, Idina drew a gasping breath.

I'm not dead. Fuck. I'm not dead. I made it!

She scrambled to her feet and laughed as she raced after her chute still partially floating away from her. If she hadn't been looking for the rest of her fellow jumpers, she would've thought the zone was empty, that she was the only person here. A few shouts echoed from somewhere behind her, muffled by the distance, and Idina stepped on the lines of her chute to keep it from getting any farther away.

Okay. Pack up the chute and get to the rendezvous point.

That part was easy enough, but now her hands shook as she detached the deployment bag from her harness and swung it around to start jamming the deflated parachute back where it belonged. A gust of wind picked up behind her, briefly making her lurch forward on her knees. Then a sharp cry made her look up.

Someone—she couldn't see who it was—prepared to land as the blast of wind caught his chute and ripped him sideways in the direction of his slip. The soldier hit the ground no more than twenty yards from Idina and dropped. His chute blew over his head. The wind picked up again, then dragged him across the ground like a race-horse pulled him and not a deployed parachute.

"Unclip!" Idina shouted.

Whoever it was let out a few more grunts and shouts of effort as he raced away. She finished packing her chute and took off after him.

"Unclip!"

The soldier roared and found his rings, pulling both simultaneously. He kept rolling over and over as the lines disconnected and the chute flapped away from him. When he stopped, he lay facedown in the grass, unmoving.

"Oh, no." Idina sprinted toward him. "Hey! You good?" The soldier seemed forever away, and he still hadn't moved as she approached. "Can you hear me?"

He should be moving by now. It looked like a good landing, but who knows?

Finally, she reached him and dropped to her knees, sliding toward him. "Hey, hey. Move or groan or some—"

"Ah!" The soldier slammed his palms against the ground and shoved himself instantly to his feet. Idina lurched away from the unexpected recovery and immediately recognized First Lieutenant McCabe. He bounced from side to side on the balls of his feet, shaking out his hands, his face red and his eyes wide. "Fuck! *Fuck* yeah! *Woo!*"

Idina laughed and slowly got back on her feet.

"That's what I'm fucking talking about!" McCabe pranced in a tight circle, shaking out his limbs. Then he leapt toward Idina and drew a hand back for a high-five. "*Hit me*!"

Grinning, she high-fived him and couldn't think of a single thing to say.

I didn't know McCabe could smile. First time for everything, right?

The wind picked up again, and Idina looked past him. "You might wanna get your chute."

The first lieutenant stopped mid-cheer, stared at her, then pivoted to see his gear rolling away in the wind. All the frenetic energy seeped out of him in an instant, and his shoulders sagged back into their usual posture. "God-damnit. This fucking blows."

With a snort, Idina tucked her repacked chute under her arm and watched him stalk away. "Hey, you made the jump, though."

"Shut the fuck up."

She laughed harder than she thought possible after doing something so insane and incredibly badass. The first lieutenant flipped her the middle finger before dropping onto his knees to furiously shove his chute into the deployment bag, and Idina turned in the direction of their predetermined rendezvous point.

Nothing against me. That's just First Lieutenant McCabe. I might be the only person in the Army to see his happy dance.

That made her laugh again, and she rucked across the brown, cold grass. McCabe's muffled cursing followed her as the rest of the trainees descended from the sky in a wide perimeter around where she'd landed.

Awesome. Now we need to do this four more times in the next four days. No problem.

A bus was waiting for the trainees once everyone reached the rendezvous point. The soldiers' expressions ranged from white-faced shock to jittery realization as the effects of so much adrenaline set in to wide grins and more high-fives. Sergeants Birch and Hutchinson doled out their rounds of congratulations, high-fives, and thumps on the back before the bus door opened and the trainees filed into their ride back to the barracks.

At least, that was where Idina assumed they'd be going. She was ready to get back to the barracks, take a shower, stuff her face with a hot meal, and get a good night's sleep before it was time to do it all over again tomorrow. That was all she could think of as the bus rolled out of the jump zone and onto a real road again, the air filled with jumbled shouts and conversation as the trainees relayed their experiences and pumped each other up for what they'd all accomplished.

"Hey, Moorfield!" Greenburg called from the front of the bus. When she found him, he shot her a toothy grin that made him look insane and gave her two thumbs-up. "Way to not fucking die!"

She snorted and returned the thumbs-up before noticing McCabe sitting in the row behind Greenburg. The first lieutenant sat perfectly still with his arms folded awkwardly over his reserve strapped to his chest and didn't say a thing to anyone.

I don't have to see his face to know he looks like his usual pissed-off self again. For a minute, though, he was like the rest of us. And he loved it.

The edge of Fort Benning's compound came into view, buildings rising in the distance. Instead of taking the road toward the training barracks as everyone expected, the driver turned in the opposite direction.

Toward the airport.

What?

"Uh…Sergeant Airborne?" Jennings called from the back of the bus. "Did someone forget to tell the driver how to get back?"

"I know how to get back," the driver replied for himself and gave the Marine an amused glance in the massive rearview mirror above his seat.

"Barracks are that way."

"You saying you've had enough, Marine?" Sergeant Hutchinson turned in his seat to eye Jennings. "Wanna bow out?"

"No, Sergeant. I just—"

"You thought we'd finished." The jumpmaster waggled his eyebrows. "Not yet, you're not."

The bus fell intensely silent as the trainees stared out the windows facing the airport before the bus turned down the entrance road stretching alongside the tarmac.

Idina drew a deep breath and held it.

No way. No. We already did our jump today. We have four more days of jump week. Why are we back here?

The jumpmasters probably wouldn't have given her a response if she'd voiced the question aloud. Because it didn't matter *why*, only that they were here to receive orders and carry them out.

The bus stopped with a gentle squeal of brakes, then the doors *hissed* and pulled apart.

Sergeant Birch stood immediately. "Everybody up and out. In case you're wondering, yes. You're jumping again. We have one C-130 and only so much time cleared to use it. So move."

In stunned silence, the trainees quickly packed into the

bus aisle and filtered out of the door onto the road, following the quick pace their jumpmasters set.

Idina stared at the airport and the hangar toward which they headed.

Again. Two jumps in one day? Shit.

She didn't notice Crimshaw stepping up beside her until the other woman cleared her throat and muttered, "Jump week, right?"

"Ha." Idina gave her a weak smile. "Fucking jump week."

There was nothing more to say.

CHAPTER NINETEEN

It was well past dark when they returned to the barracks, and the sergeants dismissed them. "You're on call," Sergeant Birch reminded them. "Your orders for the next jumps will come in as soon as it's time to move out, so don't go anywhere. And don't sleep in."

Sore and exhausted, the trainees shuffled across the yard toward the training barracks. The officers and NCOs broke away at the last minute for their respective barracks, and Idina struggled to keep her eyes open as she filtered in after the others.

I need a shower. Forget going out. I'll take an MRE and as much sleep as I can get.

That was exactly what she did. Fortunately, the small commissary inside the barracks was still open for another twenty minutes, and she purchased three MREs in case the same time constraints hit her tomorrow. Not eating all day for multiple days in a row was something she'd rather avoid altogether.

She barely tasted the MRE that wasn't anything like

whatever flavor it was supposed to be, as stated on the package. A hot shower did little to alleviate the aches and pains of sitting on the jump benches for six hours and again for another two before their second jump. It was enough to bring the rest of Idina's exhaustion creeping back in before she practically collapsed on her bunk and drifted off to sleep.

Even when Crimshaw entered the women's bay later to turn in as well, Idina didn't stir.

As it turned out, her jump school training cycle didn't have another jump the next day. She could only assume it was because the C-130 used for training was needed elsewhere for something else—or the pilot was. After a day of waiting around in the yard, running drills, and spending a few hours helping the riggers sift through other T-11 parachutes and check for defects before repacking them, the jumpmasters finally dismissed them. "Not happening today. Same time, same place tomorrow. Have a good night."

The news was halfway relieving and half annoying as hell, but nobody complained. Idina was glad she'd had the chance to eat lunch and would now have time for dinner too before they tried again in the morning. Still, a small part of her wished they had their third jump that day because having nothing else to do after getting this far through jump week only made room for all the unanswered questions and frustrations of Reggie's last email to seep into her awareness.

When she still couldn't take her mind off what he'd told her once she'd finished dinner and returned to the women's bay, she finally gave in and pulled out her phone to draw up that email she hadn't yet been able to write in response. Now, though, she didn't hold back.

Reggie,

I'm still here, in case you and Mrs. Yardly and anyone else who's read my emails were wondering. We had our first two jumps yesterday. Tell Mrs. Yardly she doesn't have anything to worry about when it comes to my survival in the field. We've been well-trained.

I have no idea when the next three jumps will be, but there was nothing today. The jumpmasters have us on call for the next three days, so it could be any time of the day or night. One of those jumps *will* be at night, and at least one will be in full combat gear. Either way, I'm ready.

I can hear you both in my head asking me what it's like, and I don't think I have the words right now to explain in a way anyone else would understand. Maybe after I graduate and earn my wings. I'll send another email next weekend when that happens.

As for the other subject you brought up in your last email, everything's all good here. Nothing to

worry about. I'll keep what you said in mind, so thanks for the tips.

Give everyone my best.

—Idina

She had to read it over one more time and grimaced at how terse and formal the email sounded.

What else am I supposed to write? 'Thanks, Reggie. I figured it was something like that. Good to know the destructive voices in my head and all the visions aren't because I'm losing my mind. Feel like talking so we can figure out what they mean?'

With a snort, Idina shook her head and sent the email before she had a chance to reconsider sending anything at all.

It won't make him feel any better about the whole thing, and he probably won't believe a word of it. Reggie knows something's *happening with my ability, or he wouldn't have written his last email the way he did. But he doesn't have the answers I want.*

She didn't feel much better about the situation when she turned in for the night, but she expected that. The fact that she hadn't had any other crazy visions of "warriors" from the past or the growling voice telling her it could *feel* her made it easier to focus on falling asleep. Whatever happened, she'd deal with it when the time came. Like she had to deal with three more jumps before earning her wings.

What she didn't expect in the least was for her dream

that night to fall into the same category as her ability acting up the way it had.

Idina dreamt she was alone in a field, surrounded by a thick forest on all sides beneath the night sky. She had no idea how she'd gotten there or why, but the pervading certainty that she was here for something urgent wouldn't leave her alone.

There was no one else around. Nothing she recognized.

Until the ground trembled, and the crumbling roar of the earth threatening to split apart drowned out the sound of her rapid breathing.

"Warrior..."

The voice was the same one she'd heard after NIC at Night at the end of basic training. Everywhere she turned, she found only a dark forest and a dark sky and emptiness.

The ground bucked beneath her, and she stumbled forward under the jolt of the world quaking under whatever force the voice belonged to.

"I know you now, Warrior. You've been hiding for so long. Time to face me." Trees snapped miles away in the forest. The canopy rustled and swayed wildly. *"Face me and know your failure. I will* finish this!"

The last part was a furious scream like wind howling through a rocky canyon. The ground shook again. Trees cracked and split, throwing massive branches that crashed all around Idina.

She spun in every direction, looking for the owner of that voice. The one who wanted to "finish this," whatever *this* even was.

"What do you want from me?" she screamed into the shrieking wind and the trembling earth.

"To end you and your line!"

A blaze of green light filled everything in Idina's vision before she looked up and found the stars above pulsing with the same color. Only it wasn't quite the color of her ability. It was darker somehow, muted, twisted into an adulteration of itself.

Without warning, the trees right in front of her burst apart and sent splintering fragments of branches and pine needles sailing toward her. Then a massive hand, glowing the same green as the stars, shot up from the forest floor to stand thirty feet above the canopy. Black-tipped claws scratched at the sky at the end of every finger.

"You are mine!*"* the voice bellowed.

Idina's body filled with the icy-hot surge of her ability coming to a head—the start of a strong and unstoppable episode she couldn't have held at bay even if she tried.

I'm not supposed to. I need *this...*

As soon as she had the thought, she knew it was true. Raising both hands, Idina tried to call up her ability the way every fiber of her being urged her to do. She had no idea how.

She had no one to show her.

As she stared in horror, the blazing green claw hurtled out of the trees and down toward her, racing faster than she could react. In one swift motion, it bashed against Idina's side and sent her flying across the field as hand after clawed green hand burst from the trees. They tore toward her, disembodied and howling with the wind.

She hit the ground with a *thud,* drew a searing gasp, and woke up.

Fighting to catch her breath, Idina stared around her and for a moment, had no idea where she was.

The bay. The women's bay at Fort Benning. I'm in jump school, and I'm...on the floor?

The blanket had tangled around her, which made it that much harder to sit up. When she finally did, she propped her back against the side of her bunk and drew long, steady breaths.

"What the hell?" she whispered.

Movement across the bay made her heart leap into her throat a second before a *click* echoed through the room. A bedside lamp switched on. Idina clenched her eyes shut against the instant glare.

"Moorfield," Crimshaw said groggily.

"Yeah."

"You're on the floor."

A wry laugh escaped Idina. "Uh-huh. I was just starting to figure that out myself. Sorry if I woke you."

Crimshaw looked at her field watch she'd worn to bed, yawned wide, then pushed herself up into a sitting position on the bunk. "I set my alarm to go off in five minutes anyway." She ruffled her short hair, stopped abruptly, then stared at Idina. "What are you *doing* on the floor?"

"Trying to run away from my dreams?"

"Huh?"

"Nothing." Idina untangled herself the rest of the way, then pushed to her feet. "Crazy dreams is what I meant. That's all."

"Hmm." Crimshaw nodded and stared blankly at the foot of her bunk. "High levels of adrenaline and cortisol can do that."

"I don't think my levels *last night* were nearly as high as the night before."

"That depends on how long you were in shock after our jumps."

Spinning around to face the medic, Idina wrinkled her nose. "I wasn't in shock."

"Yes, you were. We all were and probably will be again. It's perfectly normal."

"Huh." Idina ran a hand through her hair and finally turned on her bedside light now that her vision had adjusted. "So...the dreams are normal too?"

"It doesn't happen to everyone. But yeah." Crimshaw tossed the covers off herself and spun swiftly on the edge of the bed before standing.

Okay. If the medic says weird dreams are from adrenaline and cortisol, I can buy that. I wonder what she'd say if I told her what I dreamt about actually existed in real life three months ago and that I've been having waking visions of the same stuff too.

Idina snorted and shook her head before pulling out her OCPs to get ready for another day of being on call for their next three jumps.

"Feel free to research it on your own if you don't believe me," Crimshaw added as she changed out of her pajamas as well.

"No, I believe you. I'm just..." Idina swallowed. "Just trying to wake up all the way. You have any weird dreams last night?"

"Not the kind that threw me onto the floor." The other woman worked quickly at the buttons of her uniform shirt. "I don't dream much at all, honestly."

"Really?" Glancing over her shoulder, Idina raised an eyebrow at the other woman. "Like, at all?"

"Maybe once or twice a month. Dreams are to help us process information, experiences, and emotions. I manage to do that on my own during waking hours, which is, I assume, why I don't dream." Without another word, Crimshaw snatched up her toiletries bag and headed toward the bay doors for a trip to the bathroom.

When the doors swung closed again behind her, Idina laughed in disbelief and finished getting dressed.

Uh-huh. Private Literal doesn't need help processing her emotions and experiences. Okay. But everybody dreams.

A flickering image of her dream returned to her, and Idina clenched her eyes tightly shut.

Only a dream. That's it. A dream about things you've already kind of seen, even if nobody else on the planet has. Except for Uncle Richard...

With a grunt, Idina slammed her trunk shut with an echoing *crack* through the bay. "Focus, Moorfield. You're not dreaming now, and you have a job to do. Forget this and let it go."

Somehow, giving herself the command out loud—especially with no one around to hear her—seemed to do the trick. She drew a deep breath, stood, and grabbed her combat boots to slip them on and lace them up.

After the week is over, I'm getting my wings. That's all that matters.

CHAPTER TWENTY

Crimshaw didn't bring up the subject of dreams again when the chalks met in the yard again that morning. They'd had time for morning PT—which everyone performed in full uniform in case the jumpmasters showed up to say they were scheduled for a third jump *now*—and a quick breakfast. Now they waited for the last few straggling soldiers to make it out to the yard and await their instructions, whatever those happened to be.

The Black Hats had been out there with them all morning, looking surprisingly smug for apparently no reason at all. Then Birch informed them of their plans for the rest of the week.

"Just got the rest of the schedule for this cycle," he told them. "This has never happened before while I've been a jumpmaster, so it feels like a win. We're heading out to the airstrip today at nine hundred hours for a daytime combat jump. That includes full combat gear for your MOS, including at bare minimum your field rucksack and weapons case. No live rounds on the combat jumps. You'll get a rubber ducky at the approximate weight of your weapon instead.

"We'll distribute the lowering lines at the gear hangar once we get there. Until we move out, Sergeant Airborne and I will run you through how to rig up and deploy all three correctly. Then we're back at it for a nighttime jump at twenty hundred hours tonight. Your final jump will be nighttime combat at twenty-two hundred hours tomorrow. Any questions?"

The trainees were silent.

"All right. Sergeant Airborne?"

"The lowering line." Hutchinson bent to pick up the new piece of gear and demonstrated its proper use.

Idina watched intently with the rest of the trainees, though she repeatedly had to remind herself not to let her mind wander back to her weird dream.

No distractions. You're almost at the end, Moorfield. Focus on right now.

Hutchinson's rundown of proper lowering line use was quick and efficient, not to mention the least complicated part of their jump training so far. The chalks practiced deploying imaginary lines immediately before PLF, then received orders to hustle to the bays and grab the rest of their gear for the upcoming daytime combat jump.

As a light sapper combat engineer, Idina's stuffed rucksack held everything she needed for being dropped out with a unit in the middle of nowhere, sufficiently prepared to ruck to any rendezvous points or mission coordinates no matter the weather, time of day, or terrain.

Lucky me.

Once everyone had gathered in the yard again with

their full gear, the jumpmasters distributed the training weapons cases. They were as dented and beat up as the helmets and harnesses. Jump school didn't issue actual weapons, so the trainees had a good laugh when they discovered what Sergeant Birch had meant by "rubber duckies."

Fake weapons.

Idina had been given nothing more than a thick piece of plywood cut in the approximate shape of an M16 and affixed with a metal head and metal strips along the sides to give it weight. It fit perfectly in the weapons case she was also issued until the end of jump week. The only problem was that until they received their lowering lines that would attach their rucksacks and weapons cases to their harnesses, every soldier had to carry the packs on their backs and the weapons case in their arms.

Weapons cases that were thick enough and heavy enough to withstand hitting the ground before the soldier without sustaining any damage.

Idina readjusted hers in her arms and sighed. "I always wanted an extra hundred pounds of gear on me when I jumped from a plane."

Greenburg snickered. "Careful what you wish for, Moorfield."

"Tell me about it."

Then it was finally time to load up onto the bus and head to the airstrip for their third jump. The mood in the bus, on the tarmac, and again in the hangar once the trainees had received their lowering lines and T-11s was much more stable than their first day of live jumps. Everyone was still a little nervous, but now they knew what to expect. Just with the added weight of full combat gear.

Sergeant Hutchinson ran them through one more quick demonstration of using their lowering lines, and everyone had a chance to deploy the new gear. Rucksacks and weapons cases *thumped* and *clattered* to the ground until the jumpmasters were confident in their trainees' working knowledge.

After that, every soldier and their gear buddy helped each other rig up their distributed T-11—plus all the additional gear and the lowering line, all attached one on top of the other to the harnesses. The jumpmasters performed another necessary round of JMPI. Every helmet got a new sticker with the Black Hat's initials claiming responsibility for each soldier. Then they were led back into the hangar to the specialized benches built precisely for the bulkiness of combat jumps.

The sight of so many soldiers waddling around with their combat gear dangling between their legs was borderline hilarious. At least, they would've laughed if it weren't for the focus and physical strength required to make it to the benches like that. The Black Hats, on the other hand, had no problem snickering and tossing out joking encouragement. They weren't the ones carrying half their body weight in gear—in Idina's case, over half.

She slumped onto the bench between Major Hines and Greenburg and sighed. "I hope we don't sit here for another six hours this time."

Hines managed a weak shrug. "Wasn't as long for Jump Two."

"Come *on*." Greenburg shifted in his seat and tugged at

his OCP pants beneath the tight cinch of his harness' leg straps. He could barely get his hand to his thigh with all the gear dangling between his legs. "Of *course* they can make it more fucking uncomfortable than the first two jumps. If we're sitting here all day, someone's gonna have to get their legs amputated."

Crimshaw leaned forward with a condescending glare. "That would never happen under these conditions. The harnesses would have to be tighter around key arteries by at least—"

"We get it, medic," Jennings interrupted. "He's wrong, and you take everything literally. How about you keep the worst-case scenarios and all the details to yourself, huh?"

Crimshaw leaned back on the bench and didn't say another word.

She's not embarrassed or pissed. But she's not gonna keep talking if nobody wants to hear it. I'm glad I'm not the only one.

Then came the moment they'd all been dreading—the same anticipated moment no one wanted to discuss.

Sergeant Birch pulled the squeaky-wheeled metal cart with the beat up old TV away from the wall and out into the center of the hangar for everyone to see. The trainees groaned.

"Are you kidding me?"

"Come on. I could recite that whole video word for word in my sleep."

"We're already *recruited*—"

"Quiet!" Hutchinson barked from the table of jump-masters.

The benches fell into indignant silence again. Soldiers rolled their eyes, tried to lean back, and shifted uncomfortably as the extra weight of all their added gear bore down on them.

"What do you think this time, Sergeant Airborne?" Birch asked Hutchinson.

"I'm thinking of a number between one and twenty."

"That's not how it works. Pick one."

"Nine."

Birch snorted, turned on the TV, and pressed play on the previously rewound recruiting video before the obnoxious narrator's voice warbled through the crackling speakers.

"Airborne. Three weeks of mind and muscle pushed to the limit."

Idina closed her eyes and let out a long, slow exhale.

I can't sit here listening to this. We already made it through our first two jumps. Do they have to keep up the torture?

Every single trainee shared the sentiment as they waited on the bench for an undetermined length of time until the C-130 showed up outside the hangar door. No one had a clue when that would be, and it was still impossible to see anything through the windows or the open door because their orders were to stay on the benches and not move. For anything.

The silence in the hangar this time seemed a direct product of all the extra weight strapped to their harnesses. After shifting around through every uncomfortable position possible, Idina eventually discovered a trick. If she leaned all the way forward until her reserve hit her thighs, she could fold her arms on top of her rucksack and weapons case and at least rest her head there. It was a hell of a lot better than sitting upright and letting her gear tear down the strength in her core and back she'd managed to regain after the last two jumps in twelve hours.

I could fall asleep like this. That's the best way to pass the time. It's not like I won't hear the plane coming or miss boarding time.

So she tried to do just that. Her limbs relaxed, most of her body weight propped up by her stack of gear between her legs. Drifting off to sleep for a nap seemed entirely possible.

Until another jumpmaster approached the TV to rewind the video and put the trainees through hell all over again. The soldiers tried to muffle their groans, fighting their muscle exhaustion, the anticipation of another jump, and intense irritation at *more* video repeats all at the same time.

Idina gritted her teeth and tried to drown out the sound of the video narrator's voice restarting.

It's no big deal. Not compared to jumping in full gear. You got this far, Moorfield. You can handle Lieutenant Recruiter however many more times it takes.

By the seventh time the video was rewound and played from the beginning, Idina's "deal with it" mantra had run out of steam.

Her eyes flew open, her head still resting on her folded arms on top of her stacked gear. She glared at the TV on the metal cart, hating that recruiting video more than she could remember hating anything.

There's no point to this bullshit. The Black Hats want something to keep them entertained? Fuck that.

She was completely unaware of how intensely she glared at the TV until she got what she wanted.

Green light flared in her vision around the TV for a split second. A shower of green sparks flew from the back of the television with a loud, sizzling *pop*. Several soldiers reared back in their seats on the bench as the video narrator's voice crackled in and out.

Then a new burst of green sparks exploded inside the VHS player. The swinging flap to insert the tape tore off its hinges and flew toward the bench before clattering to the ground. Thin tendrils of black smoke billowed from the player's open mouth, the audio squealed and warbled into silence, and the TV snapped off all on its own.

"What the hell?" Hutchinson called from the table.

Idina lurched away from her gear stack and groaned when the weight of it caught on the waist of her harness and yanked her forward again.

Shit. Shit, did I do that?

One of the support Black Hats quickly walked to the TV and fanned the smoking VHS player with an open hand.

Of course, I did that. Green sparks. Breaking technology. I did it with Bryan's TVs and almost did it with the ASVAB computer. Why would this be any different?

With wide eyes, Idina looked around the hangar and saw every seat trainee staring at the TV in anticipation. The other jumpmasters scowled at the cart and the Black Hat investigating the damage. No one said a word until the officer peered into the gaping hole in the VHS player and shook his head. "Must've shorted out."

"What about the tape?" Birch asked.

The other jumpmaster punched the eject button repeatedly, but nothing came out. He turned and shook his head.

"Fuck!"

Whatever Sergeant Birch said after that vanished beneath the sudden, elated cheers of the trainees. They pumped their fists, clapped, whistled, and generally made a victorious ruckus knowing the cursed video and their hours of repeat viewing were at an end.

Birch stormed toward the cart, waved the support jumpmaster back to the table, and tried to get the TV working again to no avail. Then he spun and barked, "What part of quiet do you not understand?"

The trainees shut up instantly, though a few chuckles and barely muffled snickers broke through.

After fixing his glare onto every face seated on the benches, Birch turned back to the TV for one more attempt and finally gave up. "Dammit! I had a feeling about this one, and now it's screwed. What the hell are we supposed to do now?"

"Sit quietly and wait, Sergeant Airborne?" someone suggested from the end of the line.

Birch spun and pointed in the direction of the voice, not knowing which soldier had offered the sarcastic advice. "I wasn't talking to you, soldier. That was out of line." His warning frown only lasted so long, however, before he snorted and glanced at the ceiling with a wry smirk. "Congratulations. You're the first cycle to get out of this. Don't worry. We'll have this fixed up before your nighttime jump."

It was plain as day that Sergeant Birch didn't believe his words. Neither did the trainees. More subdued laughter and whispered relief followed the jumpmaster back to his table.

Idina couldn't stop staring at the TV. She knew she'd ruptured it with her annoyance. The power of her abilities surprised her in new ways almost every day.

It's not a vision. Not a dream. Not a creepy voice or a bunch of data and stats I have no way of knowing on my own. If that's not the best use of what I can do, I don't know what is.

CHAPTER TWENTY-ONE

The broken video seemed to rejuvenate all the troops even before they heard the C-130's engines powering up, first with a low whine, then growing higher and louder. Idina drummed her fingers on her thighs, ready to get back up in the air so they could get one more jump under their belts.

That much closer to the end. After tonight, we only have two more jumps. Almost there.

Now experienced with two successful jumps, the chalks were much quicker and more efficient in carrying out Sergeant Birch's orders. They boarded the aircraft and took their seats in nearly half the time. Every jump came with the same risks and the same nerves brought on by an awareness of those risks, but there were a lot more smiles on a lot more faces. Nervous smiles, sure, but smiles nonetheless.

Some of the soldiers had enough confidence at this point to at least try to distract themselves by conversing with their neighbors. Sergeant Birch's frustration over the fried TV had disappeared the moment they heard the aircraft's engines, and he treated this jump like any other.

Not quite like the others. This one's a combat jump. Then we do it again at night. The opposite of the other two we've done so far.

Despite that little nugget, Idina was as pumped for the new experience as she'd been for the other two—a little more excitement and slightly less anxiety. That didn't mean her third jump would be a walk in the park.

She didn't expect it to be.

By now, the trainees could practically predict the timing of the jump door opening before their ten-minute countdown. It didn't take them by surprise anymore, but when Sergeant Birch ordered them to stand, it took a little more finesse to get to their feet with so much gear dangling between their legs. The time between each soldier jumping and the one behind them was slightly longer than the two seconds of their previous jumps, just because it took longer to waddle toward the door with their gear before handing the jumpmaster their static line.

Idina moved as quickly as she could after Major Hines disappeared off the platform, sharing a gaze and a nod with Sergeant Birch before she made her jump.

She knew what to expect at this point, although the consistent, violent whir of the air buffeting her entire body at twelve hundred feet was still a jarring shock to the system for the first second of freefall. "One thousand! Two thousand!"

Six seconds in, she looked up to see her chute perfectly deployed once more and grinned.

Here we go again. Doesn't feel like an extra hundred pounds changes much of anything at all. That's helpful.

She kept grinning as her chute carried her through her peaceful descent. Another soldier below her with their chute also fully deployed slipped a hard left to avoid a shallow, muddy pond in the jump zone.

Good thinking. I should slip away from the same—

The wind kicked up and blasted against her chute, sending her swinging forward before the T-11 caught the gust and rose a bit before racing across the jump zone. Idina grabbed both right-hand risers for a hard-right slip to pull herself out of the airstream. That part was successful. She hadn't anticipated the next part.

Her chute now carried her straight for the other soldier she'd seen descending below her, who *hadn't* slipped out of the airstream and had been carried almost up to her altitude again.

Shit, shit, shit.

"Slip out!" she shouted. "Slip out! I'm coming down fast!"

Whether the other jumper heard her, she couldn't tell. His puffed-out canopy hid his face. Whether he'd tried to slip out of their impending collision didn't matter either because the wind gusted again. A second later, Idina headed right toward the other soldier's risers and *through* them. The lines of both chutes tangled, her momentum carried her through to the other soldier's far risers, then her chute drew taut, and she swung out above him.

The soldier shouted in surprise when his chute tugged him briefly in the same direction.

"Oh, come *on*." Idina grunted and grabbed her riser with

one hand and the other chute's riser with the other. Then she turned back to see the deployed chutes connected at the sides. Hers tilted a little more sideways because her center of gravity was attached to another soldier's risers too. "How you doing down there?" she shouted.

"Fucking peachy."

She didn't recognize the gruff voice, but there wasn't much time to put a face or a name to it. The other soldier's risers flashed with a green light that pulsed and raced down to the anchors on the man's harness. Their training had already prepared them for an event like this, but it didn't hurt to have the extra reminder.

Climb down. Can't disconnect the chutes, so we'll have to land together.

As quickly as she could, Idina climbed hand under hand down the other soldier's risers, fighting against the tight lines of her T-11 so she could get to her fellow trainee and reevaluate their landing strategy. Finally, she reached the guy. At the moment, with their descent taking them rapidly toward the ground and the necessity for a quick plan, she didn't register the guy's face. She didn't need to know who he was to know they had to think fast.

"Okay. We're landing together now."

"No shit."

A wry laugh escaped her as she clutched the other soldier's harness and gauged their distance to the ground. "Three hundred feet." She pulled the lowering line's ring at her waist to release her ruck, and the other guy followed suit. "Which way are we rolling when we land?"

"I roll right." His voice was raspy and clipped, and he

didn't once look away from the quickly approaching ground.

"Right. We'll go right."

Two hundred feet. One fifty. One hundred.

They were clear of any terrain obstacles, but being connected by their chutes and landing without seriously hurting themselves or each other was an obstacle in and of itself.

Idina felt the soldier beside her go almost completely limp except for his hand tightly gripping the front right riser. She gripped hers too. They both clamped the riser down across their chests and leaned into the slip. Then she felt the ground beneath the toes of her boots.

They crumpled together, both rolling right like they'd planned. However, their chutes caught slightly different wind angles, pulling Idina against him and a second later rolling *on top* of him. For the next three seconds, they both skidded across the ground at a much faster speed as she struggled to pull away from his body so he could find his release rings.

It didn't help that *both* their rucks and weapons cases bounced along the ground behind them. They nearly got tangled around Idina's legs because she couldn't control her body as much with someone else's beneath her. The other soldier found his rings first and released.

Idina picked up speed, pulled by both chutes because the lines were still tangled. With a shout, she tugged on her release rings, skidded across the ground, and let the chutes sail on overhead.

Breathing heavily, she gave herself a moment to catch her breath. Then she waited for any delayed rush of pain signaling a broken bone or any other immediately threatening injury.

Nothing. That's great after being yanked around by two *damn chutes.*

She swung her right leg in a wide arc and rolled onto her back, following her lowering line stretching from her harness behind her to the dual lumps of her ruck and weapons case resting in her path.

All of it took less than five seconds. Then she jumped to her feet and ran to grab her ruck and weapons case. After a quick inspection, she raced back toward her released chute and found the other soldier already there, repacking his gear.

"Hell of a landing, huh?" Idina croaked.

He paused and straightened slightly to look up at her.

"Hey, Jennings." She grinned at him. "What's up?"

"Fuck you, Moorfield."

She couldn't help but laugh as she dropped to her knees, removed the deployment bag, and started packing up her chute. "I told you to slip out, man."

"I *did*."

"Not out enough."

He whipped his head up to shoot her another scathing glare, then they both laughed and finished packing. "You think you're hot shit, don't you?"

Idina shrugged. "I don't know. Maybe. At least we're not *dead* shit."

With a snort, he lurched to his feet, slung his ruck over his shoulders and the rest of his gear under both arms, then trudged off across the open ground toward their rendezvous point.

Still grinning, Idina did the same and headed after him. About twenty yards to their left, someone shouted and pumped a fist in the air. Idina and Jennings returned the gesture, and she couldn't stop grinning.

Shit happens. Even on a jump. It's about knowing how to get over it in time. Yeah. I'd say that was pretty damn successful. Three down, two more to go. She looked up at the bright blue sky studded with other soldiers' deployed chutes and pressed her lips together. *At night. With full gear. We got this.*

Returning to the jump hangar and waiting for the C-130 to arrive again so they could load up for another jump was a thousand times more enjoyable than the last. To start, jump four was a regular nighttime jump—no ruck, weapons case, or lowering line. That gave the trainees a marked measure of relief, but the real joy was in seeing the TV on the metal cart shoved into the far corner of the hangar without ever being moved from its resting place.

Idina tried not to grin as she drew a deep, calming breath and closed her eyes.

Silence. Not perfect silence, but it's not that damn video either. And nobody has a clue I'm the one who killed it.

She couldn't help but look up and down the line of benches for glances at the other trainees. Clearly, they were equally pleased by such perfect timing of the TV and VHS player shorting out when it had.

I don't need to take the credit for that. Not even a little.

Nobody cared nearly as much about how long they waited for the aircraft to arrive because they weren't being driven insane by the worst recruiting video from the 70s playing on repeat ad nauseum. Despite the plane not rolling up to the hangar until almost 17:00, the trainees leapt to their feet and boarded quickly. The Georgia chill on a February night helped to keep them awake and aware, as did the knowledge that they were reaching the end.

The jumpmasters looked as eager to be finished with jump week as their trainees. They weren't as bright-eyed and straight-backed as they'd been for the last three jumps, and they spoke to each other even less during takeoff and their ascent to jump altitude.

Idina studied her instructors, and focusing on them instead of her anticipation of the next jump brought her a whole new appreciation for the sergeants who'd led the entire cycle through rapid-pace training and experiential learning only a live jump could bring.

They're exhausted too. They have to train us and *jump with us. Who knows how many times they've run these cycles over and over? Plus they're responsible for every single soldier on this aircraft. A little over twenty-four hours to go before we're all done.*

Oddly enough, the thought was both exhausting and reenergizing. No matter what anyone felt about the next twenty-four hours, there was no turning back.

Idina's first nighttime jump was as successful as the others, *without* any added obstacles of hitting trees or getting tangled in another soldier's risers. Her senses were extraordinarily heightened by the dark and seeming quiet of a night jump compared to the daytime. She briefly entertained the idea of whipping off her night vision gear to take in the view unassisted. That was a disaster waiting to happen, so she didn't.

The troops were contentedly silent when they headed back to the rendezvous point. Once they gathered outside the bus, though, Idina caught wind of sharp bursts of laughter and multiple voices speaking up all at once.

"You fucking nailed it, Greenburg," someone shouted. "Should've seen your face."

"Man, there's only one kinda face you can make when you're flapping around like a chicken on a string behind that thing." Greenburg tried to sound pissed, but he was laughing along with the rest of them.

"First time I've seen Sergeant Airborne laugh," someone else added.

Everyone turned to look at Birch, who folded his arms and smirked at Greenburg. "Happens to all of us at one point or another."

"Oh, yeah?" Greenburg scoffed. "You too?"

"Yep." Birch stuck his thumb out toward Hutchinson standing beside the bus doors as they opened. "Sergeant Airborne was the one who had to cut me loose. I'll tell you right now. He let me dangle behind that aircraft a hell of a lot longer than five seconds."

The soldiers around them burst out laughing, and several clapped Greenburg on the back before he shrugged them off. "Yeah, see how much *you* like it when it happens to you, assholes."

Laughing and shouting, they filed onto the bus, ready to get back to the barracks and call it a night.

Idina laughed as she caught snippets of what had happened to her gear buddy right after she'd jumped out of the plane.

His static line didn't release, and Sergeant Birch let him dangle beside the plane for five seconds. Shit, that would've sucked. And Greenburg still made it.

When he turned in his seat and caught her gaze, she gave *him* two thumbs-up this time. Greenburg playfully rolled his eyes and flipped her off in return, but they were both laughing.

CHAPTER TWENTY-TWO

That Friday was their last day of jump week with only one final jump to make before the troops who completed it would graduate and earn their wings. That thought seemed to be the only thing Idina could keep in mind as the trainees and jumpmasters met in the yard to go over protocol again for the final jump, get in their PT and two meals, and amp themselves up for one last drop from a C-130.

After he'd gotten over his initial frustration with tangling their chutes on jump three, Jennings had taken it on himself to tell the story of how Private First Class Moorfield had slipped right into his risers and climbed down to play "hero." The way he told the story—and the way the other soldiers repeated it to her when they made fun of both Idina and Jennings—only made her laugh.

She didn't need the Marine to give her a thank you or explain that he was only joking around. That was part and parcel of being in the same chalk in the same training cycle. They all put their lives on the line in equal measure, and the fact was Idina and Jennings had done a hell of a job working with their circumstances during that jump.

Still, the stories caught Sergeant Birch's attention, and right after dismissing them for lunch, he called her by name.

She jogged toward him and stood almost at attention. "Sergeant?"

He nodded at the group of Marines heading out together for lunch. "Tell me what happened with you and Jennings."

"What happened?" Idina fought not to laugh in the jumpmaster's face. "He caught a thermal and didn't slip out in time. We both slipped hard in opposite directions, and I came in between his risers."

"Uh-huh. Then?"

Pressing her lips together, she looked over her shoulder, but no one was watching her conversation with the Black Hat. "Then I climbed down his risers, gauged three hundred feet to drop our lowering lines, and asked him which way he wanted to roll. That's it, Sergeant."

"Yeah, I thought so." Birch snickered. "The way he tells it makes it sound like you did it on purpose."

"A thermal's pretty hard to anticipate when you're not the one hitting it, Jumpmaster."

"You're telling *me*. Good work out there, Moorfield. Thanks for the report."

"Anytime, Sergeant."

He nodded toward the barracks, not needing to dismiss her formally after a fairly casual conversation. Idina turned and only let herself smile with her back to her instructor as she hurried across the yard.

'Good work, Moorfield.' Feels like I've heard a lot of that lately. It's probably what got me to jump school in the first place. Who knows where it'll get me next? As long as I don't get a big head about it, right?

Laughing, she slipped through the barracks' door to head for the dining facilities. She'd already had a huge breakfast and would probably pare down for dinner with their final jump in ten hours. For now, she was happy enough with the luxury of time to eat what she wanted in whatever quantities she wanted and enjoy it.

We've almost finished. No point in thinking about what happens next until we get there.

The rest of the day passed a lot more quickly than she'd expected with their fifth and final jump only hours away. Morale was high even as a nighttime combat jump. The anticipation filled the trainees with renewed excitement to get this over and done with and move the hell on.

Idina and Greenburg teased each other about their respective "obstacles" during the last few jumps, but it was all in good fun.

"Got any plans after this?" he asked when 22:00 rolled around, and the chalks followed the jumpmasters toward the bus waiting for them for the final time.

"No way." She shook her head and hauled her rucksack over her shoulder. "If I think any farther ahead than this jump, I'm pretty sure my brain will explode."

Greenburg snorted. "I feel ya. Feels like we've been jumping for a whole goddamn year."

"You know where you're heading once Private Greenburg earns his wings?"

"Nope. I'll get my orders like you and every other sad sap on base, and we'll go where they tell us to go."

Idina looked over her shoulder at the training barracks and the external lights glowing in the darkness. "Hapton's gonna cry when you leave."

Greenburg laughed and playfully shoved her away by the shoulder. "Yeah. Tears of joy. Especially when it's *both* our asses getting shipped out of Benning."

She clicked her tongue and exaggerated a thoughtful stare. "You're right. He'll cry *extra* hard when I'm gone."

They boarded the bus, found their seats, and got ready for the drive to the airstrip and everything that came with their final jump of the week.

Idina smiled the entire time, even when hauling her ruck off the bus, hustling into the jump hangar, and gathering the extra combat gear for a full combat jump.

Last one. Damn. It's insane how much can happen in three weeks, and now it's almost over. She took her seat on the specialized bench between Major Hines and Greenburg, trying one more time to find a comfortable position that didn't exist. *Yep. Not gonna miss a single thing about these stupid seats.*

Whether it was because this was their last jump of the cycle or the C-130's pilot was running particularly on time, the chalks only waited an hour for the aircraft to taxi up to the hangar. The jumpmasters shouted for everyone to board the plane, and each chalk moved quickly up the loading ramp into the hull.

Idina's entire body buzzed with excited energy, which

seemed to hop contagiously from soldier to soldier as the aircraft's engines kicked up a notch and they taxied down the tarmac.

Here we go. Nothing can stop us now. This is it.

While the trainees waited through takeoff and ascent with wide eyes and the kind of confidence that came with experience, Birch and Hutchinson looked flat-out done. Idina couldn't blame them.

They've probably jumped more than all of us in this cycle combined. And they're not stopping anytime soon.

The aircraft wobbled a little when they hit a bit of low-altitude turbulence, but it wasn't anything new. It wasn't strong enough to throw the trainees off their groove now that they were ready for the final jump.

When Sergeant Hutchinson opened the door, Idina's pulse quickened and her stomach fluttered with the nervous excitement of knowing what a jump would bring. *It's pretty fun. Which might mean I'm losing it a little, but I'm totally okay with that.*

They sounded off the ten-minute countdown, clipped in, and did their gear check. Then they had the green light, and Stone was the first out of the aircraft. Idina moved forward along the static line cable after each of the four soldiers in front of her, waddling with her ruck and weapons case dangling between her legs.

Major Hines turned and jumped out into the cold darkness beyond, and Idina handed Sergeant Birch her static line. The jumpmaster briefly checked to make sure Hines' jump was successful—and no soldiers were left dangling behind the plane by a static line that hadn't fully disconnected from a soon-to-be deployed chute—then Idina had the all-clear to go.

She would have jumped. Her knees were bent, legs together, and she gripped her reserve at her chest like she'd done a thousand times in training and during all four previous jumps. The second she looked away from her jumpmaster and scanned the darkness outside the aircraft, the last thing she expected happened.

The last thing she wanted, especially now.

A blaze of green light illuminated everything in her vision. Then it wasn't her vision she experienced but someone else's. Some*thing* else's.

She was moving through the trees in the darkness. Rumbling and growling. *Hunting.*

Then the tree line broke, and she surged forward, opening her jaws to catch the tasty, terrified morsel dangling from the tree branches overhead. She was so hungry…

"Moorfield!"

Idina jolted, blinked, and returned to herself in an instant.

"Make the jump, soldier!" Birch shouted.

She reacted automatically, turning to leap off the deck before her jumpmaster had finished calling her out on what couldn't have been more than two seconds of hesitation.

Two seconds was still two seconds too long in the Army, especially with an entire C-130 of military soldiers waiting to make their final jump before graduating.

Her breath caught in her throat as the cold night air

whipped all around her, rushing in her ears and battering every inch of her.

"One thousand! Two thousand!"

Idina made her countdown like every other jump. The roar of freefall crushed every other thought from her mind until she looked up behind her to see her chute fully deployed the way it was supposed to be. Catching her. Safely lowering her in a somewhat controlled descent toward the jump zone and whatever else awaited her below.

The next twenty seconds of momentary peace was plenty for her mind to return to what had happened on the aircraft.

What the fuck was that? Another vision? Some other part of my dream? I was in *somebody else's head?*

Her breathing picked up, the rapid inhale and exhale competing with her pounding heartbeat for the loudest sound.

That wasn't a person. It was a...monster.

If she hadn't been rapidly descending toward the ground with her gear strapped between her legs, a T-11 parachute overhead, and her successful PLF to focus on, she would've laughed at the thought.

Monsters aren't real. There's no way. Soldiers who hesitate because they have visions *of monsters aren't real either. Except for me.*

Idina looked down and found the tops of the trees through her night vision gear, gauging them as maybe three hundred feet below.

Focus on the landing. That's all that matters.

She slipped left to turn the chute as far as she could

away from the tree line. Fortunately, the wind was on her side this time, and she didn't have to worry about getting tangled in anyone else's risers and having to share a PLF with another soldier.

Three hundred feet.

She released her ruck, then her weapons case.

Two hundred feet.

One hundred.

Clapping the left riser to her chest, she leaned into the slip and prepared to roll away from the trees and whatever other obstacles might've been waiting under cover of the canopy. Her boots hit the ground, she jerked her arms up beside her head, and the rest of her body crumpled as she rolled.

Her chute dragged her forward less than two yards before she found both release rings and unclipped. Then she was on her feet, breathing heavily and scanning the darkness around her before she'd had the chance to scan her body for signs of injury.

At the moment, though, her body didn't matter.

Because despite the brisk chill at almost midnight in February, the soft drone of the C-130 passing overhead until every soldier had jumped, and her senses on high alert with adrenaline pumping through her, she *felt* something.

A presence.

The feeling sent ripples of goosebumps across her flesh beneath her OCPs despite her rising core temperature and the hot flush in her cheeks.

Something's out there. In the woods. Something's waiting for—

Another vision hit her, this one almost as strong as the unexpected awareness through the eyes of some *creature* in the trees. It was Idina's reality and nothing like it at the same time. The images from her dream two nights ago raced back to her.

The darkness. The tree line. The glowing green hand tipped with black claws bursting into the sky before sweeping down toward Idina.

In between every image returning to her, she blinked through her night vision gear and viewed the landing zone around her.

Holy shit. Those trees are the same. The fist came from right there. She spun. *And another from over there. That pine tree exploded and crashed toward me, and I was standing...*

She couldn't fathom how it was even possible to be in a completely different part of the jump zone for the first time and still recognize where she was—that she'd seen this location in her dream without ever viewing it with her waking eyes.

I wasn't standing here in the dream. I was standing over there. A hundred paces out where the forest juts into the field and—

A shout of alarm and effort echoed toward her on the wind, garbled and muffled by distance.

Instantly remembering her entire purpose for being here—as an Army soldier, a Twelve Bravo, and a jump school trainee with a responsibility to her entire team of trainees—Idina spun and found her lowering line stretching behind her across the ground. She raced after it, gathering the line until she reached her weapons case first, then her ruck.

I don't have time for goddamn visions. I'm on a jump. Get it together, Moorfield. It's a high-stress situation. You know how to handle those.

She tore off her chute's deployment bag and replaced it with her ruck, strapping it over her shoulders before grabbing the bag and her weapons case to ruck back to the rendezvous point with both.

Another shout came from the opposite direction she was supposed to go—away from the rendezvous and back toward the trees. Idina still hadn't found her chute, but that hardly mattered.

Because her vision, the dream, and the warning in Reggie's last email all raced back to her in the same instant.

It's all real.

From the direction of someone's next shout came another sound that made her blood run cold.

A rumbling, grating growl like breaking stone filled the air. The trees ahead of her groaned, snapped, and cracked. The earth beneath her feet trembled.

Fuck.

Idina burst into action without thinking and raced toward all of it.

No, no, no, no. If it's real, that means there's something out there. Something coming closer. Something I don't know how to—

A blaze of intensely bright light exploded in her vision. It blinded her and made her stagger sideways in her breakneck run. For a moment, she thought she had another vision—or maybe an aneurysm—until she remembered her night vision gear and whipped it off her head.

Part of her wished she hadn't. What she saw with her own two eyes in the forest ahead didn't make sense.

It wasn't possible.

But it's all real...

The blinding light in her night vision gear wasn't blinding at all. Not now. But it *was* a blazing, sickly green like in her dream. It grew brighter between the trees as the rumbling and roaring grew closer and louder—bright enough to illuminate the silhouette of a soldier and his parachute caught in those trees halfway between the ground and the canopy.

The lines twisted around him, keeping one arm pinned behind him. The other dangled uselessly from a dislocated shoulder. He couldn't reach his release rings to unclip his chute.

The blazing green light drew toward him like a moth to a flame.

No. Like the flame hunting down the moth. Holy fuck.

CHAPTER TWENTY-THREE

"Hey!" Idina shouted. She ran as fast as she could toward the light and the soldier trapped in the trees. "Release your chute!"

The man didn't respond, but even without her night vision gear, Idina saw him struggling to turn and face the green light flashing and pulsing brighter through the trees behind him. Coming closer.

It's hungry.

She only knew this because she'd felt the same thing before she'd jumped. The feeling hadn't belonged to her, but the knowledge did.

"Shit. Hold on!" In her haste to unlatch her weapons case and prepare to engage an oncoming enemy she had no idea how to recognize, Idina forgot what was actually in the case.

Her hands closed around the hard shape of an M16, and she lifted it at chest height to support it as she would've supported an actual firearm in combat. Except the sight didn't work. A fake weapon didn't have a working sight, or live ammo, or any use whatsoever beyond bashing somebody over the head.

"Fuck!" Idina hurled the rubber ducky aside and raced toward the trees.

The rumbling and growling grew closer. More and more trees cracked and splintered as the source of that blinding green light hurtled toward the soldier caught in the branches and Idina heading toward him with all the speed she could muster.

"What is that?" the soldier shouted.

She ignored him and finally made it to the tree where he was tangled. "Can you move either of your arms?"

"No," he growled.

"Okay. Hang tight. I'll—"

The trees behind him exploded, sending bark and thick boughs in every direction. The soldier—who she still couldn't name—cried out and ducked his head against the barrage of splintered wood. The green light blazed brighter, the roar of whatever *thing* headed toward them fractured the night air with a vengeful howl, and Idina stared in mute shock at the fist of green light shooting up from the forest canopy toward the stars.

That fist opened, revealing black-tipped claws tearing at the night sky.

Then another voice entered her head. One she'd already heard before. It was only a memory, but it returned to her as clearly as when she'd seen the woman and two men standing in front of the mist-shrouded castle.

"Rise, Warriors of the Moors! They cannot stand against us!"

Idina didn't question it. There was no time. Still, she had to get the soldier down first.

Her hand slapped a front pocket of her combat vest, and she drew out the utility knife she'd bought after basic. She hadn't used it yet.

She used it now, flipping out the blade before shouting up at the soldier, "You're coming down!"

"How? I can't even—"

Idina's green lights flared to their full effect, racing in an ascending line like a glowing, pulsing rope from her right arm to the soldier's harness. Her arm blazed with the intensity of icy-hot tingling brought on by another almost episode, but this time, she didn't have to stop it.

She drew back her arm, aimed exactly as her lights had shown her, and let the knife fly. It hurtled through the air, flipping past the other branches in the way without hitting a thing until it reached the tangled soldier.

Time slowed. Idina watched her knife turn with precision, the blade glinting in the pulsing light of whatever *thing* had thrust its fist into the air before it sliced down again on the one chute line pinning the soldier's good arm behind his back. It didn't sever the line completely, but it frayed the thing enough that any good tug would rip it apart.

The blade thumped into the tree trunk past the soldier's head. He jolted in his tangled harness, stunned by a fellow soldier's knife whizzing past his head. The movement ripped the tangled line the rest of the way, and he sagged a few inches in the branches.

Then everything moved again in real-time. Trees

crashed. The pulsing fist of nauseating green light opened even wider toward the sky. The ground trembled fiercely beneath Idina's feet, and she struggled to keep her balance.

"Release!" she screamed at the soldier.

With a shout of effort, he freed his good arm the rest of the way and used it to yank first one release ring, then the other. His chute was gone, and he dropped, bashing his dislocated shoulder against another branch before spinning and finally crashing to the floor on his other side.

Idina raced toward him, ignoring the tree branches clawing at her face where her helmet didn't protect her, ripping at her OCPs and snagging at her boots. "Get up."

She grabbed the soldier's good arm from beneath him and yanked him back. He cried out in pain and snarled as she hauled him to his feet. "Out. Get out of the trees."

"Did you cut my chute with a—"

"Out!" Idina would've liked to pretend the urgency in her voice and the no-bullshit glare she gave him was what spurred the man into action. Then she would've been lying to herself. Because as she screamed at him, a burst of glittering green fog rose from her fingertips and swirled around her.

Neither of them could ignore it. Fortunately, the man had enough sense to know Idina was on his side. She'd come to get him out of his tangled chute lines, and she was here to...

What? What the hell am I supposed to do against a ghost-fit of green light I've only seen in my dreams?

The soldier's desperate footsteps crashed through the underbrush, growing fainter behind her. The open claw of green and black light rising a hundred feet above the tree line surged down toward Idina, just like in her dream.

In reality, right here and now, she stood her ground.

The monstrous voice from months ago bellowed all around her. *"You are* mine, *Warrior!"*

The green fog she'd spent her entire life trying to suppress and hold back—even from her family who knew what it was and couldn't stand the sight of it—thickened around her clenched fists.

"Rise, Warriors of the Moors! They cannot stand—"

The monstrous claw hurtled down toward her like a glowing guillotine. Idina screamed.

The burning, frigid, searing energy coursing through her limbs burst out of her because it had nowhere else to go and no fake prescription of Anagracin to keep it at bay.

Green light surged away from her body and up toward the clawed hand hurtling toward her. The light drowned out everything else in her vision. She couldn't see her hands, or the trees, or the *thing*. Everything was blinding green light and surging heat flowing through her and glimmering shards reflecting in the darkness.

The deafening *crack* of trees splintering, breaking, and toppling to the ground in a rush of decimated branches almost overpowered the blood-chilling howl of the *thing* that wanted her.

Then it was over.

The brilliant light faded. A few straggling tree trunks splintered again and slid apart, the fragmented tops crashing to the ground. Beyond that, the night was silent again save for the low hum of the C-130 quickly fading in the distance.

And Idina's heavy breathing.

The monstrous claw of light was gone. The ground had stopped trembling. Even the wind had died, leaving no distractions to get between Idina and the evidence of what she'd done.

A full-blown episode right here in the landing zone of Fort Benning, Georgia.

In the presence of another soldier who had no idea who or what Idina Moorfield was any more than she did.

She turned in a slow circle and surveyed the wreckage.

The trees had been crashing toward her and the tangled soldier before she'd gotten him down. Now everything around her was blown in the opposite direction, toppled away from Idina as if she'd gone out to the demo range and simultaneously detonated every explosive she'd learned to handle.

The only thing that proved it hadn't been a real explosion was the lack of a crater in the earth. Everything else?

Oh, fuck.

She blinked a few times in the darkness and was glad she'd removed her night vision gear.

I don't want to see this. I don't want to know what I did.

Her fists weren't smoking with glittering green mist anymore. That was probably the only thing she had going for her when she turned fully around for a clear view of the soldier she'd cut down from the trees just in time. Because the tree cover between them was gone too.

The man had also removed his night vision gear, which now dangled from his good hand. His dislocated shoulder slumped forward and to the side. His black mustache bristled over his twitching lips, and his eyes were wide in the darkness.

Major Hines. Idina swallowed and couldn't draw a new breath for another three seconds. *Fuck. I'm done. He knows I'm a freak. He saw what I can do. He'll have me kicked out of the Army faster than I can say, 'I have no fucking clue what happened.'*

Hines tilted his head to glance behind her at the perimeter of destroyed trees circling Private First Class Moorfield. Then he sniffed.

She stepped toward him, not knowing how she would explain *this* but determined to try. "Major Hines—"

"We previously covered that your background experience was in finance and not medicine," he said calmly. "But I need you to reset my shoulder, PFC Moorfield."

Pausing in confusion, Idina looked at his shoulder and nodded. "Yes, sir."

"Have you handled a dislocation before?"

"No, sir."

"Then I'll talk you through it." He pressed his lips together and watched her intently as she hurried toward him across the splintered branches and fragmented tree trunks between them.

The man's bad shoulder pulsed with the green light only Idina could see. A glowing wraith of Hines' arm that wasn't his arm at all rose from his physical body out in front of him, then jammed straight back in.

Great. I should've told him I know what I'm doing.

"Take my arm. Bicep and just below the elbow." The major gestured toward his arm with his good hand.

Idina did as he instructed.

"Lift it a little to get a good straight angle," he continued. "Then you'll want to—"

She jammed his arm back into the socket with a sickening *crunch* and *pop*. Major Hines growled through gritted teeth, turning away from her in his pain because she'd already released his arm.

"Sorry, sir."

"Don't..." He'd doubled over to collect himself and now straightened all the way, inhaling deeply through his nose. "Don't apologize. You... You were very helpful, Private First Class Moorfield. With...everything."

"Sir?" Idina waited for him to face her. She wanted to look into the man's eyes and at least try to figure out what was going on behind them. If he thought she was some kind of monster too that needed to be stripped of rank, cuffed, and hauled away—some kind of abomination unworthy of the Army.

Hines gave her the courtesy of looking her dead in the eye before he glanced behind her at the destroyed forest. "I've seen plenty of combat in my time. More than I like to admit sometimes. But that? I have no idea what that was."

"Honestly, sir, neither do I." She couldn't believe how strong her voice sounded. Confident. Sure. Like she'd done this a million times before and still had no idea why or how.

"I see." The major cleared his throat. "For reasons I'm sure I don't have to spell out for you, Moorfield, I suggest we keep this...event between the two of us."

A wave of relief washed through her.

He doesn't want to be branded as a lunatic by his superiors either. The guy's a combat veteran trying to earn his wings. No idea what they'd do with me, but they'd probably throw him *in room after room for psych evals and stick him behind a desk. Forever.*

"I have no objection to that, sir."

The man let out a weak chuckle and nodded. "I'm glad to hear it. Then that's what we'll do." He looked her up and down and raised his eyebrows. "I do have one question, though. After that, there's no need to bring this up again in the future. Ever."

"I'll try my best to answer, sir."

"Well, that's... Yeah." Hines cleared his throat. "That's about as much as I can ask of you at this point. Beyond wanting to know... I..." The man looked like he had something stuck in his throat, then looked over his good shoulder to scan the jump zone. Apparently, they were the only two trainees who'd landed anywhere close to Idina's little episode, and that was only a lucky twist of fate. "Private First Class Moorfield, what *are* you?"

Idina widened her eyes and blinked furiously in surprise. "What am I, sir?"

"That's the only thing I'd like to know. No other questions. The rest doesn't matter."

She studied the major for a moment, racking her brain for the right thing to say.

I can't tell him I have no clue. What do I say? I'm a freak? Another kind of monster? Some weirdly superpowered Moorfield who got stuck with a shitty gene that does all this?

Without fully meaning to, Idina drew herself together and stood at attention in front of the officer. Her jaw clenched over and over until she steeled herself to give the only answer that made sense. "I'm a United States Army soldier, Major Hines."

He huffed, laughed, and nodded. "Good answer. I think it's time to get to the rendezvous point, don't you?"

"Yes, sir." Idina turned and surveyed the darkness of the field around them beside one inexplicable demolition of the trees. Two different points on the ground pulsed slowly in her vision with green light—her weapons case beside the abandoned rubber-ducky weapon and her night vision gear. "Did you retrieve your ruck and weapon, sir?"

"Ah. You have a point." Hines looked down at his lowering line still dangling from the waist of his harness and grimaced before following it back into the fallen trees to collect his gear.

Idina hurried toward her weapons case to pack up the fake M16 and latch the case down tight again. Then she scooped up her night vision gear and strapped it on over her helmet.

I have to act like everything's back to normal. That's basically what he said. Jesus, this takes 'Don't Ask Don't Tell' to a whole different level.

Hines had finished collecting his gear and repacking his lowering line when she returned to him. "Find your chute?"

"No, sir. I'll repack it if it shows up on the way."

He nodded silently, his mustache twitching back and forth as he clenched his jaw and scowled at nothing in particular. As if afraid he'd say something stupid the next time he opened his mouth, the man turned stiffly in the direction of their rendezvous point and glanced at his field watch.

Idina was momentarily distracted by one more green light pulsing in her peripheral vision. She turned toward it and realized it came from her knife buried to the hilt in the broken half of the tree trunk where the major had hung.

As a tasty, terrified morsel...

She shook her head to push away the memory of her vision at twelve hundred feet and headed toward her weapon.

Stick it all in one glowing green box and bury it deep down where it won't be able to come back up again. That's where the visions belong. And the dreams. And two *voices I'm hearing in my head at the same time. Fuck. I thought things were complicated before all this.*

"Moorfield?" Realizing she wasn't walking beside him, Hines turned and tried to find her in the darkness, completely forgetting his night vision gear. "Are you—"

Idina wrenched her knife from the tree trunk, wiped it briefly on her uniform pants, then trudged out of the destruction toward him. "I'd rather not leave this behind, sir."

"No." He stared at the blade as she snapped it shut and returned it to the pocket on her vest accessible through the straps of her harness and fortunately not blocked by her bulky reserve. "No, if I were you, I'd want that knife at my side at all times."

I have no idea what he's trying to infer with that, but fuck it. I don't need to know. We survived, and I made a deal with a major to keep this screwy little secret to ourselves. Because I saved his life, and we both know it. Doesn't matter that neither one of us will ever be able to say what I saved his life from...

She chose to nod at Major Hines instead, and together,

they rucked back across the jump zone to rendezvous with the rest of their cycle.

Neither of them said a word. They didn't have to.

We made it through our five jumps. We'll get our wings. Then we'll go our separate ways and never have to talk about it again. Fine by me.

CHAPTER TWENTY-FOUR

The jumpmasters didn't miss a thing when Idina and Major Hines made it to the rendezvous point to ruck the rest of the way as an entire team toward the bus waiting for them. Birch and Hutchinson shared a curious look, but fortunately, they waited for most of the soldiers to pile into the bus before bringing it up.

"Moorfield," Birch called.

Idina hustled toward him, well aware of the way she looked—wide-eyed, maybe even pale in the scant starlight, with a severely battered weapons case, an empty deployment bag, and rips through her OCPs to match the scratches on her face. "Sergeant?"

"Have a hard landing?"

"Nothing I couldn't handle, Sergeant."

"Any injuries?"

"No, Sergeant Airborne."

He looked her up and down and gave her a crooked smile. "Looks like you got hung up in a tree. That where you left your chute?"

"I..." Idina swallowed, knowing it made her look even more suspicious, but she couldn't figure out how to answer that question.

Either I tell him the truth and try to leave out the really fucked up parts, or I lie directly to a jumpmaster's face. The same jumpmaster who has the power to sign off on my graduation and my wings. Or not.

"Actually, Sergeant Airborne, that was me." Major Hines joined them with a tight smile, favoring his bad arm despite having had it perfectly relocated almost an hour before. "My chute's in the tree. Private First Class Moorfield found me stranded there and didn't hesitate to come to a fellow trainee's aid."

"Huh." Birch squinted at her, then nodded. "Lucky landing, then."

"Lucky for *me*, yeah." Hines chuckled. "You ever need a dislocated shoulder popped back into place, go to Moorfield." He brought a hand down on her shoulder for a reassuring pat, then continued past them toward the bus.

"You did that?" Birch muttered.

"Yes, Sergeant. He walked me through it."

"If this wasn't your last jump, Moorfield, I would've told you to let med bay handle medical issues."

"Yes, Sergeant."

"All right." The jumpmaster looked back at the bus but didn't move to join Sergeant Hutchinson or the rest of the chalks. "What happened up there?"

"Sergeant?"

"Before your jump. I know this cycle's only three weeks, but it's enough time and pressure to get the measure of a soldier. You hesitated."

Shit. Now he's calling me out for that too, and I don't have an answer for anything.

"Honestly, Sergeant, I don't know what happened. But I made the jump. I'm good."

"You did." He studied her a moment longer, then shrugged. "It sounds like you were fast enough on your feet to aid Major Hines. That's good enough for me. If any other problems crop up after a jump week like the one you've had, don't wait to see someone about it, huh?"

"See someone, Sergeant?"

"A doctor. Or a shrink." Birch shrugged. "No shame in talking through some shit to get it out of the way."

"I'll...remember that, Sergeant. Thanks."

"Yeah. Get on the bus."

Idina broke into a jog to put as much space as possible between her and the jumpmaster.

So he thinks I'm either injured or mentally unstable. Fuck. It's better than the truth, but what if he blocks me from graduating? He could do that if he was really worried enough, right?

Idina approached the open doors in a daze and hauled herself up the stairs.

"Moorfield!" Greenburg shouted, already in his seat. "Where the hell were *you*?"

"Hit a few obstacles," she replied numbly before slipping into an open seat at the front of the bus.

"Huh? Hey! Moorfield, I didn't—"

Birch stepped onto the bus and scanned the faces of every soldier in the seats. He'd already taken a headcount after Idina and Major Hines were the last two stragglers to reach the rendezvous point, but now he looked a little worried that he might've missed somebody.

Hutchinson stuck two fingers in his mouth to let out a piercing whistle. "Quiet!"

The trainees did exactly that, and the bus fell silent but for the idling rumble of the engine.

Idina grimaced. *I don't want to hear another rumble of anything in my whole damn life.*

"Jump five." Birch looked over the rows of seats. "You made it. Congratulations, soldiers."

The bus erupted into cheers, whistles, and laughter as soldiers thumped their buddies on the backs and gave themselves a moment to let the knowledge sink in. Sergeant Birch patiently waited for them to quiet down again, which happened quickly without another whistle from Hutchinson.

"I'm only gonna say this once because it's late, and I'd honestly rather be in my bed than standing here in a bus that smells like ass." The soldiers chuckled. "Graduation's on Sunday at seventeen hundred hours. I expect to see every single soldier in that ceremony room to receive their wings. You've earned them. Until Sunday, though, I also expect not to see any of your ugly mugs for at least a full thirty-six hours. Understood?"

"Yes, Sergeant Airborne!" the trainees cried in unison. Most of them were still grinning like lunatics and laughing through the reply.

Birch turned to the driver and nodded. "Get us out of here, huh?"

"Sergeant Airborne." The driver smirked and stepped on the gas before Birch had a chance to sit.

The jumpmaster quickly slipped into the empty seat across the aisle from Idina. She felt his gaze on her for a long time but couldn't bring herself to do anything except stare at a small tear in the plastic covering the seat in front of her.

He wants to look at me and make sure I'm all good. I'm not. I don't even think I can pretend *to be all good after what happened.*

She tried not to think about it and focused on Birch's unofficial speech.

He did say he wants to see all of us at the graduation ceremony. Including me. So that's something.

After that, her mind went blank for the duration of the ride back to the airport, where the trainees returned their training T-11s, reserves, harnesses, lowering lines, and weapons cases. Then they were shuttled back onto the same bus for a final time to be dropped off at the barracks and call it a night.

The last night of jump week. The last night of their training.

The last kind of night Idina Moorfield ever expected to deal with, especially in the Army. Especially as a soldier.

She shuffled like a zombie through the barracks toward the women's bay, moving on muscle memory alone because her brain seemed to have shut off sometime after recounting her jump to Sergeant Birch. Once inside the bay, she had no idea she wasn't alone until Crimshaw's voice came from a few bunks down.

"You look like hell."

Idina stopped dead, blinked, and slowly turned her head to look at the other woman. "Thanks."

"It wasn't a compliment." Instead of turning back to

whatever she was doing, like she usually did, Crimshaw smirked. "But you're welcome."

As she stepped back toward her bunk, ready to strip off her ripped OCPs that she would have to replace, she stopped again when the realization finally sank in. "Crimshaw."

"Moorfield."

"Did you just…make a joke?"

The other woman looked at the bay's ceiling and tilted her head from side to side. "I'd call it more of an amusing observation based in part on facts. If you want to call it a joke, I won't stop you."

"Huh." She didn't have the energy to laugh, but half of a flickering smile was apparently enough to do the trick before Idina unlaced her boots with a few swift tugs and hauled them off her aching feet. "Guess it only took five jumps to get you this far."

"What can I say? I like throwing myself out of a plane."

They shared an exhausted, surreal laugh that died off instantly. After that, neither had anything else to say.

What else is there? We survived jump week. We're getting our wings and getting the hell out of here. Crimshaw has a sense of humor buried somewhere deep down after all. I'm…

It was too much to think about. So she undressed, folded her OCPs despite the massive rips in the arms and legs, and pulled out her usual tank top and cotton shorts for nightwear. As she crawled into her bunk, her muscles so fatigued she could hardly feel them even when holding herself up, Idina's last thought came completely unbidden and without warning.

It started as a brief, flashing image from the first true

vision she'd had where she wasn't directly a part of it. The woman and two men stood before a massive stone castle in the middle of nowhere. The thick mist glistened in the moonlight as it wafted across the open field below the hill. The woman lifted both hands glowing the same green as Idina's bursts of quickly snuffed-out episodes. Her black hair. Wide, determined eyes. Her voice.

Warriors of the Moors. By a castle. In a field. Warriors of the Moors. In a field. Moorfield...

The puzzle pieces slipping into place as Idina slid over the edge of consciousness should've been enough to bring her to full awareness again. It should've ripped her out of her exhaustion enough to cement the unlikely connection in her mind.

Somehow, though, it had the opposite effect. Putting two and two together only intensified her exhaustion. A surprising heaviness of warmth melted into her tight, aching muscles, relaxing everything beneath the thin, Army-issue sheets.

Because the realization made sense. It fit.

Idina was a United States Army soldier, as she'd claimed. She was a Moorfield, through and through. Maybe not the way her immediate family understood it or embodied their name, but in a different way.

Older. Fiercer. More capable of rising for their people and the oath they swore to uphold.

Whatever that meant.

CHAPTER TWENTY-FIVE

That Saturday between the last day of jump week and their quickly approaching graduation the next day, Idina felt like she was walking through a dream. She showered, got dressed, brushed her hair and teeth, and stared at her reflection in the mirror for at least five minutes after she finished. The only thing that broke her out of it was the *squeak* of the bathroom door as a woman she didn't know hurried inside and disappeared into one of the stalls.

You can't stand here all day staring at yourself, Moorfield. Move.

Her breakfast in the dining facility was tasteless and dry. Or maybe that was her current mood. She moved like someone who'd forgotten where they were and how they'd ended up there, although she studied every crack in the wall, chip in the paint, and scuff on the floors as she moved through the barracks toward the next thing in her day.

She had nothing planned. The idea of doing anything felt like way too much work. The only reason she didn't worry about it was that she had the weekend off to do whatever she wanted until she reported to the ceremony room tomorrow to receive her jump wings. Whatever she wanted was to do nothing at all.

Her attempt to sit with her sketchpad and charcoal failed in the first three minutes because she didn't want to look at lines—charcoal-gray *or* green. Eventually, she sat to draft another email to Reggie and the Moorfield Manor staff, to whom she knew he forwarded everything she wrote. Even the ones she'd sent directly to her parents with the head of staff CCed in the recipients box, as always.

Those emails, however, had gone unanswered for almost six months. Reggie's hadn't.

I should tell him I made it. That I graduated. I should tell him... What? That I had a full-blown episode at the end of my last jump? Instead of hurting someone like the last time, it saved Major Hines' life and stopped a green-fist monster from crushing us in the middle of nowhere?

That was the end of trying to write her friend and family butler anything at all. So she spent the rest of the day wandering around the empty training yard behind the barracks. This was worse than the jittery time she'd spent on the manor waiting for her parents to decide her fate. Worse than waiting for the call from Staff Sergeant Johansen about the ASVAB test. Worse than sitting around in reception for almost ten days and thinking she'd go insane before ever getting to basic.

Jump school was worse. So much worse. This time, I might be losing my mind a little. I had an episode *in front of a decorated combat veteran. Up and showed him the whole damn thing because I wasn't thinking. What the hell is* wrong *with me?*

Eventually, she ended up sitting at the picnic table in

the small side courtyard beside the training barracks. It was chilly out here in the middle of the day but not cold enough to seep into her bones the way it did during the New England cold snaps this time of year. Her light jacket was enough to keep her warm while she sat and stared and let the time pass without bothering to check it.

Or maybe the jacket had nothing to do with it.

Maybe I can't feel anything anymore because it's all real. The lights. The visions. The dreams. The monsters. As real as this fucking picnic table, and I'm still *losing my mind.*

"Hell-*o*? Earth to Moorfield..."

Jarred out of her warped thoughts, Idina turned to see Greenburg jogging down the barracks steps leading up to the second floor. She jerked her chin up at him, feeling like she was moving through molasses. "Hey."

"Did you really not hear me the first time?" he joked as he reached the concrete of the bottom landing. "Or the second? Or the third?"

She shrugged. "I guess I tuned out."

"Uh-huh. Swiss Army Moorfield's getting a little dull around the edges, right? You expect me to believe that shit?"

"Not really." She sniffed and swiped the back of her hand beneath her nose that wasn't runny or red and didn't need to be touched. *I don't have the energy for this. Talking to anyone. I can't...*

"So." Greenburg plopped onto the opposite bench and folded his arms on the table before leaning forward over them. "What the fuck are you doing?"

"What?"

"Sitting out here in…what? Forty-eight degrees? In *that*?" He gestured toward her light jacket. "That'll kill you."

A slow smile broke through her foggy disconnect, and she shook her head. "No, it won't."

"Yeah, maybe you're right. You know, I've heard people say jumping out of a plane can kill you too, and here you are."

"We both made it."

"Sure. Yeah. Plus everyone else in our cycle." Greenburg narrowed his eyes and stared at her, waiting for her to say something. She had nothing. "Seriously, though. What's up?"

"I don't know, man. I'm just…done. You know?"

"Don't beat yourself up about it. Jump school's over. You're supposed to be."

"Right."

He'll never understand. No one will. Major Hines included, and he didn't even want *to know.*

"Dude…" Greenburg grimaced. "You're in the grieving process, aren't you?"

"The…*grieving* process?"

"Yeah. Best three weeks of your life right here, and now they're gone." He slapped the table and spread his arms. "All you had to do was ask for my number, Moorfield. I would've given it to you no problem."

"Ha." Idina shifted on her seat and looked around the empty courtyard. "So *that's* what this is about."

"Hey, I'm trying to help a friend. And a hell of a soldier. So give me your phone."

Failing to hide another smile, she pulled her phone out of her pocket, unlocked it, and tossed it across the table.

Greenburg swiped it up and paused. "Promise me one thing."

"What's that?"

"Don't call me only to brag about all the awesome shit you're doing wherever the hell they send you next. I already have confidence issues, okay? That's not gonna help."

Idina chuckled and drew an X across her chest with one finger. "Cross my heart, Greenburg. Because yours breaks so easily."

He snickered and focused on typing his number into her contacts before tossing the phone back to her. She caught it and looked at the new contact he'd made for himself. "Reilly."

"You got a problem with my name, Moorfield?"

"Nope. I guess I would've pegged you for a Jacob. Or an Elijah. Or maybe an Ezrah—"

"Yeah, yeah. I get the fucking joke. Jewish last name, so the rest of me would follow suit, huh? Fuck you."

"I'm just saying." Idina created a quick text from his saved number, entered a middle finger emoji and nothing else, and sent it. "I won't forget who it is when I see your weird name pop up on the screen."

"Funny." They stared at each other for a second, then his phone went off with a *ding,* and he jerked it out of his pocket. With a snort, Greenburg jammed his elbow on the table and held his phone between them. "What the fuck am I supposed to do with this?"

"Treasure it forever?"

"From the Swiss Army Asshole, or do you have a first name?"

She smirked and waited, knowing it would make him squirm because he'd asked what few soldiers tended to ask of each other in active duty. "Idina."

"Hey, bless you."

"Fuck off."

They both laughed as he saved her number. "What kinda name is that, anyway? It's…different."

"English. I think."

Pulled from the nation that trampled all over my Scottish ancestors and their lands, but hey. Sounds pretty, right?

She blinked quickly, frowning at her thought.

Why am I so pissed about that all of a sudden?

"English, huh?" Greenburg continued, completely oblivious to her brief confusion. "Does it mean anything?"

Idina tried to smile again, but the thought of smiling felt like some kind of betrayal—to whom or for what reason, she had no idea. "Rich."

"Shit." He chuckled. "You said your family was—"

"In finance. Yep. Investment bankers. All of them. At the same time in the same company."

Greenburg burst out laughing. "And you're *here*!"

"It's not that funny."

"It's fucking hilarious, Moorfield. They set you up to be something totally different. I mean, it's in your goddamn *name*. You're blazing a trail of glory, man. Hey, listen. When you get all kinds of service medals and commendations and shit, don't forget about this." He jabbed his thumb against his chest and sat up straighter. "*I'm* the one who called it. So I get credit for that."

"Yeah, okay." She playfully rolled her eyes. "I'll buy you a cookie."

Their laughter quickly died out into a subdued, expectant silence again, and Greenburg cleared his throat. "Still no idea where you're going after this?"

"Not until I get my orders, no. You?"

"Fuck if I know. I wouldn't say no to more training. Extra salary, more tabs on my OCPs, a few bragging rights..."

"Well, you're getting all that tomorrow with your wings."

"You and me both, Moorfield." He scanned the courtyard again, then pushed himself to his feet. "I got a few errands. Wanna take shotgun?"

Idina closed her eyes and sighed.

"What?"

"Hell's freezing over."

"I don't—"

"No, Greenburg. I don't wanna go *shopping* with you."

The guy burst out laughing again and rubbed the back of his neck. "'Cause you're the wrong chick to ask."

"That's right."

"Ha!"

The door at the top of the stairs swung open with a *creak* before Hapton, Rorden, and one other Ranger buddy of theirs stepped out onto the platform. Hapton pulled out his cigarettes and lit up as he followed the others down the stairs.

"You know what, though?" Idina nodded toward them and grinned. "I bet if you ask Hapton, it'll make his day."

Greenburg fell into another fit of snorting laughter he tried to cover up as his Ranger buddies spotted them and headed their way.

"Fucking yukkin' it up over here, huh?" Hapton called. "What are you doing?"

"Nothing," Greenburg muttered.

"Talking shit about you," Idina added with a grin.

Rorden guffawed and shoved Hapton's shoulder. The short, ridiculously muscular Ranger staggered forward before turning and pushing his much taller friend right back. "Fuck off. And *you*." He spun again to point at Moorfield. "I won't miss you one fucking bit when they ship you off base."

"The feeling is *so* mutual."

Everyone laughed before Hapton leaned over the table to extend his hand toward her. "You didn't die this time, Moorfield. Keep it up."

"Yeah, you too." They shook, then the guys headed down the edge of the courtyard toward the front of the barracks and the parking lot.

Greenburg hung back for a second. "See you tomorrow."

"Have fun shopping."

He snorted and shook his head as he turned to follow his friends.

Idina sat there at the picnic table and watched the closest thing to friends she'd made here disappear around the corner of the barracks. She stayed a good deal longer after that too, going over all the weird interactions she'd had with various soldiers at Fort Benning who'd changed more than she'd expected in the last three weeks.

Crimshaw's not all black-and-white hardass. Hapton got over himself, if not over all the shit-talking. Major Hines...

Thinking about the man and their undiscussed secret made her grimace.

Well, he won't forget Private First Class Moorfield. I know that much. Neither of us will forget what happened anytime soon. That doesn't change the fact that I'm a soldier and have a job to do. So I better do it. Green lights or otherwise.

CHAPTER TWENTY-SIX

The next morning, Idina woke feeling refreshed and ready to take on whatever the day had in store for her. For the most part, that included preparing for the jump school graduation ceremony. She had little else going on, as far as she knew.

She went through her daily routine, starting with choosing not to skip morning PT even though jump school trainees weren't technically required to participate. Or graduates.

That'll change once I get my new orders out of here. Until then, I'm pretty much a floating name and number.

The base around the training barracks was fairly quiet, at least for the first part of the day. A certain level of activity picked up after lunch and the closer it got to seventeen hundred hours. Civilian contractors working as staff and a few NCOs set up the ceremony room. People bustled left and right all over that side of the barracks, and conversation picked up as Fort Benning opened its doors, so to speak.

Family members and close friends invited by the graduates of this most recent jump school cycle were allowed onto the base and led toward the ceremony room decked out with banners, the Army seal, flags, and insignias. Idina tried to ignore the growing noise in the barracks as she put on her dress blues and brushed her hair before tying it back in a tight bun.

I don't blame anyone for inviting their families to something like this. It's a big deal. Way bigger than graduating from basic. Still doesn't change the fact that I probably won't ever have anyone from my past showing up at one of my *ceremonies.*

She briefly thought of Reggie and Mrs. Yardly, who were the most likely to have received invitations. If Idina had felt like inviting anyone. No one from Moorfield Manor would dare leave the grounds to fly down to Georgia of all places, and especially not to see the youngest Moorfield graduating from any form of military training.

Her family, for obvious reasons, wouldn't deign to entertain such a request. The staff members were too terrified of the consequences if Harold Moorfield I discovered where they'd gone for an extended vacation and why.

Everyone already knows I followed in Uncle Richard's footsteps by not fitting in with the rest of the family. By being different. *Having some kind of weird ability that makes me that much more...extra. I bet none of them have any idea what those abilities do. What they* can *do...*

She ripped herself away from that line of thought and finished tying back her hair.

Can't think about any of that now, Moorfield. It's showtime.

Crimshaw hadn't appeared in the women's bay after her early disappearance that morning to start her Sunday.

That only made Idina more grateful for the solitude and quiet before she had to stand up in front of her officers, whichever company or battalion commander oversaw graduation for jump school, and all the smiling faces of family who'd come to support their soldiers in the armed forces.

I've gotten this far on my own. I'll keep going the same way.

At 16:45 hours, she left the women's bay and headed through the halls she'd come to know over the last three weeks, turning down corridor after corridor until the sound of friendly, hushed conversation rose from the open doors into the ceremony room.

On the other side of the doors, the chalks from her training cycle had gathered in neat lines to wait until it was time for them to enter. Sergeants Birch and Hutchinson were there, along with the other support Black Hats and NCOs who'd joined them for various stages of this cycle's training.

Birch met Idina's gaze and nodded. She returned the gesture before slipping past the door to wait with everyone else.

"Big day, huh?" Greenburg muttered when she found a place beside him.

"I don't know." She feigned indifference. "Feels the same size as every other day."

He snickered. "You got any family waiting in there for you?"

"Me? Hell no." Idina made an exasperated face and rolled her eyes. "The Moorfields I know wouldn't be caught dead on a military base."

"Even to watch you graduate?"

"*Especially* to watch me graduate."

"Damn." Greenburg puffed out his cheeks. "Sorry."

"Don't be. It's better this way. For everybody. Mostly me."

They stifled their laughter before he gestured toward the open doors. "My parents and sister made it a point to come. I didn't invite them. They asked when graduation was and where to go, and here they are. Hell, I'll loan you *my* family for the day."

Idina glanced at him sidelong and barely shook her head. "And block them from the full Greenburg Effect? No way."

"Yeah. You're probably right. They see you, badass Swiss Army Moorfield, and they'll forget all about the son they never wanted."

She knew he was joking, but Idina didn't know what to say to that. *At least they came. That has to count for something.*

A few minutes later, the jumpmasters gave everyone a countdown to the start of the ceremony, and the emcee for the small, intimate event spoke into the microphone on the podium at the far end of the room.

The words went in one ear and out the other as Idina drew deep breaths and tried not to let her nerves get the better of her. For some reason, standing in front of a room full of people she really didn't know—again—brought on a flutter of anticipation.

Act normal. You're getting your wings. You earned *them. No one's gonna freak out or spill the beans on what you can do because that's not part of the program.*

She scanned the faces of the other graduates dressed in their formal uniforms for the ceremony and found Major

Hines. His head tipped forward as he spoke to one of the airmen also graduating today. The man didn't look in the least bit uncomfortable about anything.

He's probably used to keeping other people's secrets as well as his. That's a plus for me. If it had been someone like Stone stuck in those trees, the whole damn base would've heard about my little light show by now.

Then it was time for the graduates to enter the room, preceded by their jumpmasters. The color guard kicked off the ceremony with a formal march and presented the regimental colors and flags. Idina filtered into the room with the other graduates—it was practically the same size as the ceremony room at Fort Leonard Wood where she'd graduated from basic—and stood at attention. The company commander approached the podium to give his formal speech for the occasion.

She hadn't once seen Colonel Chevalier during her time here, but he spoke about all the active service members of multiple military branches as if he'd gotten to know each one of them.

It was hard not to tune out the speeches and addresses to the small group of witnesses as she stood there among her fellow graduates. As long as no mention was made of her specifically, she could stand at attention, look as blank-faced as everyone else, and no one would know she wasn't paying attention.

Then it was time for the graduates to receive their jump wings. Her attention zeroed in on both Sergeant Birch and Sergeant Hutchinson preparing to walk down the line of soldiers and deliver those wings themselves.

More pins.

Idina cleared her throat as quietly as possible while Colonel Chevalier explained what the metal pins marking them as jump school graduates represented.

Jesus. The last time I got a tab pinned to my uniform, all vision-hell broke loose. I don't need that now. Not when Birch thinks I might be on the verge of needing therapy and Major Hines knows exactly why.

The jumpmasters moved down the line of graduates as the colonel called each name. Birch presented each soldier with their wings, pinning them to the dress uniform shirt right above the first letter in their service branch's name. Then he saluted each soldier, who returned that salute with equal pride and confidence.

It seemed to take forever until he reached Idina. She stared straight ahead at nothing as her name rang out and Hutchinson handed Birch another pair of wings to pin to Idina's dress blues.

"Congratulations, Private First Class," Birch muttered as he reached toward her shoulder. "You've earned this."

"Thank you—" She nearly bit her tongue to keep from making any other noise when the jumpmaster slipped the pin's point through her uniform shirt and jammed it even farther into her right shoulder with a quick, solid thump. The stab of the pin sent a sharp pain through her already scarred shoulder, and she grimaced. "Sergeant."

Birch saluted her. She returned it, then he and Hutchinson moved down the line.

Idina clenched her jaw and stared at the far wall behind the gathered witnesses.

Again. I got another tab punched into my shoulder. Of course, blood wings are a thing. Now what? I get visions of some kinda bird soaring through the sky and screeching for me to stand up and fight?

The cynicism of her thoughts surprised her. She gritted her teeth against the pain in her shoulder and the idea of trying to clean as much blood as possible off the inside of her shirt—again. However, the vision she expected didn't come.

She was Private First Class Moorfield, now with her wings, standing at attention and graduating with everyone else in the cycle.

Huh. Okay. So there's no rhyme or reason to visions or dreams or episodes. Perfect.

A small smile flickered across her lips before she snuffed it out.

I guess I'll have to be happy that Sergeant Airborne and Sergeant Airborne thought I deserved a little extra recognition for my performance.

The thought almost made her laugh, but she pulled herself together until the end of the ceremony.

She thought she'd be able to get away afterward, but Greenburg found her and practically dragged her toward his family to make introductions. Idina had difficulty focusing on the conversation with Mr. and Mrs. Greenburg, who felt now was the most appropriate time to regale Idina with stories of their son when he was still a minor living under their roof.

Idina smiled politely and threw in an occasional joke at Greenburg's expense, which his family found hilarious. He seemed more than happy to have her standing there with *his* family when hers would never dream of making it out to show their support and pride.

Only when she finally tugged at her uniform shirt to unhook the pin of her wings from her flesh did Greenburg notice anything weird about how she was acting. He glanced at her, looked down at her wings, and squinted.

His parents had mingled with the other family members and soldiers, and Greenburg leaned toward Idina before lowering his voice. "Are you fucking kidding me?"

"I didn't say anything."

"You didn't have to, Moorfield. You got your blood wings, didn't you?"

She looked at him with raised eyebrows. "No idea what you're talking about."

"Bullshit." Greenburg laughed and rolled his eyes. "Unbelievable. You're not the one who got dragged behind that C-130 for five seconds of eternity."

Idina smiled at someone else's mom or sister or aunt walking past them, then shrugged. "You're right. Guess I got lucky."

"Uh-huh. Next you're gonna tell me it's *all* luck with you, huh?"

She turned her smile onto him and pointed across the room. "I'm gonna get a cookie. Want one?"

Greenburg stared at her, then finally scoffed and headed toward the table. "Yeah, what the hell?"

Halfway through the following week, Idina received her next orders after passing jump school. An NCO she didn't know delivered them, although she'd been checking in every day with reception at the training barracks for word of what happened next.

"You'll report to the 3rd Brigade, 82nd Division," he told her. "They'll process you there and tell you where to go. You fly out tomorrow."

"Thank you." Idina took the paperwork with her new orders and looked it all over.

Fort Bragg, North Carolina, huh? Okay. I guess that's where I'm heading.

She had the opportunity to say goodbye to the few friends she'd made during jump school before another NCO drove her and three other soldiers off base and to the airport for their cheap, late-night flights from Georgia to North Carolina. Then she used the flight as an opportunity to write the email to Reggie she'd been avoiding since the last one.

It took her almost the entire flight to make it sound exactly the way she wanted, but when she finished, the email contained everything she needed it to say.

Reggie,

I officially completed jump school and received my wings. One more accomplishment under my military belt, I guess. We had the graduation ceremony on Sunday, and I received my new orders yesterday. I'm reporting to the 3rd Brigade, 82nd Division at Fort Bragg in North Carolina. That's as much as I know right now, but eventually, I'll be attached to my FORSCOM unit. That's active

duty. No more training unless I find something else I want to try.

I'll keep you updated on where I end up as soon as I know. It's hard to tell when that'll be or how long it takes to process anyone through to their new unit. That's the way the Army works, I guess. I don't mind. It gives me plenty of time to think about where I've been and where I'm going next.

Your last email got me thinking. You didn't specify how much you know about the Moorfield family or "what we were" before we settled in the U.S. If you have any other history on the Moorfields, going back however far, please send it along. Everything's going well here for me, and at the same time, it feels a little irresponsible not to prepare in case I come across certain scenarios like those you mentioned.

I hope you and Mrs. Yardly are doing well. It sounds like you two have been spending more time together since I left. I'd call that a good thing.

—Idina

Sending the email as the plane touched down on the tarmac in North Carolina made her stomach flutter with expectation again. Maybe Reggie would read deeper into the email than he was supposed to and sniff out the lie—that Idina wanted to be prepared proactively instead of as a consequence of having a full-blown episode during her final jump. Then again, maybe he'd take her email at face value and appreciate that she was finally showing an interest in her family history.

He said I could reach out. That's what I'm doing. I don't have to tell anyone about what's happening to me. Not until I exhaust every resource I have to figure it out on my own first.

In-processing at Fort Bragg took a lot less time than she'd expected, mostly because she was sent straight to reception to fill out all the necessary paperwork. It wasn't anything like reception before basic, and luckily, they officially processed her into the 82nd Airborne Division in less than thirty-six hours.

She stayed in reception another two days.

Her very short meeting with another NCO delivered her next orders. "As an engineer, you're attaching to the 307th Battalion. Report to in-processing again, and we'll get you passed through."

As her next round of paperwork went through the system to produce her orders for her first unit, Idina found it particularly amusing to sit and watch all the brand-new incoming trainees reporting to reception for the very first time. She'd officially been an Army soldier for a little over six months now, but the endless stasis of reception before basic training felt incredibly far behind her.

The looks on the fuzzies' faces as they gaped at the med lines closing for lunch chow or tried to fathom how anything could take so *long* were priceless.

When she finally got her last set of orders, she was more than ready to leave the reception barracks. "Report to Bravo Company," another NCO told her, pulling out a photocopy of a map they must've created before computer programs could draw and print straight lines. He uncapped a red pen and drew a massive circle around one of the buildings. "The Bravo barracks are here. They'll tell you where to go once they've processed your orders there."

"Thanks."

With her packed duffle bag, all her gear slung over her shoulder, and a crude map of Fort Bragg, Idina left reception and headed across the base to find the Bravo Company barracks.

There was plenty of activity in the middle of the day when she arrived. The soldiers passing in the halls gave her quick directions to in-processing before moving on to their destinations. The woman behind the reception desk there—a Sergeant Brunswick—took at least half an hour to run through Idina's paperwork and new orders before coming back with the only other information Idina still needed to receive.

"Here we go, Private First Class Moorfield. We've assigned you a room. Here's the key and your bedclothes. Barracks commissary is right down the hall that way. Once you settle in, you'll report to First Platoon and First Lieutenant McDurvey. Any questions?"

"No, Sergeant. Thank you."

"Welcome to Bravo."

The signs made it easy enough to find her room, and when Idina unlocked the door, she paused for a moment to take in the sight.

An actual room. I mean, yeah, I have a roommate, but privacy's a real thing now. Awesome.

She shut the door behind her and got to work unpacking her duffel bag and gear. Then she made the bed —a real bed with a mattress on a frame and not a flimsy bay bunk. Not even ten minutes later, a key turned in the lock, the door opened, and in stepped the woman who was Idina's new roommate.

"Oh, shit. Sorry." The woman paused, glanced down at her phone in her hand, then stepped inside and closed the door. "Didn't know I was getting anyone new today."

"Surprise." Idina turned with a broad smile and stopped. "Wait. We've met before."

The woman looked up from her phone, half-distracted, and squinted. "For real?"

"I mean, kind of." Idina shrugged. "Reception at Leonard Wood back in August."

The other woman widened her eyes and snorted. "That's right. You're the smartass."

"And you never gave me your name." They both laughed, and Idina stuck out her hand. "Moorfield."

"Yeah. Cameron."

They shook, and Idina glanced at the rank insignia on her roommate's OCP shirt. *Sergeant. They stuck me in a room with Sergeant Cameron. Looks like she got over whatever issues she was having that sent her back through reception six months ago.*

"So where'd you come from, Moorfield?" Cameron walked across the room to her side and plopped into the rolling office chair in front of the desk.

"Benning."

"Ugh. Georgia."

"It was all right." Idina turned back to her duffel bag to keep unpacking.

"All right, huh? Sure. What you *really* want is something you can get excited about."

Idina snorted and didn't bother to correct the sergeant's misconception. "I guess that's what *you've* been up to."

"Hell yeah, it is!" Cameron swiftly typed a password into her laptop, and the screen blinked from plain black to the desktop background of a white sand beach at sunset. "Just got back from training with the M728. You know what that is?"

"Not a clue." Idina tried not to laugh to let her roommate carry on with her awesome story. Pressing her lips together, she kept unpacking.

"Well, shit. It's the engineering tank, basically. The Combat Engineer Vehicle. They crammed us in like fucking sardines and essentially left us alone to figure that shit out on our own." Cameron chuckled. "Man, that was a crazy couple of weeks. Best training I've had so far, I can tell you that much."

"Sounds pretty badass." Idina unpacked her art supplies and stuck them into the drawer of her nightstand.

"Of course it's badass." Cameron spun in the desk chair to face her new roommate. "I mean, was the cannon tiny as shit? Yeah. The thing gets cramped like you wouldn't believe. But it can take a hit. That's my favorite part."

"Doesn't surprise me at all." Idina pulled on her OCP shirt to get started for her first day of work as a Twelve Bravo combat engineer at Fort Bragg with her first real orders that weren't training.

"What did *you* get up to before landing here?" Cameron asked. "'Cause you were going right into basic from reception, weren't you?"

"Yep." As Idina fastened the buttons and tucked the shirt into her pants, she turned to give Cameron a casual smile.

"So you must've gotten into something good if it took you this long to…" The other woman's eyes widened when she saw the new silver pin on Idina's uniform shirt right there above the "A" in Army. Cameron sighed, sagged against the back of her chair, and pointed at Idina. "Well, fuck *me,* Moorfield."

"I didn't say anything."

"No shit. You didn't have to. I'm over here bragging about this bullshit with M728s, and you got your fucking wings."

"Oh. Yeah." Idina looked down at her Airborne tab right beside her castle tab—both of which she'd earned in the last month—and smirked. "It was a hell of a time. I can tell you that much."

Cameron rolled her eyes. "Fucking E2 showing me up with her goddamn wings. Shit."

Idina rolled her shoulders back and nodded, thoroughly enjoying messing with the other soldier who hadn't given her the time of day or even her name when they'd first met in reception. "E3, actually."

Cameron narrowed her eyes, then leapt out of her chair. "Yeah, you're hot shit. I get it. Quit talking and let's go to work."

Unable to hide a small smile, Idina snatched her

uniform cap off her nightstand and slipped it into her side pocket.

Yeah, I'm doing pretty okay for myself so far. Feels like the best part is still ahead of me.

As soon as she had the thought, a blur of foggy green light flashed across her vision and momentarily made her pause. She glanced around her room, waiting for another vision, voice, or anything that would mark her as way too different from the rest of her platoon. Even more than her jump wings already did.

I thought I got through this...

"Moorfield!"

Cameron's shout ripped her out of her expectation, and the green film instantly faded.

"I don't give a shit if *you're* late, but it makes me look bad when my roommate keeps standing around like she's losing a million brain cells a minute. Let's go."

Idina sighed and hurried out of their room before locking up behind her.

Doesn't matter. I handled it in the middle of a jump. I can handle it on base with my FORSCOM unit. Hell, I've been through the worst of it already. Everything else is a piece of cake, right?

Get sneak peeks, exclusive giveaways, behind the scenes content, and more. PLUS you'll be notified of special **one day only fan pricing** on new releases.

Sign up today to get free stories.

Visit: https://marthacarr.com/read-free-stories/

AUTHOR NOTES - MARTHA CARR

WRITTEN DECEMBER 8, 2021

The holidays are upon us and if you're keeping track of this sort of thing, Advent has begun, and purple is the in color till mid-January. It sparks the start of the Twelve Days of Christmas, at least for me.

Little backstory for you. I grew up on the grounds of a seminary and my late father was an Episcopal minister. That's right, I'm a preacher's kid – who writes about a swearing troll. Tracks for me.

If you've read any of the Leira Chronicles, you'll see my old home featured in them. Nobody tell the dean that I said he's really an Elf. The tall, lithe, powerful kind. Not the lawn ornament kind.

My childhood was spent hanging around scores of young men, and then finally women who wanted to become ministers. Mix in the ghost stories dating from when the place was used as a field hospital during the Civil War. Sprinkle all of it with how easy it was to build a soft-ball team at a moment's notice, and it was a pretty good childhood. But I digress.

This is more about redoing the Twelve Days of Christmas to suit well, the troll. That's right, Yumfuck Tiberius Troll. Why not?

By the way, one more aside. I'm giving up on Italy as a backdrop for The Leira Chronicles, for now. I found a substitute closer to home that will work just as well so more books will be coming out before you know it.

Now, back to our revised Twelve Days.

On the FIRST day of Christmas, Yumfuck went out in his mask and cape and found a small mouse abandoned near an old house and went searching through the sewers for a Willen he heard about that lived near the subway. The Willen agreed to watch out for the mouse, a very distant cousin of Willens, and named him Ralph.

On the SECOND day of Christmas, Yumfuck crept quietly into the kitchen, darting between Correk's feet with a quick lick of some crumbs on the floor. He quietly opened a panel he built under a cabinet door and slid inside, squeezing through where he found two bags of Cheetos hidden behind the trash bags. He saved some to share with Ralph on his next visit.

On the THIRD day of Christmas, Yumfuck hung his stocking carefully on the mantel and got inside waiting patiently for Santa. Leira finally came to get him after three hours when he fell asleep. She found a small mouse curled up next to him covered in Cheetos dust and thought better of it, leaving both of them alone.

On the FOURTH day of Christmas, Yumfuck made his Christmas list. It had only four items. A new mask and cape for Batfuck, in yellow this time. A tiny bike to go in his room with an updated obstacle course. New supplies for the vending machine, also in his room. And a Ouija board to see if anyone in the World In Between could send a message. Leira looked at the list and back at him and called her grandmother to ask if that was really possible. Yumfuck went in search of a larger stocking. Correk noticed the orange paw prints and went to check on his stash, now almost depleted. Ralph was picked up by the Willen and they headed down the alley toward home.

On the FIFTH day of Christmas, Yumfuck binged on Christmas movies. His favorites in no particular order were Die Hard, A Christmas Story, It's a Wonderful Life, Elf, and Klaus. He went back and added, *some more Oriceran playing cards* to his Christmas list for Mara, hung his smaller stocking back up for Leira, gave back some of the Cheetos when he heard that Santa is always watching (some of them still damp where he licked them), and found a matchbox just Ralph's size for a bed that he wrapped with a bow.

On the SIXTH day of Christmas, Yumfuck visited the Donut Run on 4th Street in DC with his pal Samuel who bought him two mango coconuts, a cookies and cream, one French toast donut, a strawberry, and two Boston cream. They strolled back to their favorite park where Samuel put the box under the bench and smiled to himself, listening to the sounds of a hungry troll burrowing his way through six donuts all at once. Followed by a satisfied and loud burp. Samuel heard the tsk of a woman passing nearby and tipped his hat, still smiling. Yumfuck finally joined him on the bench and told him the plot of Elf, partially mixing in the story from Klaus. He also shared his Christmas list and asked if it was true that Santa was some kind of new magical that could see everyone all the time and knew who was naughty and who was nice. Samuel said that was the rumor. Best not to test it. Yumfuck wondered if his large stocking might end up with only coal and asked Samuel if they could stop by the store on the way home to buy some Cheetos for Correk. He rode in Samuel's pocket along the way and told him all about Ralph.

On the SEVENTH day of Christmas, Yumfuck went out again in his blue Batfuck outfit and found seven dogs roaming through the alleys behind his house. Six large dogs and one chihuahua riding on the back of a pit bull. Yumfuck pulled a sharp thorn out of the paw of the large German Shepherd and was quickly added to the pack. They showed him where all the best dumpsters were in town behind the fast food joints and he climbed up with one tiny paw on the back of one dog, and another tiny paw on the back of another and guided them to the dumpster behind the Donut Run. Yumfuck climbed in and threw out donuts, taking his share in a few bites of each one. He told them all the entire story of the Grinch Who Stole Christmas, slowing down when he got to the parts about the mighty little dog, Max who could pull that giant sled and stuck by his friend, the Grinch, no matter what. The dumpster behind the Safeway had some smashed Cheetos still in the box, which were just as tasty. Just as the sun was starting to set, Yumfuck climbed up onto the back of the pointer mix and held onto his collar, directing him to the sewer for a short visit with Ralph.

On the EIGHTH day of Christmas, Yumfuck mailed seven Christmas cards and one long letter to Hagan.

Correk took the letter with a promise to hand deliver it on his next visit with Harkin. There was scratching at the back door and Correk opened it to see six large dogs and one chihuahua standing on the back of a pit bull, barking at Correk. "I think it's for you," said Correk, arching a brow. The German Shepherd had a greasy, crumpled bag from Donut Run in his mouth with two day old donuts inside. Yumfuck waved them in, grinning at Correk showing all his tiny, pointed teeth. "They're here to watch a movie." Before Correk could stop them, they had all trooped past him, the chihuahua still barking, and headed for the living room. The chihuahua took his favorite spot on the couch. Leira came walking in carrying Yumfuck's list. "What is this about dog food? Since when do you…" Leira looked up startled at the crowded, furry living room, a crooked smile growing across her face despite her surprise. "Never mind, I think I get it." Yumfuck clapped his paws, starting the TV. "And a few more stockings please."

Correk noticed the large bowl of Cheetos and started to point but Leira stopped him. "Let it go. There's always more."

"But is there ever enough?"

A squeak could be heard at the back door and Leira opened it to reveal a small mouse grinning up at her. Yumfuck appeared at her side, his arms raised over his head. "Ralph! Come on, we're just getting started."

"Why do I still get surprised?" asked Correk, scratching his head.

"You're a Light Elf from Oriceran who's got a couple hundred years at least under your belt and have battled hairy monsters but you're thrown by a troll and a dog party with a small mouse. Think about it."

On the NINTH day of Christmas, Harkin came to visit and Yumfuck showed him around his room. There were nine little potted ferns along a shelf waiting for another visit from his friends. Harkin had brought two new ferns to add to his collection and helped him build another shelf. Correk handed him the letter for Hagan while Yumfuck put Christmas stamps on the other seven. Only the reindeer ones were applied to his chest. "Can we invite my friends to Christmas dinner?" he asked. "Sounds like fun," said Harkin. "I'm in."

"My grandmother will love this." Leira patted Correk on the back as he gave a resigned shrug. "Sure, why not."

"I brought these just for you," said Harkin, handing over the pink box of donuts from Voodoo Donuts. "Aloha motherfucker!" squealed the troll, digging his claws into the side of the box and vaulting toward the top.

"Remember your Christmas list and who's watching," said Leira, as the troll stopped mid-chomp of a Gorilla Grape. He paused long enough to offer a donut to Harkin and Correk who wisely declined, and he happily went back to tunneling his way through a chocolate covered one.

"Want to watch a movie?" asked Harkin, startling his son. "You watch movies?"

"Lily has been catching me up." He glanced over at the mantel at the long line of stockings in a wide variety of sizes. "You have new tenants?"

"Kind of," said Leira, checking her list of gifts she still needed to buy. Something for Correk was at the top, and even Ralph was included.

On the TENTH day of Christmas, Yumfuck startled ten older ladies waiting for a bus to take them to their regular Bingo game. "A talking mouse!" exclaimed one of the ladies. "And he's holding a… what is that? A fern?" asked another.

"Why are there pictures of reindeers stuck to him?"

"I think those are stamps. Do you think he was mailed somewhere like that?"

"Why do I keep smelling donuts. Damn, now I'm hungry. Dolores, do you still have that Kind bar in your purse?"

"We're gonna be late for the movie, Lucy. Where's that bus?"

"I still have things on my Christmas list to get. I wonder if my grandson would like a talking mouse."

"Would fit neatly in a stocking."

"A mouse with an iPhone. You think you've seen everything. Look, he's taking our picture. Smile, girls."

"Look! The mouse is eating a Cheetos. Or is that a worm? Hard to see that far away."

"No kidding. That's not a talking mouse. It's more like a hamster. That's a mouse," said Delores, pointing at Ralph, who was busy hugging Yumfuck.

On the ELEVENTH day of Christmas, Yumfuck opened all his presents – eleven of them all carefully wrapped. His present to Correk were eleven bags of Cheetos. Leira got some new Oriceran playing cards with pictures of older ladies smiling. Yumfuck got a gift card to the gardening store for more ferns and some nice stationery with a new pen to write to Hagan. Six large dog bowls, with one smaller one tucked into the last one.

Correk gave him a gift card to Donut Run with a wink. Leira gave him Die Hard two and three. Everything on his list was there! Even the stockings were filled with M&M's and Snickers and candy canes and red vines. "I must have been really good this year," he exclaimed, as Leira rubbed his soft, furry head. Mara gave him two large cases of Cheetos, just the right size for his vending machine. And at last, there was a small present of cheese just right for Ralph.

On the TWELFTH day of Christmas, Yumfuck invited over twelve of his cousins from Oriceran (and one small mouse). Eleven slept in the ferns and one at the top of the slide. He showed them all his presents, sharing the red vines and Snickers. His cousin, Phil left a sticky paw print on his newly framed picture of the bus ladies who took him and Ralph to the movies with them, riding in Dolores' purse. Nine of his cousins were perched in their ferns, watching from the shelf. Cousin Mitch was dipping his paw into ink and dancing across a piece of paper. "Mail this with your letter," he squeaked.

"Are you guys ready? We're catching a ride with the dogs downtown," said Yumfuck, as he zipped over their heads on the wire.

"You promised donuts, right?"

"Always!"

"I think I like this Christmas thing," said Phil, smearing chocolate across his fur.

"Remember it's not Christmas till Hans Gruber falls off the Nakatomi Plaza building," cackled Yumfuck. He waved his hand at the line of furry, blank faces. "I'll show you later. You'll love it."

A head topped with neon yellow hair popped out of his stocking, the cheeks stuffed with M&M's. "Can we make lists too?"

"Sure! Why not?"

A troll leaning against the vending machine, rubbing his belly let out a loud fart as a perfect orange circle floated toward the ceiling. "That's gonna leave a stain," muttered Yumfuck, letting off one of his own. Yumfuck headed out the door followed by his twelve cousins – and one small mouse named, Ralph.

Happy Holidays everyone! More adventures to follow.

AUTHOR NOTES - MICHAEL ANDERLE

WRITTEN DECEMBER 17, 2021

Thank you for not only reading this book, but these author notes as well!

So, when Martha...

Told me she was doing the 12 Days of Christmas with Yumfuck, I thought she was going to re-write the song.

I wonder if the words are around here somewhere?

"11 Potted Ferns..." (singing to myself.)

I read Martha's author notes while sitting here in Cabo San Lucas, where (unfortunately) there are not any donut stores near me.

Really sweet items aren't a national thing here in Mexico. Their sweet bread isn't very sweet at all to an American, and I'm jonesing for heavy-duty cinnamon rolls with gobs of frosting.

My sweet tooth has gone catatonic.

My weight is getting better ever-so-slowly.

I just figured out writing about this is causing my cravings to get worse. I'd kill a box of donuts right now, I swear on a Bible. This craving sucks horribly. When I tell Martha about this, will she have any pity?

Not an ounce, trust me.

BACKYARDS

Martha is working on her backyard with plants and trees and stuff. She calls it a forest. I think of it more like a Druid's Grove. Either way, it's really nice from the pictures I have seen and very Zen.

My backyard view (here in Cabo) is out to the Sea of Cortez, and to the right is the Pacific Ocean. If you look on a map and find the Baja Peninsula under California, you take your finger and go to the very bottom. That's where I live when not in Las Vegas.

Last week in Vegas, I dealt with 32-degree nights and 60-degree days. Now I'm doing 60-degree nights and 70-degree days.

For those of you closer to the North Pole, you have my sympathy. Unlike others, I can't STAND being too cold.

Well, unless I'm reading. Then, I like it to be so cold I need blankets as an excuse to just read. "Too cold to go outside. Too cold to move around. I need blankets and a book."

When those times happen, I prefer a tablet so I can buy another book when I finish the book I'm reading. Just open up Kindle… find a book…download a book…keep reading.

That isn't going to happen here in Cabo. Well, it could happen if I crank down the air conditioner to 21 Celsius (about 70 degrees Fahrenheit) and pay a lot of money for the electricity… and possibly burn out the AC.

Yeah, I think I'll skip that.

It's about to be the holidays here, and that means for a couple of weeks, we stop having scheduled meetings and while I never stop 'working,' things are a bit easier as we take the winter holidays as a time to rest.

I hope you get a chance (no matter the temperature) to enjoy a few good books and enjoy yourself.

Have a fantastic weekend or week, and I look forward to talking in the next story you read from us!

WAKING MAGIC

Solve a murder, save her mother, and stop the apocalypse?

What would you do when elves ask you to investigate a prince's murder and you didn't even know elves, or magic, was real?

Meet Leira Berens, Austin homicide detective who's good at what she does – track down the bad guys and lock them away.

Which is why the elves want her to solve this murder – fast. It's not just about tracking down the killer and bringing them to justice. It's about saving the world!

If you're looking for a heroine who prefers fighting to flirting, check out The Leira Chronicles today!

AVAILABLE ON AMAZON AND IN KINDLE UNLIMITED!

BOOKS BY MARTHA CARR

THE LEIRA CHRONICLES
CASE FILES OF AN URBAN WITCH
SOUL STONE MAGE
THE KACY CHRONICLES
MIDWEST MAGIC CHRONICLES
THE FAIRHAVEN CHRONICLES
I FEAR NO EVIL
THE DANIEL CODEX SERIES
SCHOOL OF NECESSARY MAGIC
SCHOOL OF NECESSARY MAGIC: RAINE CAMPBELL
ALISON BROWNSTONE
FEDERAL AGENTS OF MAGIC
SCIONS OF MAGIC
THE UNBELIEVABLE MR. BROWNSTONE
DWARF BOUNTY HUNTER
ACADEMY OF NECESSARY MAGIC
MAGIC CITY CHRONICLES
ROGUE AGENTS OF MAGIC
THE EVERMORES CHRONICLES

OTHER BOOKS BY JUDITH BERENS

OTHER BOOKS BY MARTHA CARR

JOIN THE ORICERAN UNIVERSE FAN GROUP ON FACEBOOK!

BOOKS BY MICHAEL ANDERLE

Sign up for the LMBPN email list to be notified of new releases and special deals!

http://lmbpn.com/email/

For a complete list of books by Michael Anderle, please visit:

www.lmbpn.com/ma-books/

CONNECT WITH THE AUTHORS

Martha Carr Social
Website:
http://www.marthacarr.com
Facebook:
https://www.facebook.com/groups/MarthaCarrFans/

Michael Anderle

Website: http://lmbpn.com

Email List: http://lmbpn.com/email/

https://www.facebook.com/LMBPNPublishing

https://twitter.com/MichaelAnderle

https://www.instagram.com/lmbpn_publishing/

https://www.bookbub.com/authors/michael-anderle

Made in the USA
Coppell, TX
28 July 2023